THE SLAVE TRADE

Justin sensed Varus moving to stand right behind his spread-eagled body, and he felt the legionary's rough hand pulling the skirt of his tunic halfway up his back. Justin shivered, even though the autumn afternoon was still warm. He was wearing pants underneath his tunic. In one fluid motion, Varus lifted up Justin's legs and ripped off the thin material, flinging it into the far corner of the market square with a contemptuous grunt. He lowered Justin's legs and gazed at his bared backside, smiling in appreciation.

While Varus began to pull and knead Justin's arse with one hand, Gaius moved round until he stood in front of him. The legionary pushed his crotch almost casually into Justin's face, and the boy realised that the Roman was already hard beneath the strips of his leather skirt. Unable to move, Justin was forced to breathe in the heady aroma of man and leather – and discovered that he liked it. There was something deep inside him, a desire to let the two men take him in any way they chose, that he could no longer suppress.

SAFER SEX GUIDELINES

These books are sexual fantasies – in real life, everyone needs to think about safe sex.

While there have been major advances in the drug treatments for people with HIV and AIDS, there is still no cure for AIDS or a vaccine against HIV. Safe sex is still the only way of being sure of avoiding HIV sexually.

HIV can only be transmitted through blood, come and vaginal fluids (but no other body fluids) – passing from one person (with HIV) into another person's bloodstream. It cannot get through healthy, undamaged skin. The only real risk of HIV is through anal sex without a condom – this accounts for almost all HIV transmissions between men.

Being Safe:
Even if you don't come inside someone, there is still a risk to both partners from blood (tiny cuts in the arse) and pre-come. Using strong condoms and water-based lubricant greatly reduces the risk of HIV. However, condoms can break or slip off, so:

* Make sure that condoms are stored away from hot or damp places.
* Check the expiry date – condoms have a limited life.
* Gently squeeze the air out of the tip.
* Check the condom is put on the right way up and unroll it down the erect cock.
* Use plenty of water-based lubricant (lube), up the arse and on the condom.
* While fucking, check occasionally to see the condom is still in one piece (you could also add more lube).
* When you withdraw, hold the condom tight to your cock as you pull out.

* Never re-use a condom or use the same condom with more than one person.
* If you're not used to condoms you might practise putting them on.
* Sex toys like dildos and plugs are safe. But if you're sharing them use a new condom each time or wash the toys well.

For the safest sex, make sure you use the strongest condoms, such as Durex Ultra Strong, Mates Super Strong, HT Specials and Rubberstuffers packs. Condoms are free in many STD (Sexually Transmitted Disease) clinics (sometimes called GUM clinics) and from many gay bars. It's also essential to use lots of water-based lube such as KY, Wet Stuff, Slik or Liquid Silk. Never use come as a lubricant.

Oral Sex:
Compared with fucking, sucking someone's cock is far safer. Swallowing come does not necessarily mean that HIV gets absorbed into the bloodstream. While a tiny fraction of cases of HIV infection have been linked to sucking, we know the risk is minimal. But certain factors increase the risk:
* Letting someone come in your mouth
* Throat infections such as gonorrhoea
* If you have cuts, sores or infections in your mouth and throat

So what is safe?
There are so many things you can do which are absolutely safe: wanking each other; rubbing your cocks against one another; kissing, sucking and licking all over the body; rimming – to name but a few.

If you're finding safe sex difficult, call a helpline or speak to someone you feel you can trust for support. The Terrence Higgins Trust Helpline, which is open from noon to 10pm every day, can be reached on 0171 242 1010.

Or, if you're in the United States, you can ring the Center for Disease Control toll free on 1 800 458 5231.

Prologue

Ganymede stood just outside the throne room, trying to hear what was going on. The raised voices were enough to give him a fair idea: Jupiter and Juno were rowing again. He smiled in anticipation – he knew what the usual result of one of their rows was, there was no succour that Juno could offer when Jupiter was in such a mood. The only answer was for Juno to retire to her own chambers, and leave Jupiter in the company of the one person on high Olympus who could satisfy him. Ganymede, cupbearer of the gods, and Jupiter's favoured manservant.

He smiled. It was going to be a good night.

As Juno left her husband's throne room, she saw Ganymede waiting beyond the curtained arch to the bedchamber, his boyish looks as enthralling as they had been countless centuries ago, when Jupiter had spotted the youth at rest in the groves of Athens. Dressed in a simple white cotton tunic edged with gold, Ganymede's body was lithe yet muscular, his skin smooth with a light golden sheen that spoke of his early years in the olive groves that bordered his native city.

1

Jupiter had seen the boy, seen him and watched him at work and at play. He had immediately been taken with his handsome looks, his athletic body, and his purity of spirit. Deciding that he couldn't live without Ganymede at his side, Jupiter had granted him immortality and brought him to Olympus. And Juno simply had to put up with it. No one argued with the father of the gods.

'Ganymede!' The words were bellowed from the throne room as Juno walked out. Ganymede didn't meet her impenetrable stare; instead, he walked past her, his head bowed, and passed through the curtain. It didn't pay to keep Jupiter waiting.

Looking up, he saw Jupiter sitting on a bench, staring out of one of the arches that surrounded the white marble room. Ganymede could see the tension in those wide shoulders, and longed to massage them, to relieve his master's worries in the way that only he knew how.

'Ah, Ganymede!' Jupiter looked round at him, and Ganymede was once more taken by the strong face, framed with a beard of tight golden curls. To Ganymede, Jupiter appeared to be in his early thirties, but Ganymede knew that the father of the gods could appear in any form he wished. Jupiter always looked the same to Ganymede: a huge bear of a man, with broad shoulders, thick, hairy arms, and heavily muscled legs. Ganymede walked over to Jupiter, unwrapping his toga as he did so: he knew that Jupiter liked to see him naked.

'Ganymede, I am troubled. I need you to relax me.'

'Of course, my lord.' Ganymede knew exactly what to do: the two of them had been doing it for longer that Ganymede could remember, but it seemed that neither of them could ever tire of it.

Ganymede sank to his knees, catching a glimpse of his reflection in the still pool in the centre of the room. Ganymede had been given his immortality when he was only in his late teens, and that was how he still looked. His skin was as olive as the groves he had once tended, while his hair was short and jet black. His body was hairless, apart from the dark bush which framed his cock, a cock which was already growing hard with anticipation. Although Ganymede wasn't as heavily muscled as Jupiter, his dark-skinned body was taut and perfectly toned, the result of his healthy lifestyle in the groves outside Athens.

As Ganymede fell to the cold marble floor, Jupiter pulled off his own toga, but stayed seated, his thick legs parted to reveal his own cock. He too was hard: nine inches long and three inches thick, standing proudly erect from a bush of golden hair. The hair carried on upwards, covering his flat stomach and his solid, muscular chest in a blond rug which Ganymede loved to run his hands through.

Leaning forward, Ganymede took the engorged head of Jupiter's cock in his mouth, tasting the moistness which was already leaking from the slit. He slid his mouth further and further along the shaft, trying to take as much of it as he could. But Jupiter was too big even for him and, before he could choke, Ganymede drew back and looked up into the god's face. Jupiter's eyes were closed in pleasure, encouraging Ganymede. He placed his hands on Jupiter's thick, hairy thighs and pushed himself forwards, taking even more of the nine inches into his mouth. His own cock was almost painfully erect, and as Ganymede rocked backwards and forwards, sliding his mouth along Jupiter's thick shaft, his sensitive helmet rubbed against the base of Jupiter's bench, sending shivers of delight through his entire body.

Jupiter suddenly pushed Ganymede away. No words were needed: Ganymede knew exactly what was expected of him. As Jupiter stood from the bench, Ganymede lay down on it, bringing his legs up to reveal his arse.

Jupiter pulled Ganymede along the bench, so that his legs were almost over the edge; then he put one of his meaty hands on the boy's buttocks. A single thick finger stroked the tiny black hairs that surrounded Ganymede's ring – gentle, teasing strokes that made Ganymede gasp. The other hand laid itself on Ganymede's cock, seven thick inches of dark, veined manhood, the foreskin drawn back to reveal the glistening helmet; Jupiter gave it a single, firm wank, sliding the foreskin over the end and back. But Ganymede knew what Jupiter really wanted: he eased himself on the bench so that his arse and ring were even more accessible. Jupiter responded by increasing the pressure of his finger, pushing it harder and harder against the boy's ring. Slowly, he eased his way inside, and Ganymede groaned with the sensation, yet knew that this was nothing compared with how he would feel once Jupiter's shaft was inside him. Ganymede couldn't wait, and obviously nor could Jupiter: he pulled out his finger and roughly pulled Ganymede's legs apart.

Straddling the bench, Jupiter hoisted Ganymede up from it. Then he moved forward, his cock ramrod-straight and glistening with a mixture of Ganymede's spit and his own pre-come. His helmet rested for a second, brushing the outside of Ganymede's ring, before Jupiter pushed forward, pulling Ganymede closer to him as he did so. Even though Ganymede had done this many, many times before, he still gasped as Jupiter's thick penis forced its way inside him; for a moment, the burning pain threatened to overwhelm him. Then he relaxed as the pain turned into a feeling of total contentment and unbelievable pleasure. Jupiter was inside him, part of him; Ganymede tightened his muscles, squeezing his arse around his master's cock. He relaxed then tightened again, and carried on for long moments, aware of Jupiter's heavy breathing, aware of Jupiter's huge hands gripping his thighs tightly. He looked at Jupiter's face, rapt with pleasure; Jupiter's solid hairy body, now glistening with a thin layer of sweat. Then he relaxed his arse for one final time. He knew exactly what was expected of him now: nothing. All he had to do was lie there.

Jupiter took the initiative once more: he pulled his cock halfway out of Ganymede's arse before pushing it back in with all of his weight behind him. Out once more, then back inside, the rhythm of Jupiter's strokes in time with his heavy breath. Jupiter's face was now only inches away from Ganymede's own, and Ganymede pulled his head up so his cheek was resting against Jupiter's beard. Suddenly, he was aware of one of Jupiter's hands grasping his cock, pulling on it with the same rhythm as the breathing and the fucking. Ganymede knew that Jupiter was close: Jupiter's balls were slamming against Ganymede's arse with each desperate fuck, and Ganymede could sense them getting tighter and tighter as he approached his climax.

With a final, deep groan, Jupiter plunged his shaft as far into Ganymede as he could do and then he came: Ganymede could feel Jupiter's come exploding inside him, and that sensation, coupled with Jupiter's big hand wanking him with tight strokes, was enough to send Ganymede over the edge. With a yell that must have echoed across Olympus, he shot his load: gout after gout of thick white come landed on his stomach, his chest, his face, even . . . but Jupiter continued to wank him as he himself carried on shooting load after load into Ganymede's arse. Ganymede couldn't remember ever coming so much, as yet another wave of pleasure overcame him –

Marcus Lucius awoke from the dream, the wetness on his taut stomach evidence of how vivid it had been. A thick gout of semen stretched from his navel to just below his chest, indicating a release just as powerful as Ganymede's had been in the dream. To be taken by a god! He stretched, before sitting upright on the bed and looking out of the window, gazing across the manicured lawns of his family's villa towards the town square. Dawn was just breaking, and the smell of the baker's first bread was drifting in from the town. He knew that he should be thinking about breakfast, and of his daily lessons with his tutor, Cimber.

So why did the thought of another man entering him, violating him, taking him in the way that Jupiter had taken

Ganymede, excite him so much? An even more worrying consideration then crept in: men were meant to be with women, not other men. That was how the world worked. So why didn't his excitement over the far-too-realistic dream trigger any feelings of guilt?

With confused emotions running through his head, Marc wiped his stomach dry with a rag and pulled on his woollen tunic, before setting off in search of something to eat. Today was just another day: his usual lessons from Cimber, followed by his household chores. Nothing exciting, because nothing exciting ever happened in Marc's village. But you should always set off with a full stomach, his mother said, because you never knew when something unexpected might happen.

The rest of the house was quiet; his family was still asleep. Indeed, Marc himself wouldn't usually have woken up quite so early, but he knew that the effect of the dream meant that going back to sleep wasn't an option. A walk around the grounds of his family's villa was just what he needed to clear his head – and if today's lesson with old Cimber was as full of facts as yesterday's, he would need a head totally clear of fantasies of gods and their cupbearers.

As Marc walked out of his parents' villa into the dewy autumn morning, he smiled at his mother's homespun philosophy: something exciting, something unexpected? That would be the day.

One

————

Marc's mind was brimming full of his daily lessons with his tutor when the cries of terror and the acrid smell of carnage invaded the usual tranquillity of the downs. But the sounds were totally foreign to Marc: he was still too busy thinking about what old Cimber had taught him that morning to fully realise that something was happening. Something unexpected.

Marc was Cimber's favourite pupil: Marc knew that with a certainty devoid of the slightest trace of arrogance or conceit. Cimber had told him time and time again that never before had he met a Briton so skilled in the language and verse of the empire – and this was at a time when most of Marc's compatriots could barely read or write. And Cimber should know: after all, hadn't he told Marc that he had once tutored the great Nero, when he had still been known as Lucius Domitius and had not yet become the Emperor of mighty Rome? Indeed, Cimber still claimed to be one of the Emperor's closest friends, although Marc took that claim with a pinch of salt, as he did Cimber's saying that Marc's learning was almost the equal of that of the twenty-five-year-old ruler of most of the world. But it was high praise, and Marc had blushed then, embarrassed by the compliment and flattered by the old man's promise to take him one day to Rome itself. Even if they were simply the fantasies of an old man, something to dream about.

Rome was the capital of the world, the imperial hub of all civilisation, and Cimber had almost promised that he could make the necessary introductions so that Marc could meet the Emperor himself. He hadn't even minded or thought it strange when Cimber had laid a friendly hand on his upper thigh and left it there slightly longer than some might have thought proper, although it had brought back faintly disturbing memories of his dream the previous night.

His reverie over Cimber was suddenly broken as the screams and carnage became too intrusive for him to ignore. What had been a minor disturbance on the edges of his perception exploded: cries and shouts, the smoke and the choking smell of burning houses and burning flesh.

Marc stopped and looked around, trying to locate the source of the disturbance. It took him a few seconds, but, when he did, fear and terror gripped his stomach like a solid knot.

The clouds of black smoke and the screams were coming from the small town where he lived with his parents. His home. The hazy blanket that hovered above the town was like a black eagle circling its prey, or a carrion bird waiting for death. Without hesitation, Marc threw his wax tablets – with today's lesson scratched on their surfaces – on to the grass and raced down the hill and into the valley. A small voice told him that he was being stupid, that he was putting his own life at risk, but he knew where he had to be and what he had to do. His family and his townsfolk needed him, and he needed to be there with them.

People were streaming through the village gates in all directions, trampling over their fallen neighbours in frenzied attempts to flee from the marauders – but Marc couldn't see who was responsible for the chaos. He dodged the mob and tried to get closer, pushing his way through in the opposite direction to his townsfolk. To his horror, he could see that some were covered in blood, while others had their clothes ripped off their backs.

Children screamed as their mothers dragged them away; mothers screamed as their children were pulled away from them in the mad rush to escape. But there were very few adult men: Marc guessed that they were somewhere in the smoke and noise that lay at the heart of the town, giving the women and children a chance to get away.

As he made his way towards the town square, Marc could hardly hear himself think above the cries of the people and the yapping and barking of the dogs. He continued through the crowd, before grabbing hold of one of the fleeing women whom he recognised, stopping her in her tracks and spinning her round to face him.

'What in Jove's name is happening?' he shouted, his voice raised to make himself heard above the clamour. 'Tell me, woman!'

Ekka struggled wildly for a second, her only thought that she was in danger, caught by the very attackers that she was trying to escape, and knowing that, in their panic, none of her fellow villagers would stop to help her. Then she looked up to see the person who was tightly grasping her wrists, shouting to raise his voice above the cries from all around.

In spite of herself and the furore that raged around her, she gazed appreciatively at the trim and toned body which even Marc's coarse woollen tunic couldn't disguise. She recognised his soft, unblemished complexion, which made him look much younger than his eighteen years, and his brown, close-cropped hair, which fell down in a fringe above brown and long-lashed eyes. Finally, there was the full, sensual mouth which all the girls longed to kiss but somehow had never succeeded in doing. But now was not the time to think about that.

'Marcus Lucius,' she said breathlessly. 'It's you.' She let out a sigh of relief at the realisation that this was a friendly face. She had often served him in the marketplace on his daily shopping trips for his parents, and had always enjoyed his easy and polite manner. 'Marcus, we must leave here before it's too late.' Already, the sounds of death were fading: once the marauders had finished with the men, they would start with the women and children – the people whose lives were being bought with the men's sacrifice.

Marc pulled her to the side of the road so that they were out of the way of the villagers who were still streaming through the gate. Ekka wanted to go with them, but Marc was so insistent that she felt obliged to answer his question. Before she could reply, his impatience made him repeat the question.

'Romans, that's what's happening,' she said. She pronounced the name with disgust. With hatred. It was what they deserved, she thought, as she glanced back at the screen of smoke which obscured the carnage.

'Romans?' Marc frowned. 'But they're our friends.'

Ekka could see the confusion in the boy's face, but she couldn't feel any sympathy for him. Everyone knew about Marcus Lucius's family's favoured status with their imperial masters. She sneered at him, and pulled her hands away from Marcus's grip.

'To you and your family in your fancy villa, perhaps, paying lip service to Governor Suetonius and his bastard taxes,' she spat. 'Try telling that to the men and women – the *children* – that they're massacring in the marketplace. The families whose homes are being burnt and looted. Or the people who've barely escaped with their lives.' She jabbed an urgent finger towards the town square. 'Tell it to them, Marcus Lucius!'

His mind racing, Marc looked at the panicking villagers running out towards the open countryside. What Ekka had said had cut him to the core. Although there were many in Britain who

10

admired – or even welcomed – the Romans, that definitely wasn't true of everyone on the island.

Ever since Caesar's armies had first set foot on British shores over a hundred years ago, there had been an uneasy truce between Marc's people and the Romans – the invaders. Some resented living under the Roman yoke and had formed resistance groups, hiding out in Fenland or the north, making periodic assaults on Roman camps, or desperately trying to unite the varying British tribes into some sort of coherent attacking force.

But there were others who saw the value of what the Roman conquerors had brought to the Isles of Britain. A road system linking nearby Londinium to Eboracum in the faraway north; growing trade routes between this country and lands that Marc had never even heard of; culture, learning and philosophy from all corners of the world.

Marc's father had always thought this, even going so far as to adopt Roman names for himself and his family. He had been rewarded for his loyalty by a spacious residence and a lifestyle that many of his fellows envied – but that envy wasn't always well intentioned. Marc knew that he had had a favoured upbringing, and that upbringing was a direct result of his father's courting favour with the Romans. It was something that Marc believed in too, but now was not the time to argue the Roman case. He pulled Ekka out of the way as another furious knot of people ran past, trying to make sense of what was happening. He peered through the flames and the smoke, but couldn't see his family's villa on the far side of the burning town square. 'My father and mother – my sisters,' Marc gasped, with a sense of growing dread. 'Are they all right?'

'Dead, like as not,' said Ekka, her fear making her blunt. 'If they're lucky, that is . . .'

'What do you mean?'

'There're many who'd prefer the sword to what the Romans have in store for them,' she said. 'They're Romans. They take their pleasure in whatever vile way they will.' With that, Ekka stepped away from him. 'I hope your family has fared better than mine,' she called, before following the other villagers.

Marc left the woman and headed towards the village, making for his parents' villa on the small hill that overlooked the main marketplace in the town square. He met little resistance as he raced through the wide straight streets – yet another innovation of the Romans, he thought idly – since he had found the foresight to go round the outskirts of the square, avoiding the Roman attackers. Most people had now made their escape, and the outlying streets were quiet and empty. Too quiet: even the screaming from the square had diminished, and the sick thought that there was no one left to kill entered Marcus's mind unbidden.

That thought was reinforced by Marcus's realisation that empty was a relative term: the streets *were* empty – apart from the blood already congealing in the small trenches lining the road; the earthenware pots and amphorae shattered around the entrance to the marketplace, their contents spilt around them. And the bodies of villagers lying in the gutters, their blood-drained faces frozen in death masks of fear and horror. Marc swallowed, and turned his head away from the corpses. He had to find his family.

From somewhere nearby Marc suddenly heard the sound of shouting and the clashing of metal upon metal: clearly not all the villagers had panicked and fled, and a few courageous souls were putting up some kind of resistance. But he knew it would be a futile attempt: without a strong leader to organise them, no Britons would ever stand a chance against the Romans. The Roman hand was too strong, its grip too powerful, for Britain to escape. That was why it was better to follow the path taken by Marc's father and accept Roman sovereignty. It was the easiest way. But was it the *right* way? a little voice questioned in Marc's head.

But Marc was assuming that Ekka had been correct, and the

marauders *were* Roman. He still couldn't quite believe Roman soldiers capable of such carnage. The ones he had met had always treated him with kindness – affection even – although occasionally Marc would wonder why a few of the older men favoured him with their special attention. But the evidence of his own eyes and ears seemed to suggest the contrary. Had Ekka the market woman – not the brightest of people, but an honest, upstanding citizen – been right? Was he really being so naïve? Had he lived such a sheltered and privileged life that he couldn't believe the truth when it was staring him right in the face?

Marc turned the corner leading into the central marketplace and froze. The square had been ransacked: the shops lining three sides of the square had all been looted, while, in the square itself, the wooden stalls had been overturned and their wares thrown on to the ground. Earthenware pots lay shattered, their precious contents of wine and milk and oil seeping into the ground.

But, unlike the silent side streets, the marketplace wasn't empty. Ekka had been right after all. Two legionaries were standing in the centre of the square, wiping the blood off their swords on to their cloaks before replacing them in their scabbards. Marc hid behind an overturned stall before they could look up and see him. Then he carefully peered through a gap in the splintered wood and watched.

The legionaries were tall, wearing the standard uniform of footsoldiers of the all-conquering Roman army: leather-studded sandals tightly bound to naked mud-bespattered calves, made firm and muscular through hours of forced marching; scarlet tunics under which Marc knew the hardiest of legionaries wore nothing even in the harsh British climate; upper-body armour glistening like silver in the afternoon sun, reflected light accentuating biceps which Marc could never hope to encompass with his two hands. The two legionaries were wearing black-plumed helmets, and Marc risked discovery by putting his head out from his hiding place to try to take a look at their faces.

Nothing. Their faces were almost completely hidden by their helmets, leaving only their eyes in view. Hard, merciless eyes. Dark and arrogant. Roman eyes. The eyes of the conqueror. Faceless and powerful, the embodiment of dangerous masculinity.

The shorter, stockier and hairier of the two legionaries reached up and took off his helmet. Marc craned out his head even further to catch a glimpse of his face. Not a face he'd like to meet when he was alone and defenceless, with its cruel, vicious mouth and hard, callous jawline.

The hair was close-cropped, brown and thinning slightly on top, but not unattractive in a brutish sort of way, and the dark shadow of new beard growth indicated that he was of good Roman stock. Then there were the eyes, as black and hard as coals, and the scar running down the length of his right cheek. The nose was slightly out of joint, probably the result of some bar-room brawl, rather than a misfortune in battle. This was the face of a thug, hard, vicious, masculine. Yet even under the current circumstances, Marc felt an unfamiliar feeling stirring inside him: the thought of that hard, stubbled face just inches above his own, the legionary's hot breath on his face . . . Marc swallowed. These weren't emotions that he wanted to accept at the best of times – and these were hardly the best of times.

Marc continued to watch from his hiding place, risking even more the chance of being spotted, as the legionary's comrade walked over to his taller companion. This legionary was slimmer, less muscular. Unlike his fellow's, his legs and arms were hairless and honey-coloured. A North African or a Spaniard, Marc guessed, conscripted as a footsoldier when his country had been enslaved by the conquering Roman army. It had been a choice offered to Marc, until old Cimber had pleaded with the Governor to allow him to become his own special pupil.

The helmeted legionary put an arm over the shoulder of his colleague in what seemed to Marc to be more than just a comradely gesture.

Then the pair of them started to walk in the direction of the stall behind which Marc was hiding.

Marc tensed, certain that the two of them would see him any second now. He glanced nervously around, wondering whether he'd be able to make a run for it in time. It would be no use, he realised. The two legionaries would easily outrun him and trap him in their mighty arms.

He thought of what the woman from the marketplace had told him. *Dead – if they're lucky* . . . Marc felt another strange thrill, as he imagined what would happen if the two legionaries were to find him here.

The Romans were almost upon him now, and he could hear their deep, rude voices, even though his Latin couldn't quite translate some of their coarser expressions. He cowered further down behind the overturned market stall as the shorter of the two fighters came within inches of him.

Marc could smell the legionary's heavy, musty man smell: it was overpowering. Like most of his fellow footsoldiers, this legionary bathed only rarely, and he carried with him the heady and, for Marc, strangely intoxicating aroma of sweat and old leather. It was a smell so different from the scent of his mother and his sisters and the women who had raised him from a child, and he wondered why it excited him so. Another puzzle for the future – if he had a future.

The legionary was almost upon Marc now. Marc felt his heart beat faster, fit to burst out of his chest. The thought of being caught by the two men continued to excite him: despite the circumstances, he could feel his cock hardening beneath his tunic as a thrill of anticipation went through him – anticipation at being pulled out from his hiding place by those powerful hands, and submitted to who knew what experiences.

Dead . . . if they're lucky . . .

There was a sudden clattering from the other side of the marketplace and the two legionaries halted and turned around. Marc breathed a small sigh of relief, mixed with a peculiar disappointment, and peered out to take a look at the cause of the noise.

Someone else had been hiding from the Roman legionaries, sheltering, just like Marc, behind one of the upturned market stalls. Marc recognised sandy-haired Justinius, one of the market boys, whose cheeky expression and slim, boyish figure belied the fact that, at twenty, he was a good two years older than Marc himself. Justin had seized his chance and left his hiding place, falling over a pile of crates in his haste. Now that cheeky expression had transformed itself into one of abject terror as the two legionaries approached him.

'Well, well, well, and what do we have here?' the shorter and crueller-looking of the two legionaries drawled, as his hand went to the weapon by his side.

'I'm . . . I'm called Justinius,' Justin whispered.

'A Roman name for a piece of British shit,' said the stocky one.

'Another stinking, filthy Brit, Varus, that's what,' his helmeted companion replied as he approached the boy, who was cowering in a corner of the square, his route of escape cut off by a market stall. 'Shall we do him in like we did the others?'

Varus shook his head. 'Nah, Gaius. We've seen off more than enough of this barbarian scum for today,' he replied. 'We need to leave some alive to keep our reputation going. 'Besides,' he added with a knowing wink, 'these British boys have other uses.'

'General Decius won't be happy,' Gaius pointed out. 'He wants the prettiest ones for himself.'

Marc watched from his hiding place as Varus laughed, and spat on the ground. 'Decius is probably halfway back to Rome by now,' he said, hardly bothering to hide the contempt in his voice. 'We've done his bidding, we've slaughtered these animals. Now we want our sport.'

Justin tried to stumble to his feet and escape but Gaius was too quick for him. He reached out and grabbed the top of the frightened boy's tunic and dragged him roughly to his feet.

'Going somewhere?' he sneered, and held Justin by the arm. Strong hard fingers dug into pale white flesh.

Justin looked up, clearly terrified, into what he could see of Gaius's face. Marc shuddered in sympathy for his fellow villager, but there didn't seem to be anything he could do. Except watch, and imagine what Justin was going through.

The legionary's helmet, glistening in the afternoon sun, cast sinister shadows over his dark eyes. That was the most frightening thing of all, not being able to see the man's face. Not to know whether he was teasing him, merely playing with him as a cat plays with a mouse. Not to know whether he planned to kill him, or hurt him, or ... Not to know what the two legionaries had in store for him. Justin had thought that the slaughter of his village was bad enough: it was clear that he hadn't even considered that there were worse things than death.

'Please – please, don't kill me.' Justin's voice was weak, plaintive, almost a whisper. He could hardly get the words out through his terror, and his rudimentary grasp of Latin threatened to fail him any moment.

The legionary leant down as if to hear Justin better. 'Sorry? I didn't quite catch that.'

'Please, don't kill me . . .' he whimpered.

The second legionary grabbed Justin's other arm so that now the boy was pinioned between the two of them. Escape just wasn't possible.

'Don't you recognise the uniform of a Roman soldier, boy?' the other legionary barked. 'Show some respect to your elders and betters.'

Justin looked pleadingly into the man's eyes. 'Please . . .' he said again. And then a last desperate thought occurred to him. 'Please, *sir . . .*'

Varus exchanged an amused look with Gaius, before turning back to the boy. A cruel look played on his brutishly handsome features before he answered Justin.

'Oh, we won't kill you, boy,' he promised, with a note of scorn in his voice. Or was it scorn? Justin was sure that he could detect something else. Something . . . frightening.

'Thank you,' Justin sighed with relief, even though he wasn't sure what he was thanking them for. Somehow, saving his life suddenly took on a more sinister purpose.

Gaius increased the pressure on Justin's arm. The boy flinched with pain. 'Thank you, what?' he snarled.

'Thank you, *sir*,' came Justin's grateful reply. 'I'll do anything you want. Only . . . please don't hurt me – *sir*.'

Varus laughed. 'Now, you know we can't promise you that, boy,' he said. He nodded over to Gaius and the two of them dragged Justin over to the market stall that had been preventing the boy's escape from the square.

For one second they relaxed their grip. Justin sensed it with animal instinct, and took advantage of their laxity to get away. He tried to pull away, but Varus stopped him – violently, brutally. The two legionaries tightened their hold on Justin, and he gasped in pain.

'Try that again, and you're dead,' Varus promised. 'We haven't spared you just to let you go.'

Gaius laughed – a cruel laugh, a hard, sadistic laugh. 'No, boy, you've got to earn your survival.'

Justin swallowed. Perhaps death would have been better.

Marc peered out once more from his hiding place, intrigued. This was the time to make his own escape, he knew. Gaius was standing with his back to him, holding a spread-eagled Justin down by the shoulders, pinning him to the wooden boards of the market stall, and Varus was too busy verbally abusing the boy to notice him.

Yet something inside Marc made him want to stay, to watch, with a bizarre mixture of fascination and disgust. The scene playing out in front of him had captivated him, enthralled him. Without quite knowing why, his hand fell down to the swelling between his legs.

Justin was quieter now. Something told him that accepting his fate was the only chance he had of living through this. He just hoped that whatever the two legionaries had planned for him didn't turn out to be worse than death. He had heard stories of the Obsidian Legion, terrible stories that the older boys had told them late at night to stop them from sleeping. As Justin had grown older, he had dismissed them as nothing more than horror stories. The situation that he was in now was a terrifying indication that they had been anything but.

He sensed Varus moving so that he was standing right behind his spread-eagled body; Justin felt the legionary's rough hand pulling the skirt of his tunic halfway up his back, exposing his back. Justin shivered, even though the autumn afternoon was still warm. He was wearing pants underneath his tunic; in one fluid motion, Varus lifted up Justin's legs and ripped off the thin material, flinging the torn pants into the far corner of the market square with a contemptuous grunt. He lowered Justin's legs, and gazed at his bared backside. He growled in appreciation.

'We've a nice piece of boy-meat here, Gaius,' said Varus as his rough, masculine hands began to slowly knead the cheeks of Justin's arse. 'We're going to have a lot of fun with this one.'

At that moment Justin knew exactly what they meant, exactly what they were going to do with him – no, *to* him.

He began to struggle, he began to scream, but Varus clamped a solid hand over his face and another between his shoulders.

At that moment Justin really knew the meaning of fear.

Varus increased the pressure, firm fingers digging deep into soft and pliant flesh. Justin tried to call out with the pain, but Varus's hand was still covering his mouth. He swallowed and tried to hold back his fear. With any luck, it would all be over soon. He hoped. All thoughts of escape left him: paralysed with fear, he stopped struggling. Varus must have sensed this: he removed his hands and put them on Justin's arse.

While Varus once again started to pull and knead Justin's arse with one hand, Gaius moved round so that he was in front of him. The legionary pushed his crotch almost casually into Justin's face, and the boy realised that the Roman was already hard beneath the strips of his leather skirt. Unable to move, Justin was forced to breathe in the heady aroma of man and leather – and discovered that he liked it. There was something deep inside him – a desire to let the two men take him in the way he knew they were going to – and it was growing, possessing him. His own hardness increased, and he started to move back and forth in response to Varus's own manipulation of his arse. His prick, now a stiff six inches, rubbed against the wood of the broken market stall.

Gaius licked his lips. 'Boy-meat,' he agreed, 'just waiting to be filled. Begging for it, eh, Varus?'

Varus looked down at Justin's squirming figure. 'Are you begging for it, boy?'

Justin tried to turn his head around to look at Varus, but found he couldn't. Instead, he looked up at Gaius, who was towering above him, a man with no face, no personality, just the promise of cock and come, a man holding absolute dominion over him.

'Please let me go,' he implored. But he wasn't sure that that was what he wanted any more. He wasn't sure of anything apart from the stiffness between his own legs and the smell of legionary in front of him.

'You call me *sir*!' Gaius commanded, as Varus viciously slapped Justin on the arse: once, twice, three times. Brief spasms of beautiful red-hot pain coursed through Justin's body, an hard prick jerked with pleasure. He groaned, but it was out o. pain mixed with pleasure.

'This little slave needs to be taught some manners,' said Varus, and Justin was aware of his legs being pulled apart. He felt the rough leather of Varus's boots scrape against the tender flesh of his inner calves, and felt the legionary's feet on his, preventing him from making an escape. If he had wanted to.

Unnoticed by the three of them, Marc continued watching as Varus reached between Justin's legs and fondled the near-hairless balls that he found there. Marc's hand reached under his tunic for his own cock, which was already standing proud and erect: seven inches of thick warm meat. Slowly he started to massage the velvet head, his fingers flitting around it in circular motions. He shuddered with the sensation, his eyes transfixed by what was being done to Justin.

'This filthy slave needs a good fucking,' Varus announced to Gaius as he massaged Justin's full and waiting balls. 'Let's show him what it means to serve the empire.'

Justin closed his eyes in anticipation. *Gods!* His balls already felt fit to explode as Varus twisted and pulled them, cupping them in one massive hand, running a finger back and forth between them, but never straying near Justin's cock which was rock-hard and aching for release.

'Ever been fucked before, slave?' Gaius barked. He pressed his crotch once more into Justin's face, giving the lad a tantalising feel and smell of his hard-on. Justin muttered something inaudible: the words just tumbled out. Gaius simply laughed.

'Let's find out, shall we?' Varus said.

His two massive hands splayed across Justin's arse, and roughly pulled the cheeks apart, to reveal his crack and the pink and tightly puckered fuck-hole. Varus lifted the forefinger of

⌐ his mouth and moistened it with spit. Up front, ꜱᴇᴅ his leather-covered hardness into Justin's face. ꜱathed in the smell and suddenly realised that this was what he wanted. The games that he had played with his ᴊod friends – wanking and sucking one another off in the ꜰields – had been just that: games. This was real. This was what it was like to be a man.

Now only partly hidden from view, his excitement making him careless, Marc spat into the palm of his own hand and covered the head of his own solid cock. Then he pulled on it, up and down, up and down, his breath quickening as he watched Varus insert a finger into Justin's quivering hole.

Varus worked his way into the gently resisting warmness of Justin's hole, rotating his finger to widen the ring of muscle, pushing in and then out and then further in and out and in again. It was obvious that the boy was a virgin. But there was none of the struggling that Varus might have expected. It was as if the filthy little animal was enjoying it! Justin squirmed, but it was obviously in pleasure, not pain, his arse responding to Varus's thrusts as a second finger was inserted into his expectant hole, and massaged the warmth inside.

'Please, sir, no . . .' But they were play words, the words of a slave who wanted to please the empire, to serve the empire. To serve Varus and Gaius.

Varus responded to Justin's plea with a third finger up the boy's arse, stretching the hole to what surely must be its limits. He wanted to make sure that the boy could take his thick Roman cock. Then again, he didn't want him to be too loose: Varus wanted to fuck a nice, tight British arse.

'Please, sir, no . . .'

'And don't give me that "please-sir-no" shit,' Varus grunted, and rammed his fingers harder and deeper into Justin, making the boy groan with equal measures of pleasure and pain. 'You're loving every minute of it. I bet there have been hundreds up your pretty little arse. Flog it around town and the Roman camps, do you, like the nasty little soldier's whore you really are?'

'No . . .'

'No, *sir*!' With his free hand Varus slapped him hard on the buttocks, leaving a bright red handprint. Justin yelped with pain. Varus looked over to his companion, who was still teasing Justin with the promise of his as yet unseen cock.

'This piece of British trash is boring me with his whining, Gaius. Shut him up!'

'With pleasure!'

'Take my cock, slave!' Gaius grunted. Justin lifted his head at the same time as Gaius lifted up the leather skirt around his own waist. His erect cock was enormous – Varus had taken that piece of meat in his own mouth more times than he cared to remember – and he waved it tantalisingly close to Justin's face. Long and thick, buried in a dense bush of jet-black hair, the purple vein along its nine-inch length throbbing with anticipation, tiny drops of pre-come glistening on its purple head. For a brief moment, Varus wished that it was going to be his mouth that would be drinking that salty wetness.

Gaius stared down at the boy impassively, his face still hidden by his black-plumed helmet.

'Suck it.'

'Please . . .'

'You heard what he said,' Varus said. 'Suck it. Take all of it in your whore-slave's mouth. Suck it! Suck every last inch of it!'

Varus grabbed Justin by the hair, and pulled his head back so that it was on a level with Gaius's waiting cock. Justin shook his head, trying to avoid the inevitable, but Gaius's prick forced its way into his mouth.

It pushed its way right down, until it looked as though the boy might choke on its purple-red length and girth; then Gaius pulled it out, its rock-hardness wet and shining, Justin's saliva dripping off its full and gorgeous head.

'Again!' Varus commanded and forced his fingers deeper into Justin's arsehole, pushing Justin once again on to Gaius's cock, although not quite as deeply this time. They didn't want the boy to choke on it: there was still plenty of sport to be had with the young British slave.

Gaius reached down and held Justin's head, tangling his fingers in the boy's sandy hair. He moved the Briton's mouth up and down, up and down, over his trembling and erect manhood, sending shivers of uncontrollable delight throughout his entire body. Justin looked up at Gaius, whose head was thrown back in ecstasy, enjoying the sensation of his steel-hard prick slipping and sliding in a warm and moist and willing hole. The sight made Varus's prick even more eager to get inside that tight warm hole.

'Harder, suck it harder,' Gaius groaned. He pumped his cock deeper and deeper into Justin's mouth, pulling the Briton's face into his bush of pubic hair, making him breathe in the musky man smell. But now it was no longer Justin who was the captive, but Gaius: Gaius the slave, prisoner to his ecstasy, his entire being-dependent on the filthy whore-slave sucking at his cock. Varus couldn't wait for it to be his turn.

Justin pulled his mouth away, but if Gaius had thought that he was going to stop pleasuring him then he was wrong. Justin reached out his tongue and traced a line along the throbbing vein of Gaius's cock, snaking its way slowly to the tip, and teasing the edges of the Roman's hard purple helmet, before engulfing it once again with his warm mouth, sending Gaius into further ecstasies. Varus knew his comrade too well: it was only a matter of seconds before he shot his load into this slave's waiting mouth.

Then it would be Varus's turn.

★ ★ ★

Marc watched on, stroking himself, trying to hold back the flood of come that he could already feel surging and swelling up in his own prick. He reached up a hand and tweaked his left nipple, which immediately became firm and erect. The fantasies that he had pleasured himself with in those quiet night moments were coming true in front of him. And he couldn't help himself.

His legs were shaking now, and his brow was glistening with sweat. He didn't care if Varus or Gaius spotted him now; all he cared about was watching them fuck Justin both ends just as though he was some cheap boy-whore from the streets.

He knew that part of him would willingly exchange places with Justin. But that thought didn't scare him. It just made him more excited. With determined strokes, he continued to wank himself off to the spectacle in front of him.

Varus pulled his fingers suddenly out of Justin's arse, and Marc watched as the boy reached behind him with his free hand, trying to bring them back. Varus chuckled and slapped him once again on the arse.

'My turn to fuck his face now,' said Varus, and then laughed at the disappointment on Gaius's face. 'Don't worry: you get to play with this end.'

Still slightly reluctant, Gaius pulled his quivering cock away from Justin, who vainly tried to grab it back. The helmeted and faceless legionary swapped places with Varus, who looked down at Justin's expectant face with a mixture of contempt and amusement.

'Not so much the innocent now, are you, whore-slave?' he said, and spat in Justin's face. Justin raised his head, mouth open in eager anticipation, and Varus spat on him again, his saliva dripping from the boy's eyelashes.

This time it was Justin himself who reached out for Varus's cock, slipping his hand under the soldier's tunic, and pulling out his erect manhood. Varus's prick was smaller than his companion's, but much thicker, and it filled Justin's eager mouth to the limit.

'Taste my cock, you filthy whore,' Varus said, as he shoved his cock deeper into Justin's throat. 'Show me what you've just been doing with my friend Gaius. Because I'm going to fill you full of my thick spunk.'

Justin tried to reach down to touch his own cock, but his arms were suddenly pinned behind his back by Gaius. He wasn't going to be allowed to seek his own release until the two Romans had spent their own seed. At this moment, Varus's and Gaius's needs were paramount. And urgent. Gaius's cock began to probe the crack between Justin's arse, the thick purple helmet teasing at the hot wet hole. Varus watched as the very tip of his comrade's prick started to force its way inside the boy.

'Take it,' Gaius grunted. 'You're going to take all of this cock – all of it, right up to the very hilt.'

This was it: this was the moment that Justin had both dreaded and longed for. The moment when he became a real man, having a real man inside him. Justin tried to relax his arse as much as he could, as he tried to imagine what it was going to feel like with that huge Roman cock forcing its way into his arse, into his soul.

Seconds later, he found out.

He groaned as Gaius's manhood forced its way into his arsehole, not gently, but brutally, just as if he really was a whore-slave, being allowed his life only so that he could pleasure his Roman masters, only so that they could ram their meaty cocks up his arse.

A whore-slave! Yes! That was exactly what he was, Justin realised, as Gaius's huge cock thudded further inside his arsehole, and Varus slapped his face with his own mighty prick. A whore-slave, nothing more than a piece of meat to be fucked: two holes ready to be taken by the whole damn Roman army if needs be. He felt Gaius drilling deeper and deeper into him, with a pain that was almost overwhelming. Hot tears dropped from the corners of his eyes as his arse felt like it would split in two. Nine inches of Roman manhood, forcing its way further and further inside him . . . Then, as suddenly as the pain had started, it stopped; stopped because it was replaced by a feeling of exquisite pleasure, a sensation of complete satisfaction as he felt totally and utterly fulfilled with Gaius's huge cock inside him.

The pain returned briefly as Gaius partially withdrew his prick from Justin's hole, but it lasted only seconds before the indescribable pleasure returned as Gaius rammed his thick penis deep, deep inside. Gaius was fucking Justin to death, fucking him till he saw stars in his eyes, till the world started to spin around him. The pain-pleasure as Gaius's cock pounded deeper and deeper and deeper into his arse, his body, his very being, was almost too much to bear. And yet, when Gaius released him from his armlock, Justin's hands immediately reached out behind him, pulling the legionary on to him even more, wanting to be taken body and soul, arse and prick and mouth, by the enormous, red-hot cock of the man whose face he had still not seen.

'Please, *sir*, fuck me. Harder, sir, harder!' Justin pleaded, as Gaius's thrusts sent stabs of exquisite torture through his entire body, and Varus rammed his meaty cock once more into his mouth.

For a brief second, lucidity returned, and Justin glanced around him. Suddenly he saw Marc watching him, pulling on his own prick in time with the two legionaries. A look passed between the two boys, and Justin smiled, before he once again closed his glazed eyes in rapture, drunk with the sensation of being penetrated simultaneously by two fat, hungry cocks.

Varus was close to coming now – somehow, Justin could tell. Perhaps it was the tightening of the big hairy balls, or the trembling of the huge cock, or the salty wetness of pre-come which dribbled into his mouth. Justin prepared himself for his master's come, but Varus suddenly took his prick out of Justin's mouth, and started to jerk on it, teasing him with its tumescence. Justin leant forward, mouth open, tongue out ready to taste his master's seed, which he could almost see, welling up in Varus's cock. Behind him, Gaius's thrusts were becoming faster and faster and he, too, was close to release. Gaius slapped Justin's cheeks as he pushed deeper and harder and rougher inside him.

'Beg for it!' Varus grunted. 'Beg for it like the filthy little British whore-slave you are.'

It was almost too much for Justin. 'Please, sir, please,' he whimpered. 'Let me taste you. Come on me. Come all over me. Please. Now. Sir. Please. Please. Please.'

Varus shuddered as a fountain of spunk erupted from his prick, once, twice, three, even four times, covering Justin with its warm stickiness. Varus reached out and rubbed his come in Justin's face, over his eyelids, his lips, in his hair, until the boy was covered with the legionary's seed. Justin was in rapture: he greedily lapped it up with his tongue like a wild animal, licking the salty droplets from around his mouth.

From his vantage point, Marc watched as Gaius's thrusts grew longer and deeper, ploughing into Justin's arse, Gaius's buttocks clenching and unclenching as he came closer and closer to release. Gaius linked his arms around Justin and dragged him to his feet, so that he was now fucking him in an upright position. Marc could tell that Justin was enjoying it, and that small voice inside still wished that it was him standing there. His strokes even more urgent, Marc continued to wank, knowing that his own release was only moments away.

Gaius's hands slid under Justin's tunic, squeezing his nipples tightly, roughly. Justin groaned, squirming with pleasure at the pain that Gaius was causing. Varus came up to him, grabbed Justin's erect cock, pumping it up and down, before kissing him, greedily lapping the aftertaste of his own come from Justin's lips.

Nothing was said: all that remained was the final release for both Gaius and Justin.

Gaius thudded harder and faster into Justin's arse and squeezed his nipples even more tightly. Justin could feel Gaius's hairy balls slapping against the cheeks of his arse in time with each thrust, and he could feel the throbbing rise up from deep inside himself. As Varus pulled harder and faster on Justin's own cock, Gaius threw back his head and cried to the heavens for release.

Gaius exploded, filling Justin's arse with creamy white hotness. Justin sighed as he felt the stickiness drip out of him and down between his legs; then he groaned as Varus gave his prick one last wank, which brought him to orgasm, and he spurted in the man's hand and over his dark leather skirt. Varus smiled crookedly at him and raised his hand to Justin's lips, smearing them with his own come. Justin smiled back and tasted his own seed, before falling, exhausted and sated, back into the arms of Gaius, who enfolded him in firm honey-coloured arms.

As he did so, Justin stole a sideways glance at Marc, who was still tugging on his own prick, and gave him a knowing smile. Marc hastily retreated back behind the upturned market stall.

'You're a good whore, you are,' said Gaius, who had still not removed his plumed helmet. He reached out an almost tender hand to stroke the boy's hairless cheek.

'One of the best,' Varus said.

Marc watched them turn to go, the muscular cruel legionary and his mysterious companion, who still had not removed his helmet. He saw Gaius reach for Justin's arse and squeeze it, before taking his hand and leading the boy off with them. He imagined the fate in store for Justin at the Roman camp. Someone as willing and as pretty as Justin would soon be the favourite of Varus and Gaius's black-plumed legion, Marc realised, with something approaching envy – why, he wondered? At the thought of Justin's being a slave to the Romans' every sexual whim and caprice, he pulled harder on his own prick, throwing his head back in pleasure as his entire body rushed to release. He was about to come, about to shoot his milky-white spunk, about to –

'Marc! What are you still doing here, you little idiot?'

Marc tried to hide his twitching cock, but it was too late. He felt the warm stickiness trickling down between his legs, and he tried in vain to hide the swelling beneath his tunic before turning around.

A beefy-looking man, somewhere in his mid-thirties, dressed in a horsehair tunic, leather trousers and boots, was standing before him. His face was burnt from years of toil in the fields, and he wore a neatly trimmed black beard. His tunic was torn to the waist, revealing a finely chiselled chest, covered in thick black hair; the muscular frame was slightly offset by the beginnings of a slight belly. Marc grinned at the friendly face.

'Alexander, you startled me,' Marc said, breathing a sigh of relief. Alexander had been one of his father's trusted friends in the old days, before he had disagreed with the family's growing friendship with the Romans. No one had seen Alexander for months now: some had said he'd gone off to fight the Romans in the northwest of the country, near Deva. Marc had missed him, even though he wasn't quite sure why. After all, the man was little more than an educated barbarian, a Pict from the far-off northern wastes. But there was something about him that inspired trust . . . and maybe something more?

'I can see I startled you,' Alexander said and looked down meaningfully at the bulge beneath Marc's tunic and the wet stain that was spreading there.

'What's happening, Alexander?' Marc asked. 'What are the Romans doing here?'

'What does it look like, you idiot?' Alexander said scornfully. 'Taking their revenge out on us – that's what.'

Marc frowned. 'Revenge? Revenge for what?'

'Boudicca's uprising of last year,' Alexander replied, as if Marc were the uneducated barbarian. 'They want to teach us all a lesson we won't forget in a hurry.'

'But our people played no part in that,' Mac protested. 'My father refused to lend support to her forces. Said that we had to learn to live in peace with Rome, not fight against her.'

'Don't I know it,' said Alexander bitterly. 'That's why I left your father's service. Better death in the Queen's service than eking out a miserable life as a slave either here or in Rome.'

'But why attack *us*?' Marc wanted to know. 'It doesn't make sense. If they want to restore order, why attack a village that's always shown them loyalty in the past? Doing this will only stir up more resentment against Rome and the Emperor.' And why send in the Obsidian Legion? he pondered. If Alexander was correct, this was most definitely overkill – and it was making him see the Roman Empire in a very different light.

'Who knows why they do what they do?' spat Alexander. 'They're Romans, aren't they?'

Used to Alexander's dislike of Rome, Marc let that pass. 'That's still no reason to ransack our villages and rape our women.'

'*And* our men,' Alexander added, with a knowing look at the stain on Marc's tunic. 'Or hadn't you noticed that, young master Marc?'

Marc blushed. 'They caught Justinius,' he told Alexander. And then added a face-saving lie: 'There was nothing I could do to help him.'

'Justin, the cloth-seller's son?' Alexander sneered. 'He didn't need saving. He'll open his legs to anything with balls and a cock, that one. Caught him countless times in the fields at night – *playing* with his friends.' He laughed, a cold, bitter laugh. 'He'll soon find out that this isn't a game – not to the Romans. He won't be able to sit down for a week when that lot have finished with him.'

Marc shifted uncomfortably: as always, Alexander's blunt manner made him feel awkward and unsure of himself. He wondered if Alexander had seen him pleasuring himself while watching Justin and the two legionaries. It was clear that he was disgusted by Justin's willing submission to the Romans; would he think the same of Marc?

All he'd ever wanted to do was to please Alexander, and there had been nights when he'd have liked nothing better than to sleep with him in the same bed, hugging him for warmth, just the way he and his older brother had done before he'd caught the fever and died. But that had been something that he had never dared suggest to the burly, straight-talking barbarian.

'We have to find my father,' Marc insisted. 'He'll make everything right again. He'll tell the Romans that we mean them no harm.'

'How old are you, Marc? Eighteen years or eighteen months?' Alexander looked pitifully at Marc. 'Can't you get it into your thick skull that Romans are no friends of ours? Those of us that they don't kill they'll take back as their slaves.'

'Slaves?' Marc thought back to Varus and Gaius fucking the life out of Justin. Filthy little whore-slave, they had called him, and Marc's cock had stiffened when he had heard that.

'You heard. Believe me, you'd be better off dead. Especially the likes of you.'

'What d'you mean?'

'Never mind,' Alexander said hastily. Now it was his turn to blush and turn his face away.

'We have to find my father,' Marc insisted again. He started to move off in the direction of the villa, but Alexander held him back.

'I told you – there's no point,' he said. 'If he's not been killed with the rest of them then he's been taken prisoner.' The reply was blunt.

Marc looked at him defiantly and shrugged him off. 'If there's no point, then why did *you* come back?' he demanded.

Alexander tried to looked away, but Marc could still see his dark eyes, brimming with emotion in spite of himself.

'I had to see if you were all right,' he admitted gruffly. 'Now let's go and find that blasted father of yours, shall we?'

'But I thought you just said –'

'The hell with what I just said,' Alexander grunted. He grabbed hold once more of Marc's arm, and led him across the now empty marketplace and towards his father's villa. 'Perhaps we can make him see the error of his ways. He trusted the Romans, and *this* –' Alexander gestured at the wrecked town square ' – this was the result.'

Two

The streets were deserted now. Marc and Alexander guessed that the Roman raiders had given up their looting of the shops and homes, their vicious attacks on the townsfolk, and had made off back to the open countryside, taking with them whatever booty they could carry.

As Marc approached the villa that a grateful governor had bequeathed to his father and his family, his heart was pounding in his breast. But whether it was on account of his concern for the safety of his father and the rest of his family, or because of Alexander's declaration that he had returned to the village solely for his sake, he wasn't quite sure.

Smoke was rising from the centre of the villa, and Marc quickened his pace. If some Romans still remained then his father might be in danger. He thought of his mother and his two elder sisters, and tried not to think of the lustful hands of the legionaries pawing their bodies as Varus and Gaius had done with Justin. Boudicca's daughters had been raped by the victorious Roman host, Alexander had told him on the way up here. Marc couldn't bear the thought of such a fate befalling his own mother and sisters.

'Careful, Marc,' Alexander said softly as Marc ran up the steps towards the door leading to the atrium. Marc stopped a moment, looking at him strangely.

'Why are you so concerned about me all of a sudden?' he asked curiously.

'I don't want to see you getting hurt, that's all,' Alexander muttered. 'Isn't that good enough for you?'

Marc turned and raced into the atrium, across its ornately mosaic floors and into the large central courtyard. By the main fountain, jars and elaborately painted amphorae had been smashed, and what remained of his father's furniture had been piled high and set ablaze; it was this barbaric and wilful destruction that was responsible for the pall of smoke above the villa. Within the flames, Marc spotted some of the precious parchments that Cimber had lent him.

'Barbarians,' he said through gritted teeth.

'Not barbarians – Romans,' said Alexander with a bitter smile.

Of Marc's parents and sisters there was no sign, not in the bedrooms nor the dining room, not even in the *lararium,* where they worshipped their favoured Roman gods. The lares and penates, of course, were the gods who were supposed to keep a wary and protective eye on the household – much good they had done in Marc's house. All-seeing and all-powerful Jupiter, and the recently deified Augustus. And Apollo, he of the golden curls and magnificent physique, whom Marc had always thought of as his own, personal divinity, watching over him from cradle to grave.

'Forget your family, Marc,' Alexander said, and rested a hand on his shoulder, pulling him closer to him, so that their bodies were almost touching. Marc could almost feel his hot breath on his cheeks. He frowned and looked curiously at Alexander, and a frisson of forbidden delight coursed throughout his entire body.

This, he realised, was what he had always secretly longed for, from those days as a boy when he had watched Alexander wrestle his elder brother naked in the open air, and indulge in laddish horseplay. Then Marc had felt a curious sensation deep within him, but it was only today that he could put a name to those feelings. Only now, with Alexander standing so near to him, his heavy barbarian hands massaging away the tension from his shoulders, could he truly comprehend those urgings deep within him.

'Not here, not now,' he said, and gently pushed Alexander away from him. Alexander's brow darkened.

'What do you mean?' he asked defensively. 'You don't think that I – you do, don't you?'

'Forget it,' Marc said quickly, and averted his eyes from Alexander's gaze. Had he read the signs so wrongly?

'Because if you think that I'm filthy scum like Justin, then you couldn't be more wrong.' It was clear from his tone that that was the end of the subject.

'I'm sorry, Alexander,' Marc said – and meant it. 'But we have to find my father and sisters.'

'And where will you look?' Alexander asked bluntly – bluntly but sensibly. 'They're gone. Either escaped to the country or taken as slaves.' He shook his head. 'The country's a big place, Marc.'

Marc frowned, trying to think. Then it struck him. 'Cimber would know where they've gone to.'

Alexander laughed. 'Cimber? Another one like Justin.'

'What?' Marc once again had the feeling that he was missing something very important.

Alexander shook his head. 'Don't tell me you never saw the way he leered at you whenever he came to the house, or the way he used to stroke your knee when he thought others weren't looking. You were always the prettiest one. Cimber may live here in Britain now, but he's as Roman as they come. He's the Emperor's man, after all.'

Marc shook his head. 'You're wrong. He's just being affectionate, that's all.' He sighed. 'I was a good pupil, damn it.'

'Open your eyes to the real world, Marc. He's nothing but a randy old goat whose only ambition in life is to get his hands on your cock.'

'It doesn't matter,' Marc finally replied. 'We have to find him. You don't have to come if you don't want to.'

Alexander looked curiously at Marc and now there was no mistaking the affection in his dark brooding eyes. 'I'll go with you. Like as not you'll get yourself killed or even worse if I'm not around for you,' he said, although that wasn't the real reason and, in their hearts, each of them knew it.

Alexander was playing some sort of a game with Marc – that much was obvious. All Marc could do was go with his instincts and play along with it.

'I'm pretty sure that the villa's empty,' said Alexander. 'See if you can find a few provisions – we don't know when we'll get another chance to eat.' He shrugged. 'That's if those Roman bastards haven't been there first.'

The Romans had visited the kitchens: the tiled floor was a mess of broken pots and crockery. But Marc still managed to find some bread and some mutton, which he stuffed into a leather bag. Suitably provisioned, they set off for Cimber's dwelling, which was over the downs, the other side of the town from Marc's home.

As Alexander and Marcus made their way out of the town, the silence was uncanny. Even the dogs had stopped barking, bringing an unnerving sepulchral calm to the violated collection of houses and streets. Marc wondered when the other villagers – the *survivors*, he reminded himself – would return. And how they would react to see their houses looted and burning, their loved ones hacked to death or kidnapped as slaves. He took a deep breath: once they had found Cimber, they could find Marc's father. He would know what to do.

As they made their way over the downs, Marc thought about how much had happened since he had last trodden this path. His village had been torn apart, his parents were missing ... and he had stood and watched a friend of his being fucked like the common street girls who sold their favours in Londinium. Watched and been excited by it.

'That's where the old goat lives, isn't it?' said Alexander, pointing ahead of them.

About ten minutes more, and they would be at the small stone hut in which Cimber lived, alone apart from his parchments and manuscripts, and the succession of pretty young boy students who visited him there.

The day was hot, and, as they made their way to Cimber's hut, Alexander stripped off his tunic and wiped the sweat from his brow. Marc feasted his eyes on the muscles of his companion's upper arms as they flexed and unflexed, the taut chest with its thick hairy covering. He longed to reach out and touch Alexander, feel the naked power contained in those arms glistening in the afternoon sun, the strength that beat in that strong ox-heart. He wanted to run his fingers over Alexander's chest, embed them deep in his thick thatch of dark hair, already beaded with sweat, follow its tantalising course down to his waist and beyond. Once again Marc felt a swelling in his groin, and he longed for yet another release.

'Something's wrong,' said Alexander, as Cimber's tiny hut grew closer. Marc dragged his eyes from Alexander, and looked in the direction in which he was pointing. The wooden chair outside the hut, in which Cimber always liked to sit and read his scrolls and parchments – and, like as not, eye the nubile young men who often passed this way, if Alexander's theories about the old tutor were correct – had been overturned and broken. A flagon of wine lay smashed on the ground. Marc's heart sank. Despite Alexander's claims, Marc was very fond of Cimber.

'Careful, Marc,' said Alexander as they reached the edges of the small herb garden which bordered the front door, laying a restraining hand on his arm. Marc shrugged him off and entered the hut.

It was worse, far worse, than Marc could have imagined.

The Romans had shown Cimber no mercy. The teacher's precious parchments had been pulled from the shelves lining the walls and strewn across the rush-covered floor. A personal missive from the Emperor Nero, which had been the old man's pride and joy, and which he always delighted in showing to his pupils, had been torn into tiny ragged shreds. And, huddled in the corner of the room, was Cimber himself, hands clutching his abdomen, blood having stained his cream-coloured toga a deep shade of scarlet. The pendant he always wore around his neck glimmered dimly in the light, as dim as Cimber's life seemed to be. He looked up as Marc and Alexander entered the room, but the fading light in his eyes showed that he was near his end.

'Cimber,' Marc said gently, at his old teacher's side in an instant. 'Who did this to you?'

'Who do you think?' Alexander said gruffly from the door, where he was keeping a wary lookout.

'But they're his fellow countrymen,' said Marc, resting Cimber's head in his lap, the blood rapidly covering the dried stain of his earlier release. Marc found it difficult to reconcile the desire he had felt for the two legionaries with the cruel treatment their comrades had meted out on a fellow Roman. All his knowledge about the empire – knowledge that mainly came from Cimber – was now a twisted mess of confusion. But the old man shook his head.

'Not Romans,' he croaked, with his dying breath. 'The Obsidian Legion.'

That confirmed it. Marc remembered the black-plumed helmets that Varus and Gaius had worn: from that he had suspected that the Obsidian Legion was responsible. The dark secret at the heart of the Roman paradise, the secret that everyone whispered about, but that no one truly understood. But why had they done this to Cimber, a loyal servant – no, a loyal member – of the Roman Empire? He turned back to his tutor, whose eyes were flickering shut as the end approached.

'My father and mother – my sisters,' he asked, willing the man to remain conscious for just one moment more. 'Where are they? Did the Obsidian Legion take them as well?'

Cimber shook his head. 'They made for the coast when the Legion came . . .'

Marc gasped with relief. At least they were safe. 'But why the Obsidian Legion, Cimber?' Marc wanted to know.

'The empire is in danger,' Cimber said, and his head slumped back in Marc's hands. 'Warn the Emperor. Tell him . . .' He reached up and grasped the pendant from around his neck, showing it to Marc. 'Remember this token. Tell Nero. Tell . . .' Cimber's eyes closed and the death rattle came from his throat.

Marc looked up at Alexander, who was still standing by the open door. 'He's gone,' he said sadly. There were tears in his eyes.

'Good,' Alexander said, without turning around. 'One less Roman to worry about.'

'You bastard,' Marc snapped. 'Don't you care?' He pulled angrily on Alexander's arm, even as he gave one last, lingering look at Cimber's silent corpse. 'He was my teacher. The one who taught me Latin. The one who wanted to take me to Rome.'

'The one who wanted his mouth wrapped around your cock, more like.'

'For Jove's sake,' Marc exploded, 'show some sympathy for once in your blasted life!'

Alexander turned around and his face fell when he saw the tears that were now streaming freely down Marc's face. He took a step towards him.

'Marc, I'm sorry,' he said, and obviously meant it. He opened his arms to comfort Marc, and the younger man fell into them, letting himself be enfolded into Alexander's masculine embrace.

He rested his head on Alexander's shoulder, tasting the salty tang of sweat on his brown and burnished body, and put his hands around his waist, pulling himself into Alexander's wild and vibrant maleness. The muscles in Alexander's back were firm and hard, as hard, in fact, as the swelling that had now appeared between Marc's legs.

He felt the rough touch of Alexander's leathers on his naked thighs, as Alexander moved his right leg between his legs, forcing them apart. Alexander's leg pressed hard against Marc's erection, rubbing it up and down, while Marc pulled Alexander even closer to him, lowering his head to feel the firm and hirsute pectorals pressing hard against his unblemished cheeks. Hard against soft. Rough against smooth. Man against man.

Marc looked up to see a strange expression in Alexander's eyes. A wild realisation that this was what Alexander had wanted for so long, the firm knowledge that this was how the wild and surly creature from the barbarian north really felt about Marc. Alexander *wanted* Marc, had wanted him for years, and it was only now in Marc's own distress that he was giving in to the emotions that he had suppressed for so long, emotions that he had hidden behind his façade of disgust for Justin and Cimber . . .

Marc took a hand off Alexander's back, and reached down to the front of the older man's legs. Even through the leather he could feel Alexander's hard-on, straining to burst free.

Marc knew what he wanted, even though he'd never before been with a man or a woman. This was why Marc had held back from his own desires for so long, why he had even refused to acknowledge Cimber's advances to him, or the lustful looks of the others in the village. For he knew now that he wanted Alexander and Alexander alone. Not a randy old man. Not the effete young men who paraded their wares in front of the Roman camps. He wanted a real man. He wanted *Alexander*

41

with all his heart. He lusted for him with all his body, all his emotions, all his sex.

Gods, how he longed to unlace those leathers and take Alexander's rock-hard prick in his hands, bringing the man he had always adored to fulfilment, to see him loose his seed in an orgy of wild abandonment. To kneel down before the man who was his hero, his idol, and swallow Alexander whole, burying his face in the thick black bush between his legs, before licking his hairy balls, taking each in his greedy mouth, sucking them until Alexander cried out for release from this exquisite agony.

Marc looked once more into Alexander's eyes, recognising his own burning desire reflected in them. Alexander bent down his head uncertainly, and his lips brushed against Marc's: a brief touch which sent shivers of delight throughout Marc's yearning body. Stubble scratched his soft skin, and he reached out and pulled Alexander on to him, fastening his mouth firmly on to his.

Alexander's hand had found its way inside the opening in the top half of Marc's tunic. His fingers traced the outline of his firm pectorals, and then teased his hairless nipples, which instantly hardened with desire. His other hand went down to Marc's cock, still covered by his tunic, even though the fabric was tented as it tried to restrain the length and thickness that lay imprisoned beneath. Alexander squeezed hard on Marc's jailed prick, pulling on it through the cloth, making Marc squirm with breathless expectation.

Already he could feel the sap rising in his cock, but this time Marc was determined not to waste any drop of it. He would share it with the man he loved, smearing the steaming hot come over his face and lips, just as he would beg Alexander to do the same to him with his own sweet and longed-for love juice.

'Well, lads, it looks like we've found ourselves another pair of queer-boys.'

Marc and Alexander hastily separated from their embrace, and turned in the direction of the gruff voice. A gang of five Romans was standing in the doorway to Cimber's hut. Definitely not legionaries, they wore rough-looking garments, threadbare cloaks, and daggers at their sides. Their leader, pot-bellied and unshaven, his arms of steel covered with blue-black tattoos, strode over to Marc and Alexander. Alexander put himself between the newcomer and Marc.

'Lay a finger on him and I'll cripple you,' Alexander warned. There was iron in that voice; surely even the Romans wouldn't be so stupid?

The other man grinned, displaying chipped and broken teeth, and turned back to his four companions, who joined him, their daggers unsheathed and ready for action. Five representatives of the Obsidian Legion: Rome's evil distilled into a single fighting force. All five of them advanced on Alexander and Marc, forcing them to back further into Cimber's hut.

'You hear that, lads? This queer-boy reckons he'll do in your good mate Cassius,' the man mocked. 'Just so that he can protect his little pervert of a boyfriend.'

'He's not my –' Alexander began awkwardly, but his protestations were drowned out by the men's laughter. His eyes darted around the hut, looking for something, anything, with which to defend himself.

'He doesn't have to protect me,' Marc said and came out from behind Alexander's back, a slight figure compared with Alexander's muscular bulk. Alexander turned angrily to him.

'Marc, leave this to me,' he said, the concern clear in his voice.

The leader laughed again. 'Isn't it touching, lads?' he jeered. 'The two little queers want to stick up for each other.'

'Stick their cocks up each other, more like,' one of the others said.

Alexander saw red and threw himself on to Cassius, reaching

out for his neck, ready to crush the life out of the Obsidian Legionary. He would have done so, too, if he hadn't felt the sudden touch of cold steel on his skin.

'Get your filthy hands off him!' came a shout. It was from another of the thugs, one who had come up behind Alexander as he had leapt at Cassius, and was now holding a dagger at Alexander's throat.

'You think I'm scared for my life?' Alexander snarled, but released Cassius nevertheless.

'Maybe not, but what about your *friend*?' The word was laden with disgust.

Alexander turned to see Marc surrounded by the three other men. One of them had him in an arm lock while the other two were pawing him all over.

'Get your fucking hands off him,' Alexander said, but was unable to do anything. The dagger was still at his throat, and he watched in horror as the men fondled Marc's virginal body. Marc looked pleadingly at Alexander. *Help me*, that look seemed to say.

'Such soft skin,' one of the legionaries said, as he stroked Marc's cheek. He undid the laces of Marc's tunic, and traced a hand over his firm pectorals. In spite of his earlier fantasies, any thoughts of sexual arousal were suddenly banished. Watching Justin being screwed had been a fantasy, like watching a play. This was deadly serious. 'There isn't a hair on his body. Just like a girl's.'

'He takes it like a girl, that's for sure,' said the other. 'You take it like a girl, do you, boy?'

Marc frowned, and tried to ignore the man's eyes. 'I don't know what you mean,' he claimed unconvincingly.

The two men looked at each other in mock surprise. To them it obviously was a game. A very real and very dangerous game for Alexander and Marc. 'You think he's telling the truth?' one asked.

The other shrugged his shoulders. 'There's only one way to find out, isn't there?'

'Guess there is . . .'

Still held at daggerpoint, the helpless Alexander was forced to watch as the two men tore Marc's tunic open from top to bottom. The bastard behind Marc released his hold on him for a moment, while the others ripped Marc's clothes off his back. Now Marc was standing naked in the centre of the room.

'Looks like we were wrong, after all,' one of the men cracked. 'Seems there *is* some hair on him after all.'

He reached down and flicked Marc's flaccid cock hard with his fingers, before running them through the tiny patch of dark-brown hair covering the base of his prick and his small round balls. Marc's cock twitched involuntarily and he felt it start to harden as the man's fingers followed the line of hair up to his navel. It seemed that his body wanted to respond, even if his mind didn't. Part of him wondered whether the only course of action would be to submit to them: if either he or Alexander resisted, they would certainly be killed. At least this way they might stand some sort of chance.

Marc glanced anxiously over at Alexander, hoping that the older man hadn't noticed the burgeoning stiffness between his legs. Yet when he looked, he noticed the telltale swelling in Alexander's leathers. Alexander was aroused by the thought of the man he loved being pawed and abused by others, turned on by the thought of others touching the man-meat he had not yet enjoyed! It was as if both of them were excited yet ashamed at the feelings they were experiencing.

Marc shut his eyes and shuddered as fingers started to trace the outline of his pubic bone, and then, with a surprising softness of touch, glide up the side of his body. He imagined that it wasn't this brutish thug who was touching him up, but Alexander: tall, dark, masculine, the embodiment of all his desires since his days as a child. Alexander, bronzed and muscular, against Marc, pale, slim and pliant. Marc, naked and defenceless, powerless, giving himself up for love and for lust. And now, as tingles of approaching release started to course throughout his body, Marc opened his eyes.

Alexander was still there, a knife at his throat, his arms pinned behind his back by Cassius's henchman. A hardness in his groin. A wary look on his face.

'Let's see if this little cock-sucker really is as innocent as he makes himself out to be.'

The brutal words woke Marc from his reverie. No, he realised, this wasn't what he wanted. Not here. Not now. Not without Alexander beside him. He struggled to free himself from the men's grip but it was no use. They were hardened warriors, and he was little more than a boy. They could do with him what they wanted. He was at their mercy.

He felt the one behind him reach out for his backside, press his fingers deep into the tender flesh and then spread the cheeks of his arse apart. A finger inserted itself into the crack in his arse, seeking out the tender pink hole there. Marc grunted, and he felt a stabbing sensation, as the man pressed a second finger deep into his arsehole, roughly, all show of affection and tenderness now gone. He squirmed. Beads of sweat appeared on his brow. A look of fear was in his eyes. But still his cock stood firm and erect. Was this really what he wanted after all? To be used and abused and fucked by a nameless stranger? Despite his love for all things Roman, this was not how he wanted it.

'Seems this one is a virgin after all. It's a tight hole, just ready to be opened up.'

'Then let's do something about that,' his companion said.

He reached down and unlaced the front of his leather trousers, pulling out his massive cock, already hardened and sweaty with lust. He stroked it, and the purple vein along its side throbbed. 'Let's see how this little pervert likes me deep inside him. Turn him round.'

'No, please!' Marc begged, and struggled to free himself as

the man holding him turned him round and forced him to bend double, so that his hole was now exposed to the other's hungry cock. The man whacked him on the arse, and a red welt appeared on the soft white flesh of his arse cheek.

'No, please,' Marc repeated through gritted teeth.

'Don't give me that. Don't pretend you don't like it. Don't pretend that you don't love my hot hand on your hot little arse. You can't wait until my fat meat's all the way up your filthy little arse, can you?'

'No . . .'

Marc's voice was weaker now. He tried to free himself once again from the second man, who was holding him down by the shoulders, but it was hopeless. The man's fingers dug deeper into his flesh, and his crotch pushed itself towards Marc. Marc turned away and looked at Alexander, still being held at daggerpoint by Cassius and his lackey.

Marc's look of helpless desperation was too much for Alexander to bear. Ignoring any thoughts of his own safety, he kicked back at the Roman who was holding him in an arm lock, hitting him in the balls. The Roman fell back against the wall of the hut, and Alexander's right fist flew out, knocking the dagger from Cassius's hand.

He flung himself on to the Roman who was guiding his cock into Marc's arsehole, and dragged him away, whipping his dagger from its sheath, and sliding it across his throat. The Roman fell to the ground, blood fountaining from his jugular.

Alexander grabbed hold of the naked Marc, dragged him from the other Roman, and started to pull him towards the open door.

It was too late. Cassius had picked up his dagger and with one swift and practised movement had plunged it deep into Alexander's belly. Marc watched in horror as Alexander clutched his stomach, blood seeping out from between his fingers, and then crashed to the floor, dead.

'You Roman bastards! You killed my friend. You Roman

bastards!' whispered Marc, his legs turning to jelly. He staggered. Looking at Alexander's lifeless body, he wanted the tears to flow, but he wasn't prepared to give them that satisfaction. 'He was right about you Romans – you're nothing but scum.'

'Hold your tongue, boy,' Cassius said, and waved the blood-spattered dagger threateningly in Marc's direction. Marc spat in his face.

'I'll do nothing a Roman asks me,' he promised, gazing defiantly into the boss's eyes, a man now, no longer a boy. 'Not now – not ever.'

'You'll do as we tell you,' said Cassius, and with his other hand reached out and touched the cleft in Marc's chest. 'We've unfinished business with you, boy. We were only just getting started when your *friend* got in the way.'

Marc grimaced as the boss's fingers travelled down towards his groin, and his now flaccid penis. He felt other hands squeeze his buttocks. Unable to move, he winced once more as a stubby finger roughly probed his arse, sending shocks of pain throughout his system.

'By the time we've finished with you, you'll wish that you were with your friend, down there, dead on the floor there,' Cassius said, forcing Marc to look at Alexander's bloodied corpse, lying on the ground, close to Cimber's own lifeless body. He felt tears of sorrow and rage well up in his eyes as Cassius continued. 'We'll open you up like no one's ever been opened up before.'

'Ram our fat cocks down your throat, and make you swallow every drop when we shoot our loads,' said another.

'Flog you within an inch of your life. Fuck your dirty little arse till you beg for mercy –'

'And after that then we'll fuck you some more,' chimed in another, almost as if he didn't want to be left out.

Marc looked this way and that, unsure of which way to turn, knowing that, with Alexander slaughtered on the floor, there was now no escape from the Roman bastards surrounding him.

Even now, two of them were rubbing their big-headed and hungry cocks up and down, ready to plunge them deep down into his hole.

They would rape him, taking their self-loathing and repressed hatred out on him, filling him up with their cocks, one after another after another after another, stretching his arsehole wider and wider and wider, tearing his insides apart, filling it up to overflowing with their seed, till he could take no more, till the come dripped down the inside of his thighs, till the air stank with the smell of shit and sperm and sweat. Cassius was right: he'd be better off dead.

There was a sudden commotion at the open door, and the men turned around to look at the newcomer. Their faces fell at the sight of the legionary silhouetted in the doorway. Two of them hurriedly put their cocks back under their leather skirts.

'What in hell's name is happening here?' the legionary demanded, and marched into the centre of the room. Marc immediately recognised the steely thighs and honey-coloured arms of Gaius, one of the Romans he had watched earlier, fucking the life out of the compliant Justin.

Gaius took off his black-plumed helmet to reveal a head of tight dark curls which fell to his shoulders, dark-brown eyes, and hollow cheeks which tapered down to a firm hard jawline, which would have given him a menacing air were it not for his lush and thick lips. He took one final look at Marc's naked and quaking body, lingering an instant too long on his cock and dangling balls, and then turned back to Cassius.

'Well, what has been happening here?' He repeated his question, this time with a note of menace in his voice.

'We had a bit of trouble, that's all,' Cassius replied, and indicated the bodies of Cimber and Alexander, their freshly spilt blood staining the rush-covered ground scarlet. His previous arrogance was gone: it was obvious that he was absolutely terrified of Gaius.

'I can see that, fool,' he barked, and reached out and touched

Marc's naked shoulder. 'Have you touched the boy?' he demanded.

'It was only a bit of fun, sir,' Cassius said. 'We meant no harm.'

'Has he been fucked yet?' Gaius said coldly. 'Have any of you bastards fucked him yet?'

'No, sir.'

Marc wasn't sure how to take the satisfied reply from Gaius. 'Good.'

Gaius smiled and gave Marc a long lascivious look. Marc shuddered. Was Gaius going to take him here and now, just as he had taken Justin? Was he going to fuck him senseless with the others looking on, wanking over them as Gaius pushed his cock further and further into Marc's waiting hole?

Gaius undid the golden fibula, the ornate brooch that fastened his cloak, and flung the garment at Marc. Marc caught it and looked curiously at the fibula. It was expensive and delicately made – far too expensive for the purse of a common Roman legionary, even one in a position of leadership as Gaius clearly was – and depicted the great god Pan, his disproportionately large penis hanging between his goat-legs.

'Stop gawking and get yourself covered up, boy,' he commanded. Marc frowned but nevertheless did as he was instructed. 'I've plans for you.' He glanced over at Cassius. 'Be thankful that the ship is leaving tonight. Otherwise things would be the worse for you.'

'It was only a bit of sport, sir,' Cassius repeated. 'We just thought that with General Decius away in Rome we could –'

Gaius arched an eyebrow. 'General Decius is still here in Britannia.'

Cassius's voice betrayed traces of panic. 'But I thought –'

'You thought? You thought? You're not paid to think. General Decius has remained here in Britannia,' Gaius repeated and made a show of bringing his hand down to rest on the hilt of his sword in a meaningful gesture. 'He is away attending to affairs in the north, putting down the last of Boudicca's troops. You do remember that, don't you, Cassius? Or have the affairs of the empire taken second place to your *sport*?'

Cassius took the hint and nodded. 'Of course not, sir,' he said. 'Stupid of me to forget.' He looked over at Marc, who was huddled up in Gaius's cloak. 'Will you be needing the boy?'

Gaius smiled, and Marc didn't know whether to be pleased or afraid at the subsequent words. 'Of course.'

'Needing me?' Marc asked hesitantly. 'Needing me for what?'

Gaius chuckled and shared a smile with Cassius and the others at Marc's innocence. It was an innocence that would shortly be fucked out of him, he knew, and he only hoped that it would be Gaius who would be the first to taste his innocence, to take his virginity. At least he would treat Marc better than an animal – which would have been Marc's fate at the hands and pricks of Cassius and his mob.

'You'll find out soon enough,' Gaius said. 'Both of us are going on a little journey.'

'A journey? Where to?' Suddenly Marc realised that he didn't know what was going on, or what was going to happen. Gaius's knowing smile did nothing to reassure him.

'Where else?' he laughed. 'To the seat of empire, to the Eternal City.

'To Rome.'

Three

──────────

The slave galley *Cygnus* ploughed through the waters of the Tyrrhenian Sea, driven on by the winds which had been growing ever stronger and more threatening since the departure from the shores of Britain. Obviously Neptune was having a bad day. One hundred pairs of oars cut through the wind-whipped waves; two hundred pairs of trained biceps stretched and strained, as they drove the galley ever closer to its destination: Rome, imperial capital of the world. And, if the tales that Marc's fellow slaves had told him were true, debauched and decadent beyond all belief and decency.

It had been just over two days now since they had passed through the Pillars of Hercules, five days since Marc had seen the white cliffs of his homeland for what he imagined to be the first and last time. The ship was a merchant, carrying on board a precious cargo of tin and copper from Britain, oils and wines from Hispania, and corn and spices from the northernmost tip of Africa.

But on board was a cargo more precious even than that. Men, most barely out of their teens, and none older than their late twenties, bodies bronzed by the sun of the open sea, muscles aching and glistening with salt water and sweat.

Behind them, towards the aft of the ship, leather-clad galleymasters cracked their whips, ensuring that they pulled on the oars that took them closer with every stroke to a life of slavery and submission in mighty Rome. Shackled by day, and locked away in the cargo hold at night like the chattel they were, they had no future. They belonged to the slave trade now, fit only to perform whatever services their future masters might so desire. Little more than possessions to be sold to the highest bidder. Little more than hunks of prime and juicy meat.

'You'll be all right,' the oarsman beside Marc said, as he pulled another stroke on his oar, the muscles in his broad and sun-browned back flexing with the effort. A thin trickle of sweat ran down his backbone, nestling in the crack of his arse, just visible above the top of his leather shorts.

This was the first time the taciturn oarsman had spoken to Marc since he'd been brought on board the ship when it had briefly docked in Africa two days ago. However, Marc already knew that his name was Karl. Word among the other slaves was that he had been a rebel who had been trying to foment rebellion against the Roman occupiers of the Colonia Julia Carthago on the northwestern tip of Africa.

Karl was the very model of a rebel leader. He was several years older than Marc, tall and well built, broad muscular shoulders accentuating his tapering waist, on which there wasn't an inch of fat. His arms were powerful, dripping now with beads of sweat; his forearms were covered with black hairs; his upper right arm was tattooed with an elaborate ring of thorns which circled his entire biceps.

Karl's chest was slightly out of proportion to the rest of his body: two massive pectorals, hairless, save for a few wisps of black around his dark-brown nipples. The left one had been pierced with a tiny silver ring, a fashion Marc had seen in the barbarians of the north, but not among his own native Britons or the more elegant Romans.

There was also a ring in Karl's navel, and attached to that ring was a tiny symbol, like a Greek alpha or a stylised fish. Many had been the time in the past few days when Marc had gazed, fascinated by that body piercing, and the line of dark hair that trailed from it down into the brief pair of leather shorts, which was all that the barbarian wore, day and night. Karl exuded dark and dangerous masculinity from the top of his head, the thick dark hair waxed into a spiky quiff, down to his powerful runner's legs and leather-sandalled feet.

'What do you mean, I'll be safe?' Marc asked naïvely, and wondered why the older man grinned crookedly at him. When he smiled, a dimple appeared in his right cheek, lightening his hard features with something approaching a roguish charm.

'By God, but you *are* an innocent, aren't you?' Karl said.

He spoke a rough, uneducated Latin, hardly surprising for a barbarian from far-off Germanica; then again, Marc was impressed that a barbarian from one of the empire's far-off dominions was able to speak any Latin at all. Karl pulled once again on his oar, as the galleymasters cracked their whips in the air, threatening the slaves with the lash if they didn't keep up the rhythm of their rowing.

'Do you have the slightest idea of what's going to happen to us when we get to Rome?' Karl asked, his tone indicating that he knew very well.

Marc shifted uneasily on the wooden bench to which the galleymasters had chained him by the feet. Although Karl was only three or four years older than he was, he felt like a small child beside the cynical and hard-bitten barbarian, awkward with his brutal directness. He was fascinated to the point of obsession at the same time: there was something about Karl, an element in his personality and demeanour that reminded Marc of his departed Alexander, his first love, who had been taken from him before they could even consummate their emotions.

Perhaps it was that air of danger, of wild and natural strength; or perhaps it was nothing more complicated than simple lust.

'We're being taken to Rome as slaves,' Marc said bitterly. 'To do the empire's bidding till the day we die.'

Karl smirked, paused in his rowing and looked a little pityingly at Marc. Behind them, the galleymaster cracked his whip again. Karl shouted back a curse in his native tongue and spat contemptuously on the deck, before resuming his hard and steady strokes. Marc watched Karl's arms strain with the effort as his veins pumped blood to his muscles.

'And what do you think that means?' Karl asked. 'Running around after the local dignitaries, making sure that their wine flagons are full, or that they've stuffed their stomachs till they're bursting?'

'Yes . . .' said Marc unsurely. From the German's tone it was obvious that Marc was showing up his naïvety – or was that stupidity? His earlier thoughts – being surprised that Karl could speak Latin – vanished. In their current situation, all of Cimber's books and lessons meant nothing. If Marc was going to survive, he was going to have to stick close to the German.

'Grow up, little Briton,' Karl said, but not without some humour in his gruff voice. 'It's about being owned body and soul by some bastard of a Roman master, carrying out whatever tasks he wants – no matter how filthy and perverted it makes you feel. And getting the life flogged out of you when you refuse, or when you don't come up to your master's expectations.' Karl nodded over to their fellow oarsmen, toiling under the galleymaster's whip. 'Half of this lot will be dead within the year. The rest they'll probably throw to the lions in the arena. Some, if they're lucky, might get the chance to win their freedom in the Games. But, like I said, it'll be different for you . . .'

'You didn't tell me what you meant,' Marc reminded him uncertainly.

Gods, Karl's expression seemed to say: can this blasted Briton really be so naïve? Maybe it's time to teach him some of the meaner facts of life.

'You ever been fucked up the arse?' he said bluntly.

Marc turned away, embarrassed and yet aroused at the same time by Karl's bluntness. 'No,' he said, wondering why he felt half ashamed at the admission.

'You will be,' came back Karl's reply. 'A good-looking boy like you will have had half a hundred Roman cocks coming up his tight arsehole before the year's out. Your Roman master will have you on your knees, making you lick his balls, before forcing his cock down your throat until you gag. And all the while his friends will be fucking you from behind like the pathetic little dog they believe you to be.

'They'll tie you up and piss on you. Maybe worse. Imagine it. Ten rampant pricks fucking you in the mouth, fucking you up that tight, virgin arse of yours. One after another, till you think that you can't bear another prick up you. Then wanking over you, shooting their hot and creamy load all over you. Drowning you in it.

'Forcing you to lick out their own filthy holes. Squeezing your tits until you beg for mercy. Tying your balls so tightly that even though you want to come you can't. And then they'll start whipping you on that cute little arse to punish you for being their filthy little sex-slave.

'And when they've had enough of you, when they've fucked you red-raw and come all over those raw and tender tits, then they'll toss you aside like the used piece of meat you really are.'

Then Karl raised an eyebrow. 'Of course, a proper good fucking up the arse might be exactly what you need,' he sneered.

'You're wrong,' Marc said, but Karl had already noticed the hardness beneath Marc's shorts. He grinned to himself, as Marc turned his face away, and applied himself to his rowing with even more concentration than usual.

'Of course I am,' Karl said sarcastically.

'And is that what's going to happen to you as well?' Marc asked, turning the German's question back on him. 'I can imagine there's lots of Romans who'd do anything to be serviced by someone as –' He hastily interrupted himself. 'By someone like you.'

'Feel my barbarian cock up their imperial arses?' Karl asked in amusement.

'If you like.'

'My cock and my arse are my own. I use them the way I choose. When I screw a Roman, it'll be when *I* decide.'

'You might not get the choice.'

Karl looked around to make sure that none of their fellow slaves, and especially the galleymaster, was listening, and then lowered his voice.

'The moment this hulk comes into port I'm escaping,' he said in a conspiratorial whisper. 'I'll rip out the throat of any Roman who tries to stop me. I hate the whole bastard lot of them.'

Marc allowed himself a tiny sad smile, and decided to confide in the German. 'You remind me of a friend I used to know,' he said. 'He was older than you but just as much a fighter. He was a barbarian, too, just like you.' Realising what he had said, he quickly added, 'I'm sorry, I didn't mean . . .'

Karl ignored the perceived slight, and looked knowingly at Marc. 'Some fighter he was, if he let you be captured by these Roman dogs,' he sneered. 'What'd your "friend" do? Turn tail and get his barbarian arse away as soon as the Romans turned up?'

Marc's tone was quiet as he replied. 'No. He died. Alexander is dead now.' The sight of Alexander's bleeding corpse on the floor of Cimber's hut appeared in Marc's mind. They'd never had the time to tell each other what they meant to each other, and he cursed the Romans for that.

He felt Karl's hand rest heavily on his shoulder for a moment, before a warning shout from the galleymaster made the German resume his rowing.

'Marc, I'm sorry, believe me,' Karl said – and meant it. The sardonic tone in his voice had now been replaced by one of genuine sympathy. And perhaps something else as well. 'My brother was killed by the bastards when he was trying to turn the Batavi against the oppressors. I know how it feels to lose someone you love.'

'I never said that I loved . . .' Marc began, and then his voice trailed away. It suddenly struck him. 'I never told you my name.'

'No, you didn't, did you?' Karl said, and fixed Marc with a brief meaningful look of dark-grey eyes, before asking Marc how Alexander had died. When Marc had told him about Alexander and Cimber's death and the rape and pillaging of his home village, he frowned.

'Why punish your village, when you were supporters of the Romans?'

'My father did what he had to do,' Marc said loyally, before agreeing with Karl.

'I heard that Boudicca and eighty thousand of her army were wiped out last year,' Karl said. 'Your Alexander was right. Why stir further ill feelings by taking their revenge the way they did? Especially now that Rome is taking a more liberal policy towards your homeland.'

'If this Obsidian Legion – whoever they really are – treat their friends like this, imagine what they do to their enemies,' Marc said. The rumours that the Obsidian Legion were the empire's shock troops seemed to ring true, but there were still areas of doubt. There was something else going on, some other reason why the Obsidian Legion existed, and why they had attacked Marc's town. And then there were Cimber's last words: 'The empire is in danger,' he had said. 'Warn the Emperor.'

'The British tribes are a dangerous lot,' Karl continued with a worried look on his face. He carried on rowing, but it was obvious that his thoughts were elsewhere. 'They're wild, unpredictable and ruthless fighters. Boudicca and the Iceni proved that, and there are now seventy thousand widows and orphans in Rome. Push the British too much and their wrath could reach as far as the imperial palace itself.'

'I'd imagine you'd like that,' Marc said, but Karl shook his head.

'It doesn't make sense, Marc,' he replied. 'Why put the empire at risk?'

'Who knows?' Marc said. 'Gaius is a member of the Obsidian Legion. He would know.'

Karl smiled. 'And you think he'll tell us?' he asked, and pulled again on his oar. 'He's a strange one. There's something about him that doesn't quite ring true. What's a legionary like him doing on board a slave ship heading for Rome?'

'I've hardly seen him on deck since we set sail from Britain,' Marc said. Which seemed odd, he thought, especially since Gaius had shown such an interest in Marc earlier.

'He stays in his cabin most of the time,' Karl said. 'Doing gods know what. But there's one thing that I do know, Marc: whoever Gaius is, he certainly isn't a common legionary.'

Marc frowned. 'Then what is he?'

Karl fixed Marc with a knowing smile. 'Maybe you'll get the change to find out – *if* you're lucky,' he said, and, before Marc could ask the barbarian what he meant, Karl fell silent and concentrated on his oarsmanship, refusing to answer any more questions.

As Marc continued pulling on the oars, occasionally stealing a glance at Karl, who would hurriedly turn his face away, a thousand and one questions filled his mind. Who were the Obsidian Legion really? And why were they trying to stir up more anti-Roman sentiment back home in Britannia? Was Karl right about the life destined for him in Rome? And, if Gaius was much more than a mere legionary, then what was he?

And as they drew ever nearer to Rome and the oncoming storm, Marc thought back to a certain incident a few nights ago . . .

It had been the third evening of Marc's captivity and the *Cygnus* had just cleared the northeastern coast of Hispania on its way to the Pillars of Hercules, there to pick up more cargo of wine and slaves. Unable to sleep for more than a few restless hours in the cramped hold, he lay awake, listening to the lapping of the waves on the side of the ship and the murmured snoring of his fellow slaves. Occasionally he would hear a furtive fumbling in the dark, and shortly thereafter a muffled groaning, but he gave it little thought.

Although it was the dead of night, it was almost unbearably hot. The only ventilation came from a small porthole, through which the light of the moon – full and burning like a silver sun – poured in. Some said that a storm was on its way any day now and the air was dull and muggy, the smell of hot male bodies overpowering.

Suddenly Marc was aware of the door creaking open, and someone entering the cargo hold. He turned around on to his side to see who was still awake at this hour of the night. The figure was silhouetted in the light coming in through the cabin window, and he couldn't make out the face, just the man's slim and youthful body, naked in the moonlight.

'Marc?' came the whispered voice, which sounded strangely familiar. 'Marc, are you awake?'

Marc realised who it was. 'Justin? Justin, is that you?'

The last Marc had seen of Justin had been in the marketplace, going off with Gaius and Varus. He had no idea that the boy was on board ship.

'Sssh,' Justin hissed and knelt down beside Marc. 'Gaius doesn't know I'm here. I've been in his cabin ever since we left home.'

'Why?' Marc whispered, and realised just how stupid he sounded. Why else?

'Why do you think?' Justin asked. 'But he's not interested in me any more. He hasn't come near me for a whole day now. It's as if he's got something on his mind. Or some*one*.'

Justin moved closer to Marc, until Marc could smell the boy's hot breath on his face. Beneath his blanket Marc could feel himself stir at just the thought of Justin's nearness. He could also smell something else as well – the warm, dark-brown smell of freshly fucked arse. Gaius might not have been near Justin for a whole day now, but it seemed that not all the slave galley's crew had been so uncooperative.

A soldier's fucking little whore-slave, Marc remembered Gaius calling Justin. He had been wrong. It seemed Justin was just a whore, plain and simple. So why did that excite Marc so much?

'It's so lonely in that cabin, Marc,' Justin said as he shuffled on his knees until his cock was almost on a level with Marc's face. He spread his knees apart and began to tug gently on his cock. Marc turned his face away, as he found his own cock starting to grow harder and his heart beating faster.

'Go back to bed, Justin,' he said. 'You'll feel different in the morning.' It wasn't that Marc wasn't aroused: it just didn't seem the right thing to do. When Marc lost his innocence, he wanted it to be with someone special, someone who meant something. It should have been Alexander, but fate – and the Roman Empire – had intervened. Whoever it was, it wasn't going to be Justin; Marc had no intention of being just another of Justin's conquests.

'No, I won't, I know I won't,' Justin said, affecting a sad and disaffected tone. 'He doesn't treat me like he used to – not since he set eyes on you.'

Marc turned around and looked at Justin's cock. It was long and hard now, gleaming silver in the moonlight, like a spear.

Justin was stroking it fondly, circling its tip with his thumb, while his other hand played with his balls.

'Justin, no,' Marc said, even though it was all he could do to stop himself from reaching out and cupping those balls in his hands, before taking Justin's whole length into his mouth, just as he had seen the whore-slave do to Gaius in the marketplace. His body called out for it, called out for the relief that Justin could offer. But his strength of will took over: Wait for someone special, Marc, it seemed to say, or you'll regret it.

Justin continued to play with his cock, waving it tantalisingly in Marc's face. Marc tried to turn away, but found that he couldn't. The nearness of Justin's whore-cock to his mouth was almost too much to bear. Marc's lips had suddenly become dry, and he licked them with his tongue. The moonlight gleamed off his saliva. He looked up at Justin, who seemed to be towering above him. There was a knowing and manipulative look in the boy's far-from-innocent eyes.

'*Please,* Marc,' he crooned seductively. 'Just this once. Let me feel it. Let me feel your hot, wet tongue the whole length of my dick. I want it so much, you should know that. I need to feel my hot throbbing cock in your mouth, feel you lick it and suck it and love it and swallow it whole.'

'Justin . . .'

'And you want it too, I can tell that. I saw you watching me in the marketplace the other day. I saw that look in your eyes, when Gaius was fucking me with his meaty cock. You can't wait for it, can you? You can't wait to feel my long, hard prick deep down inside you.' He pulled back the foreskin, so that the head was fully exposed in the moonlight. 'Come on, Marc, you need it too. No one need ever know. Take it all, every last inch of it. Taste it. Suck it. Love it. Feel all that hardness moving inside you. Pumping away. Going in and out. Glistening with your mouth's juices. Filling you up. Fucking you. Fucking your mouth.'

Marc squirmed, so transfixed by the sight of cock that he

didn't even notice Justin remove his bedclothes to reveal his own aching tumescence. Justin spat into the palm of his hand and reached out and started to rub his hand up and down Marc's cock.

'It's so hard, so perfect,' Justin whispered seductively. 'You see, I knew you wanted it as much as me. I want to feel it inside me. Feel your cock inside me. Oh, yes, feel you rip me apart with your beautiful, beautiful prick. Feel your balls slapping against my arse as you pump deeper and deeper and deeper into me. Making me scream out with pleasure. Drawing you further into me. Feeling every inch. Feeling you shudder as you can't hold back any longer and you shoot your hot come all over me, over my arse, over my back, over my belly, till I'm covered in your spunk. Come on, Marc, you know you need it as much as me. Suck me. Fuck me. Now . . .'

Marc moaned with pleasure, not bothering if he woke up any of his sleeping fellow slaves in the hold. Who cared if Justin was a whore-slave who was prepared to fuck or be fucked by anyone? That was just what Marc's destiny was too. A fucking whore-slave, nothing more, nothing less, just like Justin, begging for it. Begging for what had been denied him so long. Begging for cock. For long, hard, marvellous cock.

Cock. That was all that mattered in the world. Men's big cocks, full of come, aching to explode. Hard, magnificent cocks, ready to tear apart his insides, sliding in and out of his body, taking him, violating him. His attention returned to his own penis, as Justin continued to pump it up and down, till he could hardly bear it any more and he was ready to explode as he felt the come rise inside him. And Justin's cock, long, beautiful and mastering, ready to shove itself into his waiting mouth.

Without taking a hand off either of their pricks, Justin moved so that he was now sitting astride Marc, the tip of his manhood just one tantalising inch from Marc's open mouth.

Marc leant forward, yearning to taste Justin's erect flesh.

Knowing that he could wait no longer. He had to taste Justin, he had to have that hard and silky flesh inside him. He had to know what a man tasted like. He licked his lips, and his tongue reached out and tentatively touched the tip of Justin's prick. Justin threw his head back in ecstasy at the contact.

'Gods!' Justin breathed though gritted teeth, and reared up, ready to plunge his prick into the moist velvet of Marc's waiting mouth. Sweat was dripping off his brow, his breath coming in short, harsh bursts. 'Take it all, you fucking hungry bastard. Every last fucking inch. Let me fill you with my load. Suck all of me into your mouth. Suck me till I'm dry. Take it, take it, take it, like the fucking little whore-slave that you are!'

On hearing Gaius's words again, those words that had excited him so much in the marketplace, Marc could wait no longer. Despite his determination to wait, his body, his senses, had other ideas. He plunged his mouth on to Justin's waiting dick, wanting to eat it all up, take it all, right up to the balls that slapped against his chin, as Justin rammed his cock further and deeper into Marc's mouth.

Justin grabbed hold of Marc's head with his free hand, pulling him further down on to him. Justin's prick had now become so engorged that Marc could hardly breathe, but that didn't matter. All that mattered was that hot, massive shaft, having it inside him, filling him up, making him squirm with pleasure and pain and ecstasy. And fucking him, fucking him, yes, *fucking him*!

Justin's hand, lubricated with spit and pre-come, continued to pump up and down on Marc's cock, and he felt exquisite shafts of painful pleasure aching throughout his prick, growing more and more unbearable, until his maddened senses could bear it no more. He sucked greedily on Justin's own tool, willing him to come with him, desperate to taste his beautiful come. Justin screamed with pleasure: he was very close to release. Probably as close as Marc was.

'Yes, oh yes, take it, take every last fucking drop of it! Take it all!'

Suddenly, Justin's cock was no longer in Marc's mouth, his hand no longer wrapped around his cock. In the moon-drenched dimness Marc felt drops of hot fluid spatter his chest. Marc reached out to draw the precious cock back, not wanting to be denied one moment of its exquisite hardness.

That was when he realised that Justin was no longer sitting astride him. He looked up, and, as if in a dream, saw Gaius drag the naked boy away from him.

Gaius was naked from the waist up, his hair falling over his broad, honey-coloured shoulders. A cruel sadistic look marred his otherwise handsome features: he was furious. But how furious? Would he have both Justin and Marc put to the sword? Marc watched on in horror as Gaius slapped Justin across the face, spat out a curse, and then dragged the boy roughly out of the hold. Before doing so, the Roman paused for one second, and looked strangely at Marc. Was it tenderness that Marc imagined he saw in those dark and long-lashed eyes? Jealousy? Or simply sheer naked desire?

Or was it something else? Something much more meaning-ful? To get to the heart of this entire mystery, Marc would have to unlock the secrets within Gaius. But there was nothing he could do now, not with the barely restrained anger that virtually radiated from the Roman.

There was fear in Justin's eyes as Gaius dragged him away: what would happen to him? His eyes pleaded with Marc to help, but he was frozen; part of him became accusatory, saying that this was the second time he had stood by and watched Gaius take Justin – stood by and done nothing to help. But what could he do? As Gaius and Justin walked through the door, Marc sat there in the moonlight, unable to move, unable to think. He stayed like that until morning.

Marc must have fallen asleep because he woke up the next morning. But he couldn't quite decide whether he had dreamt the entire incident. However, the dried stains of white on his bedclothes were real enough. It *had* happened.

But from that day on, Marc never saw Justin again. Such was the absolute power of the Obsidian Legion.

Now, some nights later, as he lay awake in the hold, Marc found himself thinking of Gaius and Justin. The storm was fast approaching, and the lurching of the *Cygnus* to and fro had kept him awake, although it was long past midnight. Even the reassuring moonlight was absent: the black thunderheads hung above them, dark and pendulous, cutting out the light.

Gaius had ordered half of the *Cygnus*'s slave crew to remain on deck, hoping to reach the Italian coast a day earlier than intended, and thereby avoid the worst of the storm. Soon it would be the fourth hour of the morning and Marc's turn to man the oars.

He had heard Karl come in an hour ago, and had turned over towards him to watch him strip down to his leather shorts: the German had been wearing a loose flaxen top to ward off the chill night air. But the barbarian had merely grunted a brusque 'goodnight' to him before slipping in beneath the covers on the wooden pallet beside Marc's own bed and turning his naked back towards him. For long, almost unbearable minutes, Marc lay listening to Karl's heavy breathing, wondering whether he was sleeping, or if he should break the silence and wake him. But then he heard Karl's deep guttural snores and knew that it was too late.

Lying awake in the darkness, listening to the sound of the waves of the Tyrrhenian Sea as they lapped louder and louder against the side of the *Cygnus*, Marc found himself once more thinking of that night when Justin had offered him his cock, and he had accepted it greedily. Had it really all been a dream, one of those special dreams that his older sisters used to tease him about when they entered his bedchamber in the mornings, when they found the sheets sticky and damp from his vivid dreams?

Whatever it had been, Marc knew that he wanted more, much more, of what had been so brutally taken away from him by Gaius. Gaius, with the long raven locks, the smooth and honey-coloured body, and the prick that he had seen thrusting its way in and out of Justin's welcoming arse. That beautiful prick, its head dripping with come, pearls of white suspended in the mound of his dark bush of hair.

Marc felt a familiar stiffness underneath the blanket and he reached down and gently rubbed the tips of his fingers up and down his cock, from its base to the tiny slit at its bulbous head. His prick twitched in anticipation, begging for release, growing harder and harder as Marc increased the pressure.

From Marc's right-hand side there came a noise. He turned on to his side. It was only Karl, grunting in his sleep. The coarse cloth that served as a blanket had fallen down his back, revealing his broad shoulder muscles, bunched and sinewy, two perfect V shapes, tapering down to his pert arse.

Karl was cuddling himself for warmth, his hands clasped around his back. In the darkness, it almost seemed as though someone else was holding him, another's flesh against his flesh, Karl's arms enfolding him, protecting him, his perfect pectorals pressed against the other's, the ring on his left tit cold against another warm body.

Satisfied that Karl was asleep, Marc continued to rub his prick up and down, feeling the shudders of delight as he remembered the taste of cock in his mouth. He started slowly, trying to control the aching in his loins, and, as the pleasure rose in him, he kicked off the bedclothes, so that his cock was exposed, upright and beautiful in the darkness of the cargo hold. The thought that any of his fellow slaves – and Karl especially – could wake up at any second filled him with a wild excitement and he fastened even tighter hold of the shaft, while his thumb circled the head, pulling down the tiny foreskin, and pressing hard into the purple helmet.

Suddenly Marc heard a clicking sound from the far end of the hold. He froze, his cock still enclosed in the firm embrace of his fist. Then he breathed a sigh of relief and relaxed: it was only the creaking of the ship's timbers, struggling to weather the approaching storm.

Marc's other hand reached for his left nipple, tweaking it as the slave traders had done in Britain, but gentler, as he could somehow imagine Karl doing. His nipple responded instantly, stiffening at the touch, and he twisted it harder, flicking it with his index finger and sending unaccustomed sensations of pleasure-filled pain throughout his youthful body.

His cock replied in kind, growing harder and larger until Marc thought it would burst, until the whole world had concentrated down to the feelings running up and down the length of his prick. He increased the speed of his hand, and he started to move his groin rhythmically up and down, fucking his fist, just as Justin had fucked his mouth, just as he had seen Gaius's cock shove its relentless way up and into the boy's arsehole.

Marc closed his eyes, tugged even harder on his left nipple. He imagined a man's lips, lush and hungry, kissing his tits, hard dark stubble scratching his smooth skin. Then he felt the lips open, and a tongue snake in a circle around the areola.

Then teeth, tugging at the tiny chest hairs, gently, playfully even, before turning their attention to the nipples themselves. Teasing them at first, pecking at them, before coming full down, and biting them so hard that it was all Marc could do not to shout out loud. To shout out and beg the faceless stranger to stop, to stop . . . But he didn't want him to stop, he wanted him to continue, to take him, to fill him with his manhood and hot salty load. He wanted to be taken by a real man, not someone like Justin, but someone like Alexander . . . or Karl.

He splayed open his hand and encompassed his left chest muscle in his palm, digging his fingers hard into the firm pectoral and massaging it. He moaned with delight, and pumped harder and harder on his cock, faster and faster.

Now his free hand was trailing its way down the side of his body, along the defined abdominal muscles, over his flat belly and past his cock, where it fondled his balls, cupping them and squeezing them gently in time with the jerking of his cock. He could feel the come in his swollen balls, ready to shoot out its milk-white load, ready to drown the whole fucking world in his seed.

But shit, he wasn't ready yet. No, this was too good ever to end. As he felt the come rise in his balls, he squeezed his cock tightly at its base. He slowed the pace of his wanking: he was on the brink, but he wanted this moment, this feeling, to last.

He inserted a finger into his arsehole, feeling the sphincter muscle resist momentarily, before allowing him into its warm moistness. Gently he moved his digit up and down, as he searched out the gently quivering bud that he knew was in there.

When he found it, spasms of pleasure filled his insides, as he tweaked it, and pushed it and circled it till he felt the sperm rise towards his prick-slit.

Gods, it felt so good. Fucking his own virgin arse, with Karl and fifty other slaves asleep beside him. Running the exquisite risk that any of them might wake up at any second. Fucking his own hole, his own fist, showing no mercy to himself. Pumping himself till he thought he would scream. His arse moving up and down. Thrashing around on the bed like a dog on heat. Feeling the come, that beautiful love juice, force its way up his cock.

Thinking of cock, thinking of arse. Thinking of Karl's thighs, Karl's tits, and his piercings, and his tattoo. Thinking of his arms, of his hands, large and heavily veined, strong powerful fingers ready to grab his prick in an iron embrace.

And his cock, that massive slice of meat that he had not yet seen. Feeling that barbarian prick inside him. Up his arse. In his mouth. Two cocks. Rock-hard and relentless. Two cocks, fucking him at the same time. *Karl* fucking him at the same time. Cock in his mouth. Cock in his arse. *Karl* inside him. Deep, deep inside him. Pushing in and pushing out. Further and further. Cock glistening, hard and hot and wet. Karl on top of him, Karl behind him, throwing his head back in ecstasy. Screaming for release. The final thrust. Deeper and harder and more painful and more glorious and more fucking perfect than anything else in the world. Karl spurting out all over him. An ocean of come over his chest. His belly. His hair. Karl inside him. Karl all over him.

'*Fuck me, Karl! Fuck me!*' Marc growled through gritted teeth. He could bear it no longer. He bucked and jerked on the bed, and his back arched, as thick fountains of come shot out from his cock, as he wanked himself into oblivion. Once, twice, three, four, five times. Over his tits. Over his face. In his hair. Drops of come on his eyelashes.

He fell back on to the bed, exhausted, and gently took his hand away from his trembling cock. In the half-light of the suddenly revealed moon through the port window, he could see the come strung between his thumb and forefinger. He brought his hand to his belly and smeared the stickiness all over his chest, over his face and mouth, bringing his fingers to his lips, tasting the sweet, salty fluid.

With a contented smile, Marc finally fell asleep, oblivious to the wind now howling outside, or the sound of the waves as they crashed against the hull of the *Cygnus*.

And as Marc did so, beside him, Karl, now fully awake, grinned knowingly to himself, and turned back over to sleep, his own erection hard and wet in his hand. And at the far end of the hold, unnoticed by either Marc or Karl, the door clicked shut, and Gaius, who had seen everything, left the cargo hold.

* * *

As the legionary made his way back to his cabin, he moved uncertainly on his feet. Gaius had never been a good seaman – in fact, until his secret mission to Britain, he had barely ever set foot outside Rome before – and he made yet another silent plea to Neptune and Aeolus, the Wind Lord, that they would reach land safely. The wind was battering the weathered timbers of the ship, and even the galleymasters and professional seamen were looking worried, as it whipped the sea into a maelstrom worthy of the death waters of Charybdis itself.

In his dreams, Marc was visited by a stranger, tall, and naked save for a brief white loincloth and golden sandals, which rose to just below his knees. A band of gold encircled his upper arm, and about his neck there hung a charm or amulet which gleamed with the brilliance of a thousand stars. Marc frowned. It reminded him of the pendant that Cimber had always worn. But whoever this stranger was, it certainly wasn't his old teacher.

The sun was behind the stranger, so Marc could see him only in silhouette. He was broad-shouldered, and slim-waisted, and walked with the effortless agility and assurance of a dancer or a swimmer. Or a big cat, stalking its prey. Although not as broad or as sturdy as some of the slaves on board the galley, the mysterious stranger gave forth a power and a strength that seemed to Marc to be almost superhuman.

He couldn't see the face of the man – if he was a man, that was, and not some spirit sent down from the home of the gods. Golden light shone in his tousled curls, which were the colour of the rising sun itself. He approached Marc, and Marc felt the man take his hands in his, drawing him into his warm and welcoming embrace. He offered no resistance, longing to give himself up totally to the spirit. The world seemed to spin around Marc and from somewhere far off he heard a familiar voice call out his name.

Marc . . . Marc . . .

71

It was the stranger, calling him to him. Drawing him to him as surely as nectar draws the bee, as the siren lures the unwary seaman. Marc smiled dreamily to himself, willing himself to succumb to the mysterious stranger's advances, ready to surrender, body and soul, to his arms. The stranger's firm hands caressed his face, traced the outline of his lips with a touch that burnt with the fire of heaven, moved downward, past his neck, down his chest and his heart, which seemed ready to leap out of his breast, towards his waiting cock, erect and ready.

Marc . . . Marc . . . Marc . . .

And then the stranger abruptly grabbed him by the shoulders and shook him roughly. Marc felt a cold hard slap on his face, which brought tears of salt water to his eyes, a red welt to his cheek.

'Marc, wake up!' A familiar voice barked in his ear. 'For all that's holy, wake up!'

Marc opened his eyes: Karl was peering down at him. It was the German who had shaken him awake and was even now roughly dragging him out of bed, seemingly ignorant of Marc's erection, which pushed against his shorts. And the slap Marc had felt had been the cold splash of seawater on his face, salty, sudden and bitterly cold.

For a half-second Marc thought he'd overslept and that the man brutally dragging him to his feet had been his galleymaster. And then the shock of another cold splash of seawater knocked him to his senses, and he took in with horror the scene before him. Seawater gushing in through the hole in the side of the cargo hold. Slaves scrambling towards the door, which was no longer manned by the guards, who had run off to save their own lives, who must have been falling over each other in their efforts to reach the top deck and jump ship, before the sea claimed the galley as her own. Panic and confusion reigned all around him, and Marc was rooted to the spot, unsure of what to do or where to go. Suddenly, Karl grabbed his arm so forcefully that it was almost ripped out of its socket.

'We've hit the rocks – we're going down,' he called out, raising his voice to be heard above the screams and shouts of the other men, the roar of the storm on the upper deck, the thunderous rush of water pouring into the hold.

Already Marc could feel the boat start to lurch and keel over, knocking him off balance. The water had obviously broken though into other parts of the hull as well, and the vessel was becoming top-heavy. As Marc and Karl climbed the creaking wooden steps leading to the upper deck they heard screams of terror from the oarsmen. Shackled to one another by the feet, they had no chance of escaping the ocean surging in through the gaping holes in the hull, now that their galleymasters had abandoned them to their fate.

They staggered towards the open hatchway, trampling each other in their efforts to save themselves. The raging waters had reached their chests now; the weaker ones had already fallen under the water, their drowned bodies pulling down and slowing their stronger companions.

'We can't leave them here,' Marc protested, and then coughed, as salt water gushed into his open mouth.

'We can't *not* leave them,' Karl grunted, and dragged Marc roughly through the hatchway and on to the open deck, as the waters rose faster and faster now, and the ship started to keel over at an even more acute and deadly angle.

The storm was in full force now, wind and rain mercilessly lashing the mainsail, and the steering sail at the fore-end was already half submerged. The top deck was cracking up under the strain, as the galley foundered in the rocks that lurked near the Italian coast. Within seconds, the entire ship would go down, Romans, cargo, slaves and all. There wasn't a moment to lose.

Wind blasted and seared Marc's and Karl's eyes, the salt water making them sting, as they saw those slaves and Romans who had escaped make the sickening jump off the starboard side and into the churning maelstrom below. Few of them had any chance of survival: in that watery hell only the strongest swimmers would be able to survive.

The night was still dark – although Marc guessed it was way past the fourth hour – and it was becoming more and more difficult to see, with the salt water spray and the thunderous clouds overhead. But as Karl dragged Marc up towards the side of the *Cygnus* Marc thought he saw a man in legionary's garb head not for the chance of safety with his compatriots but towards the open hatch leading down to the oarsmen's quarters. He had no time to question Gaius's apparent suicidal intention, for Karl had grabbed hold of him tightly with both his hands, and they were even now jumping off the side of the ship and into the murky waters below.

The impact as they hit water took the breath out of Marc, and he felt himself become dizzy. It was only the knowledge that Karl's strong arms were wrapped around him that kept him conscious, as they went down for a first, and then a second time.

Karl started to swim away from the *Cygnus* and indicated that Marc should do the same. Arms aching, muscles stretching beyond all endurance, they moved away from the sinking ship with long powerful strokes, anxious to avoid being dragged down by the swell that Karl knew would follow as soon the *Cygnus* sank beneath the waves.

They paused for a second and turned around, treading water as they watched the mighty galley finally give itself up to its watery grave. Prow first, it plummeted beneath the sea, until all that was left of it was its stern and the once-proud figurehead of a swan, wrenched from its position of honour on the bow, now broken and pitiful. And then that, too, sank beneath the waves, along with Gaius, and the shackled slaves, and all those others who had escaped but had stayed too close to the sinking ship.

Far off in the distance they could see a few faint lights and the dark shape of nearby land, silhouetted against the blue-black starry sky. It was at least an hour's swim away, and the cold waters of the Tyrrhenian Sea were already starting to numb their arms and legs.

They were free men at last, Marc realised wryly. No longer Roman slaves, but free.

Free to die beneath the all-conquering waves.

Four

M arc awoke, to feel the touch of warm sand against his face, the burning heat of the sun on his bare back. His lips were dry and crusted, his throat parched. His arms and legs were aching, and there was a stinging just above his right shoulder blade.

A hand touched him gently on the shoulder, and, for a moment, Marc thought he was dreaming again. Was it the golden-haired god from the night who had returned for him? And then he remembered the shipwreck, and how his body had started to fail him when he and Karl were almost within sight of land. He had become delirious, he seemed to recall, his arms and legs moving numbly and instinctively.

He must be dead. Yes, that was it, he was dead, and the golden-haired god was one of the servants of the Lord of the Dead, come to escort him on the long journey down into the Underworld.

'Marc?' The god's voice was deep and dark. He shook Marc lightly by the shoulder. 'Marc, wake up.'

The god gently turned Marc over on to his back, and Marc

squinted, shielding his eyes from the sun, which was overhead, silhouetting the god once more in its light.

No, it wasn't the god. It was Karl, kneeling over him, his hard and handsome face now etched with worry. The sun cast shadows on his body, highlighting his firm chest muscles even more, and, as he turned, the ring in his left nipple glinted in the light.

Karl bent down closer, until Marc could almost feel the barbarian's breath on his cheeks. He tried to speak but Karl silenced him with a finger on the lips.

'Not yet,' Karl said, his voice softer than Marc had ever heard it before. 'Drink some of this.'

Karl brought a small hollowed piece of tree bark, filled with water, to Marc's parched lips and made him sip. The water was fresh and cool, as sweet and as refreshing as he imagined nectar must taste to the gods. Marc sipped thirstily on it, and then coughed and spluttered. He looked up to see Karl grinning at him, and once again he felt like a child in the older man's presence, a little boy who had been much too greedy for his own good.

'You swallowed a lot of salt water out there,' Karl said and nodded out to the sea, now so peaceful and calm after last night's storm. 'Drink this slowly. It's fresh water. It'll make you feel better.'

Karl reached out and helped Marc to sit up, supporting him with his right arm, the one with the tattoo encircling the biceps. Marc leant against him for support, his head resting against Karl's shoulder.

'Where are we?' he asked, once he felt strong enough to speak. His voice was rasping, though, so he drank some more of the water.

Karl shrugged. 'Who cares?' he said, and moved away from Marc. Marc's body shuddered involuntarily, longing for the touch of Karl's skin against his again. 'Rome.'

Marc looked around, at the scrub which lined the beach, and

the thick wood of cypresses and sycamores beyond that, and, even further in the distance, the green-covered hills, and then the faraway mountains, purple and blue in the midday haze.

'This isn't Rome,' said Marc, trying to remember the engravings of the Eternal City that Cimber had shown him. 'We're probably near there, though. That would have been where Gaius was heading, and I doubt that the *Cygnus* would have veered that far off course.'

'And you'd be the one to know, would you?' Karl said and stood up. 'As far as I'm concerned, any place in their blasted empire is Rome. The whole place stinks of Roman. They're like cats, pissing to mark their territory. Everything they touch reeks of their corruption.'

Marc finished the last of the water and then tried to stand up. Much to his surprise, he found he could, although his legs felt distinctly unsteady. Karl looked strangely at him, but made no attempt to help. It was as if he considered his earlier act of kindness some sort of weakness, and he wasn't prepared to repeat it.

Marc smiled at Karl. 'Thank you,' he said.

'For what? For giving you that water? There's a small freshwater stream that runs into a small lake just beyond those trees.' Karl seemed almost embarrassed by Marc's appreciation.

Marc shook his head and gave a shy smile. 'No. For saving my life out there.'

Karl looked at Marc as if he were mad, and then laughed. 'You think that *I* saved your life?' he asked incredulously.

'Of course you did. I must have blacked out in the sea. If not for you I'd be dead now: drowned like those other poor slaves.'

Karl turned away slightly, so that Marc couldn't see his face. 'It was *you* who saved *my* life. I was hit by some driftwood from the *Cygnus*. Got myself knocked out. You swam us both into shore. Then you collapsed on the beach. Don't you remember?'

Marc rubbed a hand across his brow: it was hot. Perhaps the sun had affected him more than he thought. 'No,' he said finally. 'But it was you who woke me up when the *Cygnus* was going down. I'd be dead without you.'

'Then we're quits now,' Karl said and turned back to Marc. 'Thank you,' he muttered, the embarrassment clear.

Marc shrugged. 'It was no problem. Back home in Britain I used to swim every morning in the river,' Marc remembered fondly. 'I'm a strong swimmer.'

Karl nodded. 'It shows.'

Marc felt suddenly awkward as Karl's eyes travelled the length of his taut swimmer's body. He was naked, apart from the brief pants around his waist, and he wondered whether Karl – naked, too, but for those tight leather briefs – would notice the feelings that he was causing inside him.

'We'd better get ourselves some clothes,' Karl said with a knowing look at Marc. 'And some food and drink. Remember those lights we spotted when the galley was going down? There'll be a town nearby. We can get some stuff from there.'

'Aren't you forgetting something?' Karl's simplistic enthusiasm was all well and good, but there were practical matters to attend to.

'I am?' Karl asked.

'What are we going to do for money?' Marc said smugly, pleased to have one over on the otherwise worldly-wise Karl. Rome may have been the legendary Eternal City, but it still rotated around money. Without that, Karl and Marc wouldn't stand a chance.

'The day I give a Roman the smallest sesterce is the day I rot in hell,' Karl declared. 'I'll steal it, just the way those bastards stole our countries away from us. Fair exchange, I say.'

'But that's not right . . .' Marc blurted out automatically, and then realised just how foolish he must sound. Karl sniggered.

'You're a virgin, aren't you?'

Marc wasn't sure what to say. The conversation had suddenly taken a very different turn. 'I mean, yes . . . well, I . . .'

Karl smirked and laid a reassuring hand on Marc's shoulder. 'A virgin to the ways of the world, I mean,' he said.

'You're making fun of me.' Marc reached up to take Karl's hand from his shoulder, but found that he couldn't. Karl kept his hand there, strong fingers massaging the soft flesh.

'Stay here and rest,' Karl said. 'I'll go off and check the lie of the land. I'll be back within a couple of hours.'

'I can go with you.' Something inside him told him that he never wanted to be parted from Karl. Alexander had been taken away from him. So had Cimber, and his father, and his sisters. He didn't want the same thing to happen to Karl. The very fact that they had saved each other's life had forged a bond between them that Marc hoped was unbreakable. Something told Marc that Karl was going to play a very important – if not the most important – role in Marc's life. At least, he hoped so.

Karl shook his head. 'You're too weak. You need to get your strength back,' he said. 'Besides, you'd just get in my way.'

Marc looked resentfully at Karl, wondering what gave him the right to treat him like a child. But finally he allowed that Karl was right. A few years of age might be all that separated them, but Karl had the experience of a rebel, of fighting against the enemy, which Marc, back in his cosy villa in Britain, could never have known.

'All right – I'll wait for you on the beach.'

'That's the first sensible thing you've said,' laughed Karl. 'I'll be as quick as I can. Whatever you do, don't stray too far from here; I don't want to waste my time having to search for you – not if there's a chance that there'll be Romans around.' With that, the German moved off towards the row of trees, promising that he would be back soon with a slightly embarrassed wave.

Marc watched him go, until he was little more than a moving

speck of brown amid the green of the trees. Then he was gone, and Marc was alone on the beach.

His first thought was to find some shade. The cruel Italian sun was high in the sky, and was beating down on his bare back and neck. The pain in his right shoulder was still there, and he craned his neck, trying to identify the injury. He wondered whether he should have told Karl about it – strange that, after knowing the barbarian for so little time, he should think about sharing his worries with him – but realised that if the injury had been serious Karl would have surely noticed it.

Rather than seek out some shade immediately, he chose to walk along the beach in an attempt to sort things out in his head. All of it was confused, a nightmare blur that made no sense: the Obsidian Legion, Gaius, Justin, Alexander, Karl . . . and Cimber's last words. Why was the empire in danger? What was the threat?

With these thoughts colliding in his head, the waves were almost mocking him with their tranquillity now; the only signs of the storm of last night were the occasional pieces of flotsam from the wrecked *Cygnus*, washed in on the morning tide. Shards of wood. Salt-encrusted rope from the riggings. A smashed amphora that might once have contained wine or spices, but now served as the hiding place for a crab who scuttled away at Marc's approach.

Initially Marc thought he might be able to salvage something from the wreckage, but, as he walked the length of the beach, it soon became apparent that there was nothing useful there. The enormity of his and Karl's situation slowly began to sink in. They were alone, practically naked and defenceless, in enemy territory. He had no idea how far they were away from Rome but he'd be surprised if there weren't any military forts or camps in the area. If they were to come across a band of legionaries, perhaps out to investigate the wreck of last night, then Marc dreaded what might happen to them. Not even

Karl, his body lithe and well trained in battle, would be a match for some of Caesar's finest.

Marc rounded a corner and found himself down in a small, secluded bay, cut off from the rest of the beach by a steep, gorse-covered incline. As Marc scrabbled down, he noticed that more wreckage from the *Cygnus* had been washed ashore here – where the current was obviously much stronger – than further down the beach.

He looked about excitedly, like a little boy surrounded by toys. At last he could do something useful! If he could find something valuable – a golden pin, perhaps, or a brooch which they might be able to trade for money or food, a leather pouch of sesterces or denaria, or, better still, a dagger or some kind of weapon – if he could find something like that then how Karl would be impressed with him. That would show him. That would prove to Karl that he wasn't just an effete product of the Roman colonisation of Britain. That would prove to Karl that he was just as good as he was, that they were equals in everything. That would gain him Karl's approval, make Karl look at him in a different way. The way he wanted Karl to look at him.

As Marc combed the beach for spoils, a flash of silver from the far end of the bay caught his eye. He shielded his eyes from the sun and looked. A body had been washed ashore, along with all the other flotsam and jetsam from the *Cygnus*.

And not just any body, Marc realised, as he raced towards the motionless form. He recognised the metal breastplate – it was the sun glinting off it that had caught his eye in the first place – the red woollen tunic, and the knee-length leather boots. It was Gaius, more dead than alive, eyes closed, scarcely breathing.

Marc approached him carefully, instinctively looking down to the Roman's belt. His dagger was no longer in its sheath; the legionary had probably lost it in the sea as he struggled to swim to shore. If Gaius should wake up, then at least he would be in no danger. As for a physical threat, he doubted that Gaius had the strength to attack him.

If Gaius posed a threat to him at all, that was. Marc still clearly remembered how the handsome legionary had stopped the slave-traders from raping him in Britain, and he could still see Justin and hear what he had said to him about Gaius in that dream-that-might-not-have-been-a-dream: 'He's not interested in me any more. It's as if he's got something on his mind. Or some*one*.'

And what about how Gaius had dragged Justin away from him, depriving him of the sweet and heady taste of another man's dick. And that look in Gaius's eyes: tenderness? jealousy? or sheer naked desire?

No, Marc decided, as he looked at the unconscious Roman, somehow he knew that he had nothing to fear from Gaius.

The legionary was breathing fitfully, his chest heaving up and down, and Marc reached down to loosen the leather thongs that fastened the metal strips of his breastplate together. Unusually for a legionary, Gaius was wearing nothing underneath his breastplate, and Marc reached out and traced the firm contours of the soldier's chest, lingering in the small cleft which went up and down with the beating of his heart.

It was only now that he was this close to the sleeping Gaius that Marc realised how different he was from the other legionaries he had encountered before. It wasn't just his darker complexion – legionaries were conscripted from all parts of the empire, and Numidian horsemen had even helped Rome win the great Punic Wars – nor his mass of raven curls, the length of which went against all military discipline. Although certainly far more muscular than Marc – even than Karl's big barbarian frame – he was hardly the overmuscled type of thug who constituted the major part of the Roman army. Marc thought back to Varus, the legionary who had presumably been left behind in Britain. He and Gaius were as different as chalk and cheese.

'He's a strange one,' he remembered Karl saying of Gaius. 'Something about him that doesn't quite ring true . . .'

Satisfied that Gaius was out cold, Marc reached up and touched his neck: long and sinewy, the corded muscle noticeable even in this relaxed state. Tentatively he reached out to Gaius's hair, entwining his fingers in the jet-black curls. They were still wet, and Marc gently teased apart the matted locks, lifted them and then let them fall back on to Gaius's face.

His fingers lighted on Gaius's cheek. There was just the hint of stubble there, but otherwise Gaius's skin was as soft and as smooth as the silks that came out of Egypt. Which also was unusual for a legionary, used to day-long marches in the unrelenting heat of the sun, Marc realised: Gaius was obviously very careful about his appearance. This was another factor that set him apart from the others he had seen of the Obsidian Legion.

Marc's fingers travelled further, touching Gaius's closed eyelids, and the long dark lashes there. Gaius twitched in his sleep, and Marc swiftly withdrew his hand, before placing it back down on the legionary's full and fleshy lips. They were dry and cracked – hardly surprising in this heat, after hours in the sea.

Marc removed his hands from Gaius's lips, and brought a finger up to his mouth and licked it, before bringing it back down to Gaius's own lips. He ran his moistened finger along the legionary's lips, and then prised them lightly apart, feeling the warm fleshiness within. How he longed for Gaius to wake up now, and gently nibble on his finger, before sucking that and then each other finger in its turn.

Gaius grunted and shuffled in his sleep. Marc moved back, fearful that he was about to wake, especially when his eyelids flickered open for a half-instant before closing again.

Marc stood up. He had to go, he had to get some help for Gaius. No matter that he was a Roman legionary, they couldn't just leave him like this, alone and weaponless on the beach.

Besides, hadn't Gaius saved *his* life? Hadn't he rescued him from rape and almost certain death at the hands of those murderous thugs from the Obsidian Legion?

Then he saw Gaius's cock, and other thoughts took over. His tunic skirt had rucked up around his thighs, exposing his long manhood, semihard and nestling in his thick bush of hair. Marc ran his fingers up and down the long shaft, and sighed with pleasure as Gaius's cock responded to his touch, stiffened and grew until it was its full, hard nine inches. Those same nine inches as Marc had watched fucking Justin's face in the town square.

Marc licked his finger again and outlined the tiny slit on Gaius's bulbous head, rotating his fingertip around it in ever-decreasing circles. Gaius groaned softly, and there was the hint of a half-smile on his face. Marc didn't care whether he was awake or not. All he knew was that he wanted to pleasure the Roman legionary, bring him to release, and watch him thrash with pleasure as his mighty balls pumped out every last drop of their sweet seed. He needed to see that beautiful prick jerk out of control, wanted to feel it as it slapped against his face, covering him with its white-hot come.

He took Gaius's cock in the palm of his hand and stroked it till tiny beads of pre-come appeared on its tip. Gaius was still sleeping, and Marc knew what he wanted to do.

He wanted to, no, he *had* to, take that big Roman shaft in his mouth, swallow it up whole, swallow Gaius up whole. Make him come without his ever knowing about it. Make him wonder who had approached him in his dream, and made him spill his seed all over his hairless and bronzed chest. Make him wonder about the stickiness between his legs. Make him question the aching pleasure in his arse, after Marc had inserted one, two, three, four fingers up his hole. Fingers . . . or maybe more.

Gaius was moving his groin gently now in time as Marc pumped him up and down. He squirmed on the sand, still asleep, but his half-smile was now full and ecstatic. Mac gazed, fascinated by Gaius's juicy and inviting cock, and the way he could bring a sleeping man so close to the brink of ecstasy. Who was the slave now, and who was the master? he wondered, as Gaius groaned in his slumber.

Marc licked his lips, longing to taste Gaius's hardness, feel that cock all the way down his throat, filling him up with Gaius's juicy meat until it made him gag.

'Marc.'

Marc took his hand off Gaius's swollen cock, and turned around. Karl was standing at the top of the incline, hands on hips, regarding him with a mixture of amusement and anger. He was standing with his legs apart, and even at this distance Marc could see the hardness beneath Karl's leather trousers. He wondered how long Karl had been standing there, watching him.

'I thought I told you to stay back on the beach and rest and wait for me,' Karl said, as he came down to Marc. 'I've been looking all over for you.'

'I can look after myself, you know,' came Marc's sullen and defensive reply. He pouted like a little boy, being told off by an older brother. 'I thought I'd try to see if I could scavenge anything from the wreck.'

'Looks like you were successful, then,' he said wryly. He looked pointedly at the supine figure of Gaius on the sand, and at his erection. 'I can see that the Roman's not dead, at least.'

'We must help him,' said Marc.

'Are you mad? He's a Roman.'

'He's also a human being,' Marc protested, rising and moving to join Karl at the top of the incline.

Karl smiled cruelly. 'And a tasty piece of arse, as well. I wouldn't mind some of that for myself: looks like he could do with a good fucking. Screw the life out of him like his bastard lot did to the men and women back home in Germanica.'

Marc didn't like the tone of Karl's voice, and tried to move the conversation on. 'That's not what I was thinking,' he said, even though he knew that Karl wouldn't believe him.

'No?' Karl said and sneered. 'I was watching you. Couldn't wait to get your mouth on his big Roman cock, could you? Couldn't wait for him to ram that fat prick of his all the way up your arse?'

'You know that I've never been –' Marc began and then stopped himself. He looked the barbarian defiantly in the eye. It was time to be frank. 'And what if I did want him to fuck me? Exactly what is it to you, anyway?'

Karl shrugged his shoulders, and turned away, unwilling to meet Marc's accusing and knowing gaze. It was his turn to change the subject.

'We were right: there is a village a few miles away from here,' he told Marc. 'I saw it from the top of the hill. It should be easy enough to steal some food and clothes. We could be there in four or five hours.'

'I thought you said it was only a few miles away,' Marc said.

Karl pursed his lips. 'Some legionaries have pitched up camp nearby. We're going to have to make a diversion through the wood,' he told him, and pointed to the trees in the distance.

'Legionaries?' Marc was curious. 'What are they doing so far from Rome?'

'I'll leave you to worry your pretty little head about that. All I want is to get my belly full and some clothes on my back before night falls.'

'And after that?'

'Home, of course. Or to Gaul. Organise more resistance against the Romans. Although, if the Obsidian Legion's any-thing to go by, they're doing a pretty good job all by themselves.'

Marc shook his head. 'And you believe that one man can help defeat the whole of Imperial Rome?' Karl's arrogance was amazing.

'It could be two,' Karl said, and turned away from Marc

once again. His voice was suddenly businesslike: 'We have to make a move. I don't want to be in the wood when night comes. If it's anything like the great forest back home in Germanica, anything could be lurking there.'

'Wood demons and monsters,' said Marc, who had shuddered as a boy at the tales old Cimber had told him around the fire.

Karl smiled indulgently. 'I didn't say that,' he said. 'There are worse things than that, you know.'

Marc looked at Gaius, who was still lying unconscious on the sand, but breathing much more steadily now. Thankfully, it looked like he was going to survive. 'What about Gaius?'

'He'll live,' said Karl. But there was an odd tone in his voice. Indeed, Marc could have sworn that there was a trace of jealousy. Was it true? Was Karl jealous of Marc's obvious attraction to the fallen legionary? But whatever the reason, it just didn't seem right to leave Gaius there.

'Out here alone?' Marc shook his head. 'No, Karl, we have to take him with us.'

'Is he armed?'

'No. He must have lost his dagger in the shipwreck.'

'Then he's of no use to us,' Karl said heartlessly. 'Unless you want to stick around to be a Roman's pathetic little slave.' He arched an eyebrow. 'Perhaps you don't want your freedom, after all.'

'That isn't fair,' Marc retorted. 'You know I do.'

'Then leave him. If Gaius has survived, then so might others. I don't intend to stick around to get fucked by a gang of cock-hungry Romans.'

Marc nodded. He knew Karl was right, but that still didn't make leaving Gaius any easier. Karl's words had struck home, though: perhaps he was speaking the truth after all, a truth that Marc refused to acknowledge. Did he want to become the Roman legionary's slave? Was that what this was all about? He took one final look at Gaius, and then turned back to Karl.

There was a strange look of anxious expectancy on the barbarian's normally impassive face. He was waiting to see whether Marc chose the Roman over the German!

'You're right,' Marc said at last, although something inside him felt almost regretful. 'We have to go.'

Karl smiled – a smile of relief. 'We find food and clothing tonight,' he promised him. 'Tomorrow, at dawn, we can come back for him – if you really want to. But not now. He'd only slow us down.'

Marc nodded, and Karl slapped him on the right shoulder in a gesture of comradeship. Marc yelped with pain, a fire that burnt across his upper arm.

'You've hurt yourself,' Karl said. His voice was full of concern.

'It's nothing,' Marc lied.

Karl was insistent. 'Let me see.'

Karl turned Marc around with a surprising gentleness so that he could see the wound on his shoulder blade. It was a red, weeping gash, but thankfully not too deep or too large: about the size of a small coin.

'It probably feels worse than it is,' Karl said in blunt reassurance, as his hands massaged Marc's right shoulder. 'Some timber from the *Cygnus* must have grazed you when you were out there in the ocean. I should have noticed it earlier.'

'It stings.'

'Of course it does. Salt water's got into the wound,' Karl said matter-of-factly, still kneading gently away at Marc's shoulder. 'Why didn't you tell me about this before?'

'Didn't want to worry you,' Marc said awkwardly, his eyes closed as he enjoyed the sensation of Karl's firm hands on his back. 'I didn't see any reason for you to be concerned.'

'Of course there wasn't – it's just a scratch,' Karl's voice said from behind him. Was it Marc's imagination now, or was Karl making fun of him? 'But it needs to be cleaned. Wash away the poison.'

'Poison?' Karl was making what Marc had thought was a simple wound sound far worse.

'It's become infected. I'll clean it out and it'll be fine – you'll see.'

Karl stopped massaging Marc's back and took him by the hand. Marc's hand seemed tiny in comparison with Karl's as he let himself be led meekly away, all thought of Gaius suddenly forgotten.

Karl took him to a hidden grove, a little way off from the main beach. Here, surrounded by tall cypresses, there was a large rock-encircled pool, fed by the stream from which presumably Karl had earlier brought the fresh water to slake Marc's thirst.

Karl told Marc to sit on the edge of the pool, his bare legs dangling in the shallow water. He cupped his hands in the pool, scooping up the water, and started to clean the wound on Marc's shoulder.

Marc closed his eyes again, and leant back his head, enjoying the warmth of the afternoon sun on his face, the coldness of the water pouring down his back, and Karl's hands, easing and cleaning away the pain and the hurt from his body. He felt Karl's breath on his neck, now so tantalisingly close to him that he could have sworn that the German could hear the pounding of his heart.

'It'll be easier if we both get into the water,' Karl said, and stood up, pulling Marc to his feet. Marc watched as Karl bent down and took off his leather shorts, tossing them to the ground. The German looked up, smiled knowingly, fixed Marc with those dark and brooding eyes of his. 'What are you waiting for?' he asked – and now Marc knew for certain that he was mocking him. 'Take yours off too.'

Self-consciously, Marc stripped off his own shorts, trying hard not to stare at Karl as he walked down to the water's edge. Trying hard and failing. The cheeks of the German's arse were round and firm, as white as snow compared with the rest of his sun-bronzed body. A line of thin dark hair trailed down from the small of his back into the crack of his arse, promising hidden delights.

Between his legs, his heavy balls dangled, and, as he splashed into the water, Marc caught a brief sight of his cock. It wasn't as long as Gaius's, but even in its flaccid state it was thick and stubby. Marc found himself wondering what it must look like when fully aroused. He began to imagine its taste, the feeling of it deep inside him. He looked nervously down: his own prick was growing at the mere thought of it, and he hurriedly followed Karl into the water before the German could see his own tumescence.

Karl waded through the water towards him. The water was waist-deep, and, as he approached Marc, his cock bobbed on the surface, offering Marc a tantalising glimpse of its purple head.

'Turn around.'

A command. No longer a request, but a hint of menace in Karl's voice. Marc shivered: not with cold, because it was still warm. It was a shiver of anticipation mingled with fear. Something he had dreamt of, something he had hoped for, and it was suddenly no longer a dream. Suddenly it was only just out of reach, and coming ever closer. Without hesitation, Marc did as he was instructed, and he felt Karl's hands on his back as they scooped up water to clean his wound.

'You're tense,' Karl remarked, as he slowly bathed Marc's back with the water. 'You need to relax . . .'

Karl's hands moved to the back of Marc's neck, easing away the stiffness with his two strong hands, his thumbs pressing out all the tension of the past few days, causing tingles of delight throughout Marc's body as Karl's fingers splayed out over his shoulders, digging into him just this side of pain. Karl pulled him closer to himself, and Marc felt his whole body go limp, as he fell against the barbarian's hard and naked body, surrendering himself up to Karl, letting Karl do to him whatever he wanted.

Karl's hands moved down his back, magic fingers expertly touching centres of pleasure that he had never known existed before. Then those same hands ran up and down his side, as light as feathers, as they followed the grooves of his abdominal muscles. Marc sighed, and squirmed in Karl's embrace, crunching his arse into Karl's crotch, feeling Karl's prick, thick and hard under the water, gently probe the crack in his arse.

Suddenly, with no warning, Karl's hands grabbed both of Marc's tits and squeezed hard, so hard that Marc thought he would cry out in pain. 'No,' he muttered, half under his breath, but his protestations only made Karl increase his grip.

'You like that – don't pretend that you don't,' Karl's voice whispered into his ear. His breath was hot and exciting, as he exhaled in short bursts. Brutal. Dangerous. Animal. All the aspects of Karl that reminded Marc of Alexander. All the aspects that attracted Marc to Karl.

He dragged Marc closer to him. Marc felt the cold touch of Karl's silver nipple ring on his back, and sensed the German's cock start to push deeper and deeper into his crack. Marc opened his legs, willing Karl to fuck him there and then, begging to feel his hard, thick maleness push his arse apart, preparing to enter him, to take him ... the only thing that Marc wanted, the only thing that Marc cared about.

He reached out behind him, grabbing Karl's arse cheeks and pulling him on to him, into him, massaging Karl's cheeks while at the same time trying to reach round so that he could fuck Karl's arse with his finger.

The response was brutal and immediate: Karl grabbed Marc's wrist and roughly pulled it away. 'No!' he snapped. 'No one fucks me unless I say so.'

Marc moved his hand away, silently and obediently: he wasn't going to argue with Karl. Not when he was forcing his legs apart with his knee. Not when he was fucking the crack of his arse. Not when his hand was travelling down his brown belly, down towards the centre of all that he desired. Besides, it wasn't fucking Karl that Marc wanted with all his soul: it was to feel Karl's thick German prick inside him. Anything else could wait.

Karl unexpectedly grabbed hold of Marc's waiting cock and squeezed hard. Marc threw his head back in exquisite agony, his fingers digging even deeper into Karl's buttocks, while Karl's other hand continued to tease and torment his tits, ignoring his pleas for mercy.

Marc groaned. Karl's teeth sank into his shoulder, biting at the tender flesh, biting and nibbling until the air was full of the sounds of pleasure and the splashing of water as Karl jerked relentlessly on Marc's cock and Marc pressed his arse further and further into Karl's groin.

'This is it, isn't it?' Karl grunted, as he lifted his knee up underwater and rammed it gently into Marc's balls, which were longing for release. 'This is what you've wanted ever since you first set eyes on me on board ship. Isn't it?' he grunted.

'Yes!' Marc cried, squeezing Karl's arse even harder, while Karl wanked him faster and faster, and then slower and slower, faster, slower, playing with him, teasing him, taking him to the brink of orgasm and then pulling him cruelly away.

'A fucking British noble, after his own bit of rough – that's what you are, isn't it?'

The words excited Marc even more. That was exactly what he wanted. 'Yes. Fuck me. Fill me. Let me feel that prick of yours inside me.'

'And why the fuck should I do what *you* want?' Karl said as his engorged cock started to seek out Marc's arsehole. 'What do you think I am? Your fucking slave, or something? You do what I want, boy, only do what I say you can do. Is that clear?'

'Yes. Please, fuck me . . .'

'Yes, what?'

The words that Marc wanted to hear. The words that Gaius had used on Justin. 'Yes, *sir* . . .'

'That's better,' Karl said. He abruptly let go of Marc's cock and tit, and roughly turned him round. There were tears in Marc's eyes – tears of pain and ecstasy, fear and delight. There was danger and menace in the barbarian's dark eyes, and Marc found himself totally, utterly, under his spell.

'Look at you,' Karl said contemptuously. 'You're hardly out of the nursery. Why would a man like me be interested in a snivelling boy like you?'

'Please . . .'

Marc took a step through the water towards Karl, who backed away into the shallows. But it wasn't fear or hesitancy – Marc could tell. The German was playing with him, teasing him, and it was a game that Marc wanted to play. Karl tugged on his own fat cock, showing it off to Marc, and played teasingly with his nipple ring, driving Marc crazy with the sight of everything that he wanted – but something that was apparently forbidden. He took another step towards Karl, who climbed out of the pool and on to dry land, tantalisingly out of reach.

Karl's hands caressed his own body, his eyes closing in ecstasy as one hand played with his tit and the other lovingly fingered his cock. Marc gazed transfixed at the long stem, and its purple head, wet and shiny from the water. His fingers encircled his own prick and he licked his lips; he wanted that cock, he wanted it now.

Karl smiled: an evil, superior smile. He nodded for Marc to come near to him.

'Go on. Kneel.'

Marc looked quizzically at him.

'Kneel, you bastard! Kneel!'

Marc sank to his knees, never for one second taking his eyes off that magnificent cock, or those dangling balls, dark and filled with come. He looked up at Karl, towering above him, playing with his meat, one hand now behind his back, fingering his own arse, fucking himself. Karl looked down on Marc with contempt, as if he was little more than a piece of British trash, a hole to be filled and fucked and then thrown away.

'Look at you,' Karl sneered again, as he continued to toy with his own cock, waving it tantalisingly in Marc's face. 'You can't wait for it, can you? And I know exactly what it is that you want. Beg for it. Beg for it like the stinking little slave you are!'

'Please . . .' Marc's breath came out in short bursts and he strained forward, longing to feel his lips on Karl's thick tool, aching to feel its velvet softness thrusting deep inside him. He pulled on his own cock. He was close to coming, close to shooting his load all over Karl's naked feet.

'Louder!' Karl said, and slapped Marc's face, once, twice, with his cock. 'Beg for it, slave!'

Marc opened his mouth, tongue longing to feel the touch of Karl's meat once again, eyes tearfully pleading for another blow from Karl's rock-hard love-shaft.

'Louder!' Karl commanded again. 'Tell me what it is that you want! Tell me what it is that you can't live without!'

'Please, *sir*, give it to me: give me your prick. Let me feel it inside me. Let me feel all of you inside me.'

'Lick me, slave,' Karl said, and took a step away from the kneeling Marc. 'Lick me now.'

Marc crawled forward on his hands and knees, a slave to his lust, his mouth gaping open like a dying man in the desert searching for water. He reached for Karl's cock, but Karl cruelly pulled it away from him.

'Not yet,' he said. 'You can't have that in your mouth yet. You've got to earn that.'

'Please . . .' Marc's voice was a whimper, saying the only word that he could now say.

'Lick my balls, take them into that hungry mouth.'

Supporting himself on one arm, Marc went down on his master. His tongue reached out for Karl's spunk-heavy balls, licking each of them in turn, while, with his free hand, he took hold of Karl's cock and started to pump it up and down. Above him, Karl groaned, as much a slave to his passion now as Marc was to his.

Marc's tongue played around the balls in their sac, tasting their odour, still musky even after their immersion in the lagoon. He opened his lips, and took the first one into his mouth, nibbling and licking and breathing heavily as he grew closer to orgasm.

'That feels so good,' Karl moaned above his head, and reached down to stroke Marc's head with a surprising tenderness, while the other continued to massage the muscles of his broad chest. Marc looked up, and saw Karl's eyes closed in a paroxysm of delight. He sucked harder on first one ball and then the other, drawing them all the way into his mouth, teasing them with his tongue.

'My prick. Suck my prick – you've earnt it.'

Marc allowed Karl's balls to plop out of his mouth, kissed them in a gentle goodbye, and then trailed his wet tongue the whole length of Karl's blood-engorged cock. He held the German's massive tool steady by the base, and guided it slowly into his mouth. First the head, velvet and shiny, twitching in anticipation. He sucked on it and Karl moaned again, and tried to push Marc's head further on to his prick, wanting Marc to swallow his magnificent manhood whole and complete.

But Marc was the master now, and he resisted, savouring every one of Karl's sighs, as he circled the head, before taking more of the shaft into his mouth. He reached up and felt Karl's flat stomach, and the fish-shaped piercing in his navel, before tugging at his left nipple. Karl whimpered with pleasure. This was agony, agony of the most exquisite kind: Marc could tell that Karl was feeling the same mixture of ecstasy and agony as he had felt himself.

Marc's head bobbed up and down, licking, sucking, taking all of Karl inside him. And then he pulled back abruptly, making Karl shriek with rapture, begging for his mouth, before diving down once again on his cock, burying it in him, his jaws aching as he tried to accommodate its thickness inside him.

Reaching down, Marc started to tug on his own prick as he swung back and forth, eating Karl, sucking all his maleness inside him.

'Harder!' Karl groaned, shoving his cock further down Marc's throat. He reached down with both hands and drew Marc's willing mouth deeper on to him, mouth-fucking him in deep sharp thrusts. 'Take it, take all of it, you bastard. Feel me, fucking your hungry mouth. Coming in your mouth. Filling you with my hot load. You'd like that, wouldn't you, you greedy slut? Your mouth full of my come. Drowning in it. Come dripping from those lips of yours.'

Marc sucked harder on Karl's prick, while at the same time tugging faster at his own meat. Then he felt strong hands grab his shoulders and drag him up to his feet.

'Not yet. You're going to have to wait to taste my come.'

There was a wicked look on Karl's face, as he pressed his lips on to Marc's, and forced his tongue down his throat. One hand travelled down the small of Marc's back, resting at the top of the crack in his arse, and pressed him fast against his body till Marc thought he would be crushed against Karl's vibrant maleness. The other hand dived between Marc's legs and expertly manipulated, pumped that beautiful cock of his.

'You love this, don't you?' Karl grinned, as he continued to pull on Marc's swollen prick and press him close, closer to him. 'You love having another man use you and abuse you for his pleasure.'

'Yes, oh yes,' Marc said and raised his left leg, rubbing it up and down Karl's thigh. He clenched the barbarian's buttocks, his fingers reaching for his arsehole. Karl's hand came fast down on his. There was an angry gleam in his eye.

'What did I tell you?' he said angrily, holding Marc's wrist in a grip of iron, his other hand still pumping away at his cock. '*I* decide when I get fucked. Not you and not anyone else. Do you understand?'

'Yes, sir . . .'

Karl shook his head. 'I don't think you *do* understand,' he said, with a sly grin on his face. 'It's time that you were taught a lesson, British boy – a lesson that you won't forget in a hurry.'

Karl took his hand off Marc's erect cock and dragged him roughly away from the shores of the pool and towards a small grassy mound. He made him kneel, and then pushed him face down into the mound so that his arse was exposed and available. Marc looked behind him, at Karl fondling his own fat cock, taking in the sight of his bare arse.

'That's an arse made for fucking,' Karl said, and slapped Marc on the buttocks. He pulled his arse cheeks apart, savouring every detail of his arse, and Marc could sense his gaze, looking hungrily at the pink and puckered hole that he was presenting to his new German master.

'Please: fuck me,' Marc implored. 'Fuck me with your cock! I want to feel that big cock inside me, filling me!' What he wanted was so close, so near, that the sensations in Marc were almost overwhelming.

'I decide who and when I fuck – not you,' Karl reminded him. 'Understand?'

None of it mattered, none of it. All he wanted was for Karl to take him. Marc would put up with every insult, every verbal attack, just to feel Karl inside him. 'Yes, sir.'

Marc screwed his eyes shut, ready to feel Karl's cock enter him and fill him up with its thickness. Memories erupted unbidden: of Alexander, of Justin, of deciding to wait for someone special before he surrendered himself. He had come so close to losing his innocence to Justin, but, thanks to Gaius, his virginity was still intact. A virginity that was about to be ripped from him by the person who meant more to him than anyone else in Britain, in the empire, in the whole fucking world . . .

'It's tight and dry,' said Karl. 'A cock this size would rip you apart.'

Words meant as a warning only served to excite Marc even more. *Yes, please, rip me apart, show me no mercy, split me open with your massive prick!*

'You need loosening up, boy,' Karl said, and knelt down so that his face was directly opposite Marc's hole. Marc moaned as Karl's fingers probed the narrow crack of his arse, exposing his quivering hole to his hungry mouth.

Karl licked the rim of Marc's arsehole with his tongue, probing the ring of muscle, and then sucked on it. Marc gasped. This was a pleasure he had never dreamt of before; he had never even thought of it in his wildest fantasies, and, as Karl's tongue went in deeper, Marc pushed on to him, feeling the German's slinky wetness move inside him.

Karl's tongue started to flick in and out of Marc's arsehole, hot darting flicks that made Marc gasp with the sensation. Karl's hands pulled his arse cheeks even further apart. Karl was becoming greedy now, burying his face in Marc's arse, his tongue sucking him and fucking him at the same time. Marc guessed that he was savouring the taste and the smell of Marc's arse, young and fresh and ripe and ready for fucking. He felt Karl grab for Marc's cock, pulling it down, jerking it in time to his tongue as it probed Marc's tight hole, the two actions in perfect rhythm, in and out, up and down. His arse was now wet with Karl's spit, while his cock was soaked with pre-come.

'Don't stop, oh gods, please don't stop,' Marc begged, as Karl removed his tongue from his hole, and started tenderly kissing his bare and hairless buttocks. 'Keep it inside me. Keep fucking me with your tongue.' He didn't want that feeling to stop: he wanted to feel Karl's tongue, then Karl's fingers, then finally Karl's cock, penetrating him, taking him . . .

Karl started to bite Marc's arse cheeks, gently at first, and then, as his own excitement mounted, more and more roughly. Biting deep into the soft tender flesh that was thrusting itself into his face. Pulling hard on Marc's rock-hard stiffness. Bringing him to the heights of ecstasy. Pleasuring him. Hurting him. Driving him mad with desire. Making him fucking beg for it! It was almost as if Marc could read Karl's thoughts, sense his feelings, all of it being sent through that special bond that now existed between them. Marc had thought that he and his family had been close; he had thought that Cimber and he were close; at the end, he had known that he and Alexander were close – but none of them compared to the closeness that he felt, the strength of the relationship, between himself and the rough, savage German.

'Please, Karl, now. I need it. Now. I need it in me now!' Marc pleaded. 'Give me your prick, your beautiful prick. Fuck my arse. Fuck my hole. Drive it deep inside me. Screw me. Fuck me. Come inside me!'

The reply was like a message from the gods. 'Too fucking right I will!' said Karl as he stood up. He inserted a finger into Marc's waiting arsehole, slowly widening the resisting ring of muscle with sure circular motions. Marc wriggled his arse, pushing himself backward on to Karl's probing finger, relaxing himself to take as much of it as he could.

'Now, Karl. Please. In me. Now. Please . . .'

'Relax, little British slave. You're ready for it now,' Karl said, as he ripped out his finger. 'Tight, and wet, and begging for it. Ready for my fat and juicy cock up your tight virgin arse.'

With one hand he held Marc's arse steady, while, with the other, he gently guided his thick cock towards the waiting moistness of Marc's ring. The head of his cock pushed gently at the opening, forcing its way into Marc.

Marc yelped with the initial pain, and Karl started to withdraw: whether this was out of consideration or to pleasure himself, Marc didn't know, and cared even less. Marc grabbed Karl from behind, and pulled him on to him, ignoring his virgin's pain as Karl's cock entered him. He was in a frenzy of passion now: all he wanted was Karl's cock up his arse, pounding away at him, thrusting deep and long inside him.

'You have got a tight arsehole,' Karl muttered as he pushed further in. 'All this talk about being a virgin – I thought you were kidding.'

As if to prove that he knew what he wanted, Marc moved backwards, impaling himself further on to Karl's thick cock. The thrusts – powerful thrusts from the German's strong thighs and hips – became stronger as Marc forced the muscles of his ring to relax even more, to allow Karl free entry into his arsehole.

The feeling was indescribable: a deep pain that was so overpowering, so overwhelming that it touched Marc like nothing else had ever done before. Marc had been worried that his arse would split: now he was worried that his soul would split with the intensity of the feelings that were running through him. 'That's it,' Marc said through gritted teeth. 'Shove it all in me. Make me take it all. Fuck me, Karl – *oh gods, fuck me!*'

Marc screamed with pleasure, as Karl's cock buried itself deep inside him. This was it! This was what he had been waiting for all his life! He was being fucked! Taken from behind, a huge cock inside him. Thrusting in and out. Filling him up till he thought he would burst. Filling him up with a pain and a pleasure and a passion too much to bear. For that moment he was lifted above his cares and worries, above the machinations of Rome and the Obsidian Legion, up in Olympus where Jupiter was taking him like he had taken Ganymede in his dream . . .

But it was Karl's cock in him – big, rough Karl, the savage, barbarian German. Taking him like he was a piece of meat, a slave, there to be used. Marc could feel those heavy, spunk-filled balls slapping against his own, Karl's weight on him, driving those balls, driving that cock into him. Karl's teeth bit into the back of his neck as he plunged into him, and it was clear that the German was losing his reason to the pleasure that was now controlling him. Just what Marc wanted.

It was man-flesh on man-flesh, a prick in Marc's arse, a man *inside* him. *Karl* deep inside him. This was the factor that had been missing from his life, this was what he had yearned for.

'Can you feel me fuck you, slave? Can you?' Karl grunted as he thudded further and deeper into Marc's hole to reinforce his question. 'Can you feel my prick all the way up your arse? Feel it tearing away at your inside?'

'Yes. Don't stop, please don't stop. Faster, faster.'

Karl increased the pace and the force of his thrusts, his hands grabbing Marc's hips, pulling him closer to him, banging his meat into him, fucking the innocence out of his tasty virgin arse. Marc grabbed his own engorged cock, and started to pump furiously away at it, jerking in time to Karl's thrusts.

'Harder,' Marc screamed out in equal measures of pleasure and pain: he could feel everything building up to the one thing he wanted above everything else. 'Fuck the life out of me. Get your fucking cock all the way inside me.'

Karl threw back his head, and his thrusts became slower and more direct; through that link that existed between them, Marc knew that his German's climax was only moments away. 'I can't take it any longer. I can feel it coming.'

Although it was what Marc wanted, and he could feel Karl's prick grow even thicker inside him, he wanted this moment to last for ever. 'No, not yet!' Marc cried, even as Karl jerked out of him, sending stabs of red-hot pain throughout his arse with the brutality of the withdrawal.

'I'm coming!' Karl yelled with an intensity that almost terrified Marc: a truly savage, barbaric cry that summed up the big German. Marc looked over his shoulder and saw Karl pumping furiously on his prick. He continued to roar with ecstasy, as he finally found release: the shower of thick white come spurted out of his cock, covering Marc's back with its creamy warmth.

He hung his head, beads of sweat dripping from his brow, and squeezed the last drops of come from his still swollen cock. 'I just couldn't wait . . . That was so good. Fuck, that was so good.'

Marc was still banging away at his own prick, his arse bucking and thrusting, as he felt his own come swell up in his balls. He felt Karl's hands, wet and sticky with love juice, knead the cheeks of his arse together, willing him on to his climax.

'Feel it in you, Marc,' Karl said softly. 'Feel all that come, waiting to burst free.' Then his voice grew rougher once more 'Shoot it out, Marc, shoot it out of yourself. Shoot, for fuck's sake, you British bastard!'

Karl's hand reached around and grabbed Marc's cock. Two hands now, Marc's hand dwarfed by Karl's, jerking his cock, faster and faster and faster and faster, Karl ignoring Marc's pleas to stop, stop, stop, no, please don't stop; biting into his neck, pressing his hard, hot body against his, squeezing his balls, playing with his arse, tugging his tits; bringing him to climax, making him come, making him explode, spattering the ground, spattering the whole fucking world, the whole fucking empire, with his thick, juicy, sweet-tasting, warm and beautiful come. As the feelings finally overwhelmed him, he felt his balls tighten and then release: a huge gout of hot white come shot from his sore purple helmet, then another, then another. One last spurt of come shot from his prick before Marc was finally done. He was fulfilled. Complete.

He shuddered and fell back on the ground, panting, face pressed down into the grass, exhausted and sated. Moments later he could feel Karl's heaviness on top of him, weighing him down; Karl kissed him on the neck, and then he turned him around so that they were facing each other. His lips brushed Marc's lips and he smiled.

'So I was right,' he said. 'You are a virgin, after all.'

'*Was*,' Marc corrected him, and felt a warmth inside him that he had never known before, a beautiful aching in his arse.

There was soreness, pain – but also the knowledge that an aching void within him had finally been closed. For a second, an image entered his mind: Alexander. The big hairy Pict was smiling at him. *He'll look after you*, the rough voice told him. Then he was gone.

'You're a good fuck, whatever you are,' Karl said and grinned. 'Maybe sometime I'll let you get your greedy hands on my arse as well.'

'When?' Eagerness on Marc's part. Too much eagerness. It was clear who was the master in this relationship, and the young Briton didn't want to overstep the mark and lose the happiness that he had only just found.

Karl smiled. '*Some*time, boy. When *I* decide and not before.' And that was the end of that conversation.

Karl gave Marc a final kiss on the lips, and then sat up. His chest was covered with dried come; the piercings in his left nipple and in his navel shone in the late-afternoon sun.

After a few moments to get his breath back, Karl threw his head back. 'We'll have to be making a move soon,' he said as he looked up at the sun, just visible over the tops of the trees. He stood up and walked over to where their discarded pants lay. He tossed Marc's shorts over to him before beginning to put his own back on. 'It'll be getting dark in a few hours' time. I want to be out of those woods long before then. We don't want to be gobbled up by your wood demons . . .' Karl's tone was light, teasing even. However, there was a darker look in his eyes, and unconsciously he fingered the fish-shaped piercing in his navel. 'But, like I said, I don't believe in them,' he reminded him in a more serious tone as he finished putting on his own leather pants. Then he smiled. 'Anyway, sex and wood demons can wait. We've got an empire to conquer!'

Five

————

Night fell quickly on the wood, much faster than either Karl or Marc would have guessed: the Roman dusk was far shorter than nightfall in either Britain or Germanica – at least, it felt like that. With the breeze rustling through the leaves of the trees, and the forest animals beginning their nocturnal hunt, Marc could easily believe all those tales old Cimber had told him of the wood demons that lurked in the trees, ready to spring out and trap any travellers foolhardy enough to venture out at this time of night. Then again, it seemed that Cimber was always ready to jump out himself.

Karl had assured Marc that he would be able to find a safe way through the wood, taking them far enough away from the dangers of the Roman camp he had spotted earlier. They would reach the town before sunset, he had assured him, but now, as they stumbled over the roots of trees in the darkness, Marc began to have his doubts. Karl might have known the great forest of his native land, might have been able to survive the scorching suns of North Africa, but these woods seemed an alien country to him. It was as if the malign influence of Rome stretched out even here, thwarting their plans at every turn. It was also getting cold, and they were still wearing only their shorts. If they didn't reach town soon then they would have to find shelter elsewhere for the night.

'Admit it, Karl: we're lost,' said Marc finally, two hours after their last halt for rest. 'You have absolutely no idea where we're going, do you?'

'Of course I do,' Karl snapped angrily, and looked up at the O shape of the full moon in the dark and starry sky. 'We can make our way by the stars.'

Marc wasn't convinced by the German's reasoning. 'We're not getting very far,' Marc pointed out. 'In fact, I wouldn't be surprised if we were going round in circles: all of these trees look the same to me.'

Karl gave a short, harsh laugh. 'They would. Your cosy upbringing with the Romans and that old lech of a teacher you've told me about wouldn't have taught you very much. Learning about the gods and culture are all well and good in your safe little villa, but I've had to live on my wits since the day I left Germanica.'

Marc was getting used to this: the rufty-tufty German who didn't owe anyone anything, who was ready to stand up to the entire Roman Empire all by himself. Marc was learning to ignore most of it. 'You never have told me why you left your home in the first place,' Marc reminded him.

'No, I haven't, have I?' Karl replied evasively and pushed on. But Marc wasn't going to let it drop so easily. Karl knew a lot about Marc – indeed, Marc still didn't know how Karl had known his name before Marc had told him. It was only right that the German open up to him – especially after what they had done earlier that day.

'Was it to fight against the Romans?' Marc guessed, and followed Karl, not wishing to be left behind by the barbarian in this dark and threatening wood.

'Perhaps.'

Once again that refusal to reveal too much about himself.

What was it that Karl was trying to hide? Marc wondered. Why did he continue to maintain this barrier around himself, this fence that Marc could not breach? Had their lovemaking earlier meant nothing to him? Had it just been a simple fuck, an indulgence of both of their base and animal passions? Somehow Marc couldn't – or rather, wouldn't – believe that. He trusted his instincts: there was that special bond between them, and that had to stand for something. However, it was clear that nothing was going to come of this conversation at the moment. Marc would just have to wait until Karl felt ready to talk. If he ever felt ready to talk.

They carried on walking in silence for another half-hour or so, Karl keeping his thoughts to himself. Finally they reached a small clearing; Karl stopped and turned to Marc.

'We're getting nowhere fast,' he said. Marc knew that that was the closest Karl would ever get to admitting that he was, in fact, lost after all.

'We *are* lost then,' Marc said somewhat tactlessly, and was pleasantly surprised at the half-reproachful, half-amused look that Karl darted at him.

'I said we're getting nowhere fast, Briton,' Karl corrected him with a sardonic smile. 'And it's getting cold. I suggest we sleep for the night and start off again at sunrise.'

'Will we be safe?' Marc asked. He looked around the clearing and cast his senses beyond the walls of dark trees which both surrounded them and barricaded them. Odd noises were apparent, but they could be nothing: small animals, foraging for food. Or they could be something far, far worse.

'Safe from what?' Karl asked lightly. 'Wood demons?'

Marc scowled at him. He knew that he should never have mentioned old Cimber's ramblings. 'No. Those Roman legionaries you spotted earlier.'

'What would they be doing in the woods at night?' Karl asked sensibly. 'They'll be bedded down as well – probably with each other,' he added sardonically.

'I don't know,' Marc admitted. 'What is the Obsidian Legion doing stirring up resentment and ill feeling back home? Why did they kill Cimber, a friend of the Emperor? What's a legionary like Gaius doing in command of a slave galley? Nothing the Romans are doing at the moment makes sense.' There: all the mysteries in one simple package. Didn't make them any easier to believe, or to deal with, though.

Karl looked thoughtfully at Marc. 'You *are* growing up fast,' he said, and Marc wasn't quite sure whether he was making fun of him or not. 'Just days ago you were accepting your fate like the obedient little slave the Romans wanted to make of you. Now you're asking questions. We'll make a free man of you yet.'

'I *am* a free man,' Marc insisted, but Karl shook his head.

'You'll never be free while there's a Roman master alive to tell you what to do or think,' Karl said bitterly. 'The moment that the Romans turn up, you're going to become a liability – unless you learn to free yourself from the Roman yoke.'

Karl went over to a nearby tree and sat down, resting his back against the trunk, shuffling this way and that until he was in a comfortable position, his long, powerful legs open and stretched out before him, giving Marc a perfect view of the bulge in his leather pants – the bulge that had taken his innocence and made more of a man of him than Cimber's lessons or his love of Rome had ever done. Karl then folded his arms, hugging himself for warmth, and looked curiously at Marc.

'Why are you standing there?' he asked. 'Aren't you tired?'

'Where shall I sleep?' Marc asked and looked around for a suitable place to lie down.

'With me, of course,' Karl said with an inviting glint in his dark eyes. He unfolded his arms, inviting Marc to lie down beside him. Marc smiled, and walked over to Karl, slipping easily into his embrace, resting his head on his chest, cheek rubbing gently against Karl's nipple ring.

Karl's strong arms enfolded Marc, drawing him deep into his warm and welcoming embrace. Marc snuggled close to him, breathing out as Karl breathed in, listening to the beat of his heart. Marc's leg moved against Karl's, rubbing against his thigh, making the bulge in his leathers even larger.

'Later,' Karl said and smiled. He kissed Marc on the head, and held him more tightly. 'There'll be lots more time for that later. Sleep now.'

As Marc drifted off, Karl's promise continued to run through his mind. *Later*? Perhaps Marc did mean something to Karl: perhaps he too sensed that bond. As sleep descended, Marc found himself wishing that life could be like this for ever: no Romans, no empire. Just Marc and Karl, free and secure in their love . . . *Love*? Where had *that* come from?

Before he could decide, Marc was sound asleep under the watchful gaze of the moon.

Marc woke up with a start and looked around nervously. The wood seemed empty, but he could have sworn that he'd heard a noise. Just the wind rustling in the trees, he tried to reason to himself, but his intuition told him otherwise.

The only other noise was the sound of Karl's steady breathing. Marc glanced up at his lover. *Lover* – there was that word again. With his eyes closed, and a contented smile on his face, Karl looked strangely – wonderfully – vulnerable, no longer the hardened barbarian and fighter of Romans, but a man of tenderness, who hid his emotions behind a violent and brash façade.

Marc glanced around once more, but still there was nothing. Yet something *had* woken him from his dreamless sleep in Karl's strong embrace. Reluctantly he lifted Karl's arm from where it had been resting against his own chest, and stood up, stretching silently in the clearing.

There! A cracking sound came from behind a dense clump of trees a little way off from the clearing. That was the noise that had awoken him! His body tense, muscles steeled and ready, Marc walked off in the direction of the noise. A week ago, he would never have dreamt of being so brave, but a week ago was before he had learnt of his true desires; before he had seen his first love die to defend him; before a German barbarian had taken his innocence and replaced it with something . . . something special.

The wood was dark, the light of the full moon dimmed by the branches of the trees that towered above his head. Marc guessed that it was still at least a couple of hours before dawn.

Another crack. He stopped, his body poised to fight – or run. In the half-light he thought he could make out figures, flitting in between the boughs, teasing him with their elusiveness. He moved further into the wood, pushing aside the low-hanging branches of trees which scratched at his half-naked body. His bare feet rustled through the dry leaves that covered the forest floor.

There was someone there, he was sure of that. Always just out of reach, always seen just out of the corner of his eye. He thought immediately of the godlike figure who had visited him in his dream, powerful arms outstretched to sweep him up. Had it been Jupiter, tired of Ganymede? Or Apollo, with a prophecy to impart?

But then he thought of Cimber's wood demons, creatures of evil that could assume whatever seductive shape they so desired, all the more easy to drag their unsuspecting victims down to eternal torment. All that was rational within him told him that this was rubbish – tales told by an old Roman to frighten a young boy into his protective arms. But then he remembered the members of the Obsidian Legion who had murdered Alexander: living breathing avatars of pure evil. Perhaps monsters did exist after all.

Marc's heart started to beat faster. Karl had said he didn't believe in demons, without ever saying what he truly did believe in. But how was Marc to know that he was wrong and that Karl was right? Out here, alone in the wood, Marc truly didn't know what to believe.

Cold, cold rationalisation gave way to deep, primal fear. The demons were out there. He was certain of that now. He could hear them crashing through the undergrowth, racing towards him, ready to tear him apart limb from limb. Marc started to run, not thinking where he was heading, only knowing that he had to escape.

He was too late. A hand grabbed his arm, halting his escape. Strong, firm fingers dug into his flesh. Marc turned fearfully to confront his attacker.

'You stupid little fucker!' Karl cried. 'What do you think you're doing?'

Marc swallowed in both shock and embarrassment, but he couldn't disguise his relief. Karl was there: everything would be all right now. 'I thought I heard something,' he said, realising how lame that sounded. 'I went to look.'

'Are you mad?' hissed Karl angrily. 'The whole damn place could be crawling with Romans. You said so yourself.'

Marc lowered his head, feeling as foolish as a child being reproved by his older brother. 'I'm sorry . . .'

Karl relaxed his hold on Marc's arm. 'When I woke up I wondered where you'd gone,' he said. 'I thought you'd been kidnapped.' There was true concern in the German's voice, and Marc found that he was touched: more evidence that Karl really did care for him.

Karl took Marc's chin in his hand and lifted it so that he was looking him straight in the eye. 'Don't ever do anything so stupid again.'

Marc shrugged. 'You were worried about me,' he realised, warmed by the knowledge that Karl really did care.

'Of course I was: don't ever scare me like that again,' came Karl's reluctant and moody reply, and he released Marc's arm and took his hand. He started to lead the way back through the trees towards the glade where they had been sleeping.

Then he froze. Waiting in the glade were two legionaries, black-plumed helmets under their arms. He urged Marc to be quiet, pushing him behind a bush. It seemed that the legionaries hadn't yet spotted them: if they were careful, they might still be able to make their escape. For a second, even more relief flooded over Marc. Perhaps going off to explore had been the right thing to do: if they had still been asleep in the clearing, the Romans would have certainly captured them. And the black plumes made it very clear that these were members of the Obsidian Legion, which made their eventual fate at their hands lethally obvious.

'Going somewhere, boys?'

Marc felt the point of a blade in the small of his back, pushing him and Karl out of their hiding place and back into the glade. The two legionaries waiting there grinned and drew their swords from their scabbards.

'Well, well, well, what do we have here?' the elder of the two waiting Romans asked, as Marc and Karl were pushed into the centre of the clearing.

'Gaius said that two of the slaves had survived the shipwreck, Drusus,' his younger companion said. 'I guess we've just found them.'

Marc and Karl exchanged a look. Had Gaius really been awake when they'd found him on the beach? Marc remembered how the legionary's cock had swollen when he had touched it, remembered how his eyelids had flickered open when he had been running his finger along the warm flesh of his lips. Had it all been a ruse? The complex mystery of Gaius and the Obsidian Legion became even deeper, even more confusing.

'He never said just how tasty they were though, Sulla,' said Drusus, swaggering up to Marc. Drusus was in his mid-thirties, bearded, with cruel and piercing blue eyes, the beginnings of a belly. Like the others, he wasn't wearing any chest armour: Marc could see the thick matting of black hair which just poked above the top of his tunic. 'I think we can have some fun here.' With his finger he traced a line from Marc's throat, down his chest to the waistband of his shorts. 'And such a pretty young thing as well. A Briton, I'd guess from that pale skin.'

Marc flinched at the man's touch, and looked to Karl for support. But Karl was being held in an arm lock by the legionary who had discovered them, and was obviously powerless to help.

'Take your filthy Roman hands off him,' Karl snarled, as Sulla approached him. Smooth and hairless all over, even up to his shaved head, he was brutish and vicious-looking, with upper arms the width of Karl's thighs. There would be even less mercy from him than from his brutish comrade. Sulla waved his sword menacingly in Karl's direction. Karl refused to react, clearly determined not to give the Roman even that satisfaction. Marc felt a sudden sense of pride in his lover's behaviour: even to the last, he would refuse to bow to Roman domination.

'So, the barbarian talks Latin,' Sulla teased. 'I didn't realise that these German animals could learn new tricks.' He spat on the ground, inches away from Karl's bare feet. 'Scared we'll fuck your *friend* up his precious little arse, are you?' The word *friend* simply dripped with spiteful sarcasm.

'No Roman scares me,' Karl said, his tone defiant and hateful. 'And, from the look of you, I wouldn't think you'd be capable of fucking anything.'

Marc guessed that the comment was meant to annoy the Roman – perhaps to give Karl some sort of an advantage – but it had the opposite effect. Sulla smiled and tweaked Karl's right nipple, before groping at his cock through the leather of his pants.

'Mmm,' he said lasciviously. 'I've always wanted to try a barbarian.' He seemed to hold a short conversation inside his head before continuing. 'This one's mine, Andronicus,' he said to the legionary holding Karl. 'I want to feel his prick inside me, fucking me.' He looked over his shoulder at Marc. 'At least he's a real man.'

Andronicus released Karl and walked round to the front to look the German up and down, sizing him up like a prize piece of meat at a market. Which, to the legionary, Karl was. An escaped slave was still a slave: Karl had no rights, no freedom. Marc's heart went out to him: he could see the restrained anger, and, for a second, he was reminded of the situation in Cimber's hut, when Alexander had given his life to save him. Marc couldn't go through that again – not after finding someone like Karl. He briefly closed his eyes, willing Karl to do nothing: it wasn't as if Sulla wanted to screw him; screwing Sulla wasn't too high a price to pay for their survival. *Survival*? Yes, somehow Marc knew that they would get out of this alive: Gaius had clearly sent these legionaries to find them and bring them back, not to kill them.

He hoped. Returning his attention to Karl, he looked at what Andronicus was doing. The Roman was broad-shouldered and stocky, his hair a mass of tight blond curls. Marc guessed that he was from the northern provinces of the empire.

'You'd like to fuck my friend Sulla, would you?' he asked. Karl didn't reply, even after Andronicus punched him viciously in the small of the back.

'Maybe this one only takes it up the arse?' Sulla suggested. 'You can never tell with *barbarians*.' But there was something about the word *barbarian* that was aimed not at Karl but at Andronicus.

Karl spoke. 'No one fucks me,' he said with feeling.

Sulla smirked, and was about to say something in response, when a fourth legionary entered the glade, dressed, unlike his comrades, in full battledress, his face concealed beneath his black-plumed helmet. He took in the scene immediately, smiled, and removed his helmet.

Marc had to admit that he was impressed. Short, close-cropped blond hair, a fair and flawless complexion, and eyes the colour of emeralds. Not like a true Roman at all. He looked appreciatively at Marc, before turning to the other legionaries.

'You've done well, boys,' he said. 'A pretty one, *and* a barbarian. They'll come in handy.' He turned back to Marc and nodded appreciatively. 'An *exceptionally* pretty one, in fact.'

As he stroked Marc's cheeks, Marc noticed the brooch that fastened the newcomer's cloak. The great god Pan, Lord of Misrule. Exactly the same as the one on Gaius's cloak. The same as the one that Cimber had shown him. Another clue to the truth behind the Obsidian Legion?

'We thought you'd like them, General Decius,' said Sulla.

Decius? Marc started at the name. This was Gaius's superior officer: what was he doing patrolling the woods? Even more puzzling was his presence here, on the outskirts of Rome; the last that Marc had heard was that Decius was staying in Britain to mop up the remains of Boudicca's followers. How had he got here? And *why* was he here?

Thankfully, no one noticed Marc's reaction to the name. Marc carried on listening as Sulla continued. 'They're the ones from the shipwreck: the ones that Gaius warned us about.'

'Slaves, then,' Decius said, and dragged his eyes away from Marc. He looked at Karl, saw the fish-shaped piercing in his navel. 'What's that?'

Karl looked up at the general with a sneer. 'Go fuck yourself, Roman,' he said, and spat in Decius's face. The blond-haired man's face darkened and he raised a hand to strike him. But didn't. His voice was cold but considered when he replied.

'This slave obviously needs teaching a lesson,' he said, and nodded over to Sulla. Sulla took hold of Karl once more and dragged him to the tree where Karl and Marc had been sleeping earlier. He placed Karl's hands around the tree and then tied them together with his leather belt. Grinning, he gave Karl a playful slap on the arse. Marc swallowed hard: why had Karl reacted like that? If they had been calm about this, there would have been a chance – especially if Gaius was involved. But now?

Decius marched up to Karl, and took off his own belt, before pulling Karl's leather shorts down to his ankles. Marc didn't want to watch, but he was hypnotised by the events that were unfolding.

'You're going to learn some respect, barbarian,' he promised, and Marc continued to watch, horrified, as Decius thwacked Karl on the white cheeks of his bare arse. Karl yelped, and spat out a curse in his own language.

'Show some respect, barbarian!' Decius spat, and struck him again with the leather belt. 'Show some respect to your Roman masters!'

'I'll see you in hell first!' Karl said, his eyes scrunched up, trying to ignore the pain. Marc winced: seeing his lover like this! He wanted to break free of his captors and save him – and then he remembered Alexander: was that how he had felt about Marc? Was that why he had given up his life for him? Was that what love really meant? Marc's thoughts were interrupted by another beating.

Thwack!

Decius struck Karl once again, and red welts started to appear on the German's bare cheeks. Beneath his tunic, Decius's erection was plain to see: he was enjoying it, Marc realised, enjoying punishing the barbarian Karl, enjoying the power of dominance over another male, revelling in the ability to inflict either pleasure or pain on the German's tender, defenceless arse. Marc was sickened, but somehow excited: something told him that they wouldn't kill Karl; they would let him live, even if it was just to be their slave.

Decius increased the strokes of the belt on Karl's arse, thudding down with all his strength, and then teasing him, letting the leather barely touch the flesh, before coming back down with a force that made Karl yell to heaven for release.

'By Jupiter, you're enjoying this, aren't you, you barbarian

116

bastard?' Decius said, a maniacal gleam in his green eyes. 'You're loving it, me slapping the shit out of you, aren't you?' Decius's other hand slipped beneath his tunic and began to tug on his thick cock.

'Go to hell, you Roman scum,' Karl cried, the insult exciting Decius's anger and desire even more. He struck Karl harder, and Karl's cock responded to the force of the attack, swelling hard and erect. Marc found that his own erection was swelling beneath his shorts, and a sideways glance at Drusus showed that Karl's beating was having the same effect on the bearlike Roman.

'He's mine,' Sulla said, as he peered over Decius's shoulder at Karl's arse and the red stripes on his cheeks. Even Marc knew that this was insolence: Decius far outranked Sulla, and such disobedience was punishable by death. But Decius seemed to have tired of Karl. He dropped his belt to his side and shrugged.

'Then take him,' Decius said, before unexpectedly raising the belt once more and landing another blow on Karl's arse. Karl cried out, but whether in pain or pleasure Marc could no longer tell, and he felt his hardness grow even more between his own legs. Decius looked round at Sulla. 'He's yours, but you're going to have to share him with me.'

Sulla took out his own cock, already hard and hot. He knelt down by Karl's side, pulling away at his eight-inch prick, while taking in his mouth Karl's stiffness, and sucking up and down on it.

'You like it, don't you, pretty boy?' asked Drusus, who was holding Marc and preventing him from coming to Karl's aid. 'You love watching your boyfriend being sucked off and being beaten, don't you? Look at that cock of yours.' He flicked Marc's plainly visible erection with his hand. 'You're practically coming in your pants. You want some of the same thing, don't you?' The hulking man leant over and whispered roughly in his ear. 'I bet you can't wait for it, can you, you randy little bastard!'

The air was now full of the crack of leather on bare arse, the sound of mouth sucking and slurping on cock, and Karl's cries of pleasure-pain. 'More, you fucking Roman bastard!' he called out, as Decius whacked him once again, and Karl drove his own cock further into Sulla's open and greedy mouth.

'Come on then, you British slave,' Drusus said, and pushed Marc down to the ground and on to his knees and started to take off his own belt. 'Beg for it. Beg for my belt on your arse. Beg for my big cock up your tight, tight arse.'

'No!' The voice belonged to Decius. He had left Karl to the ministrations of Sulla, and he placed a hand on Drusus's shoulder and pulled him away from Marc before he could lay his belt on him. 'He belongs to me – me and no one else.'

Marc looked up at Decius, his face showing both fear and desire, as Decius lifted his tunic and fondled his own hard-on, long and thin, its engorged head gleaming with the pre-come which his spanking of Karl had already drawn forth. Marc was captivated by it, knowing that he wanted to take it in his mouth and drink that pre-come.

'Take off those pants,' Decius commanded, and the dominant look in his emerald eyes meant that Marc had no choice but to obey. But something inside Marc told him that he wanted to obey, he wanted to please this Roman. Had Karl been right? Was Marc destined to become nothing more than a whore-slave to the Roman Empire? At that moment, Marc didn't care: all he wanted was Decius. He wriggled out of his pants, easing them over his own hard-on, proud for everyone to see it. He started to tug on it, long slow wanks as he looked up at Decius's stiff prick. As he did so, Decius pushed Marc backward so that he was lying on the ground, before reaching down and lifting his legs high up off the ground, cupping the cheeks of his arse in his hands, gently easing them apart. Marc relaxed his ring to allow his Roman master to enter.

'You're going to love feeling my cock in your arse, boy,' Decius whispered huskily, as he guided his shaft in between

Marc's buttocks, which were already spread apart, waiting desperately for the Roman to penetrate him. 'Feeling it force its way deep inside you, filling you up with its hardness.' He placed his hands on Marc's shoulders for support. 'That's what you want, isn't it?'

Marc threw his head back, savouring the delicious anticipation of feeling the Roman general hard and full inside him. He continued tugging at his own prick, while his other hand reached out for Decius, his hand grasping the Roman's wrist, which was on Marc's shoulder, telling him that, yes, he wanted him inside him, and, yes, he wanted it now, every last inch of him deep inside and pumping away at him.

Decius smiled, mad with desire, and moved his cock towards Marc's open arsehole. Marc pushed himself forward, his body begging for it to happen.

'Yes,' Marc breathed. 'Shove it in me now, let me have all of it in me. I want to feel you inside me.' Part of Marc was saying that to appease the Roman, to ensure that he and Karl survived this, but a larger part of him wanted it – wanted it so much.

Decius laughed, and pressed his cock into the crack between Marc's arse cheeks. Marc groaned, reached out now with both of his hands for Decius's neck, pulling the Obsidian Legionary on to him, making him pierce his willing flesh with his long and ample dick. As Decius entered him, Marc grinned, enjoying the sublime sensation of another body, hot and hard, mastering and male, within him.

This time, the pain was not so acute as it had been just a few hours ago, when Karl had first entered him, relieving him at long last of his innocence and virginity. Not as acute, but just as deliriously, wonderfully, fantastically, fucking beautiful. This time, Marc's sphincter allowed cock into his arsehole with ease, before tightening itself around Decius's prick, not allowing him to leave his hungry arse, dragging it into him, wanting to keep it there, needing Decius to pump his magnificent maleness deeper and deeper and deeper into him.

'Take it, slave,' Decius said as he thrust longer and harder into Marc. 'Take every fucking inch of my cock in your arse.'

'Yes! Yes!' Marc said, and reached out, running his hands up and down Decius's magnificent arms. He groaned with the sensation of Decius's thrusts, as they became much rougher and more penetrating. Marc opened his eyes, and what he saw made his cock grow even harder. Surely this couldn't be happening?

Karl had been released from his bonds, and he was now behind Decius, fucking the life out of the legionary's Roman arse. Harder and harder, Karl was pushing into Decius's willing hole, and, as he lunged deep into the legionary, so Decius's fucking of Marc became rougher and more violent in turn. Yes, Marc thought as he surrendered to his fucking, delighting in the look of ecstasy on Decius's face, and seeing Karl mercilessly screw the Roman, burying his cock in his arse, his face in his neck. Being fucked by Decius being fucked by Karl. Was there anything more exciting in the world? At that moment everything was perfect: it was as if Decius was nothing more than an extension of Karl's cock, and it was Karl who was entering him, filling him with his thick, hard cock.

Marc wanked hungrily on his own prick, until another hand took his away. Drusus was there, kneeling down, fondling his own massive erection. The big Roman's cock was about three inches thick and eight inches long, with a huge red helmet wet with pre-come. Marc knew that he wanted that Roman meat, wanted it in his mouth and in his arse. When Drusus signalled Marc to start jerking on his cock, Marc didn't hesitate: he grabbed it, feeling its moist warm length and thickness in his hand. As Marc did so, Drusus reached down for Marc's own long and hungry prick, and Marc agreed readily. He had no idea who Drusus was: all he knew was that he was being offered cock and in Marc's world – the world that he was beginning to understand – that was really the only thing that mattered.

The feel of Decius-Karl stabbing away inside him and Drusus pumping on at his prick was almost too much to bear. Marc thrashed his head from side to side, willing them never to stop, never to stop until the end of all time, when he became aware of someone standing over him. He opened his eyes and looked up to see Sulla, his shaved body completely naked, towering over him, his legs, as thick as tree trunks, on each side of Marc's head. His balls dangled tantalisingly out of reach above Marc's head as the older man jerked on his thick, engorged cock. Marc raised his head, begging for the taste of Sulla's prick, but Drusus was pumping at his cock, and Decius and Karl were slamming into his arse: he couldn't move.

'So, you want a taste of this big cock, do you, boy?' Sulla asked, and knelt down, waving the cock above Marc's face, the shaved balls only inches above Marc's mouth.

'Please,' said Marc, hardly able to contain himself. The feel of Decius-Karl inside him; Drusus's fist bringing him closer and closer to climax; his own hand around Drusus's cock. And now this – another cock, another prick to taste and to savour. 'Let me taste you,' he begged.

'You want this piece of meat in your mouth, do you?' said Sulla, as his cock waved just out of reach of Marc's open lips, teasing him, driving him mad. 'Want it rammed right down your throat, isn't that right?'

'Fuck his mouth, Sulla,' Decius said, 'just as I'm fucking his arse. Just as his fucking boyfriend is fucking me.'

Behind Decius, Karl grunted – whether in passion or in anger at the Roman's comments it was hard for Marc to tell – and the German rammed deeper into Decius's arse, forcing the legionary's cock deeper into Marc's own aching arsehole.

'Yes, fill my mouth,' Marc screamed, and, with his free hand, reached out for Sulla's cock. Sulla let him take it, and he lowered himself on to Marc's face, letting his cock be guided into his mouth.

Marc sucked and swallowed eagerly, determined not to be deprived of one perfect inch of Sulla's marvellous cock, and those smooth, shaved balls which dangled in his face. He felt Sulla's prick push in and out of his mouth, in time to Drusus's manipulation of his prick, in time to Decius's hard thrusts into his arse, and Karl's fucking of Decius's own arse.

And then Andronicus, who had been watching the whole fuck scene, playing with his own hard tool, came over and bent down at Marc's side. He leant his face over Marc's cock, which was still being pumped up and down by Drusus, and licked the tip of the cock with his wet tongue.

Marc felt his whole body turn mad with desire, as he felt himself near to coming. Five men on him. Five men coming down on him, driving him to unbearable pleasure. Cock in his mouth. Cock up his arse. Cock in his hand. Their moans of pleasure as he serviced them, as *they* serviced *him*. Sweet gods, was there anything more wonderful in the world than arse and cock? With Decius fucking him within an inch of his life, and Drusus's big meaty hand squeezing and pulling away at his prick while Andronicus caressed his cock-slit with his expert tongue, and Karl ramming his cock into Decius's arse, greedily kissing the Roman on the lips, just as he had earlier done to Marc. Kissing him. Fucking. Sucking. Wanking. Sex, hard, hot, heavy and masculine: just as it was supposed to be.

'Take it, you bastard slave!' Decius cried, and Marc felt the legionary's balls slap even harder against the cheeks of his arse. 'Let me rip you apart with my cock!'

'Fuck yourself, Roman!' Karl cried out, and tore once more into Decius's arse. The Roman screamed in pleasure, and ploughed again into Marc's backside in response.

'Suck me off, slave,' Sulla grunted. 'Swallow me as deep as he's fucking you.'

Marc could bear it no longer. He felt the come rise in his

shaft, as Drusus tugged faster and faster on his cock, and Andronicus's tongue licked and teased his knob, while his other hand reached out and fondled Decius's balls as his cock thudded into Marc's arsehole. They were tearing him apart, screwing him like animals, their maleness in his maleness, their cocks in his arse. Fucking him. Licking him. Wanking him. Squeezing his spunk-loaded balls. Shoving their massive, hot, steaming beautiful pricks all the fucking way up him. Making him squirm with pleasure, making him sore and hot, making him groan, making him come, oh gods, yes, making him come!

Marc's come fountained out of his cock in long thick spurts, and Andronicus greedily went down on him, sucking him even harder, licking up every drop of Marc's warm load. The pleasure was too much for Marc to bear as the Roman licked the now sensitive head of his shaft, taking him to the heights of rapture.

'Gods, but he's enjoying that,' said Decius, as he pulled out of Marc and watched him shivering and naked on the ground as even more come spurted out of his cock, and Andronicus and now Drusus lapped at it like the Roman dogs they were.

Karl took his cock out of Decius's arse and the two of them stood over Marc, Decius at his side, Karl at Marc's feet. They started to tug at their own cocks, and Drusus and Andronicus licked their lips dry of Marc's spunk and stood up to join the others.

'It's our turn now,' Decius said, as he jerked harder and harder on his cock, closing his eyes in ecstasy.

Marc squirmed on the ground, and fingered his own cock, which was already growing hard again. Gods, what a feeling, to be the centre of everyone's desires, to have five males standing around in a circle, bringing themselves to orgasm, wanking themselves over him, him, just him, being the whole of their desire. Imagining their pricks in his arsehole, their big cocks in his mouth. Fucking him one after the other after the other. One cock going out as another pushes its way in. Large, firm, masculine hands, pawing at his body, squeezing his tits. Fondling his cock, stiff and proud, squeezing his balls. Forcing his legs apart. Ramming their fingers up his arse, searching out his centre of pleasure. Twisting and circling inside his darkness, bringing him more pleasure than he could ever believe, making him throw back his head in rapture, scream out in ecstasy, shout out to all the gods that this was what he wanted, this was what he needed, making him come again and again and again.

Marc grinned wickedly as Sulla's come spattered all over his face, and he licked his lips greedily, tasting the salty white spunk as it dribbled over his cheeks and chin. Drusus was next, shooting his come over Marc, which Marc then rubbed over his belly and his erect nipples while still tugging furiously on his own cock. Then Andronicus, streaks of white shooting out of his thick cock, over Marc's arm. And then Decius, yelping with release, as he brought himself to climax over Marc.

And then Karl. Naked and feral. A wild, maddened look in his dark barbarian eyes. Pumping on his prick. Thrusting hips back and forth. Imagining fucking Marc. Playing with his tit ring, crying out for release, watching Marc, on the floor, squirming and moaning, covered with oceans of come. Come on his face, come on his tits. On his belly, on his arms and legs.

Marc watched entranced as Karl came, drenching him with his wonderful, hot, creamy come. Drowning him in it. He felt a pressure rising in his own cock, and he exploded too, his come mingling with Karl's on his belly, soaking his clenched fist.

Marc fell back on to the ground, exhausted. When he looked up, he saw Karl leaning for support on Decius's shoulder. His muscled body glistened with sweat. Decius gave Karl a brief peck on the lips, and then walked over and pulled Marc to his feet. He kissed him full on the lips, and gently tweaked his nipple. There was something about Decius's bearing, thought Marc, a gentleness that put him apart from the other members of the Obsidian Legion – but reminded Marc of Gaius.

'I thought you were begging for it,' said Decius. 'And it seems I was right.' He nodded over to where the legionaries had tossed Marc's and Karl's shorts. 'Put them on.'

'You're letting us go?' Marc asked incredulously, as he stepped into his pants. Decius laughed and shook his head, before ordering Sulla, Drusus and Andronicus to pick up their discarded swords.

'Whatever gave you that idea?' Decius asked, and held Marc firmly by the arm while the others drew their swords on to Karl. 'We're taking you with us. Your barbarian boyfriend will help the lads to pass the time.'

'A pair of sex-slaves you'll be,' Andronicus said, and smiled malevolently. 'Living only to service us. To pleasure us in whatever way we say.'

Drusus looked challengingly at Karl, whom he was holding at swordpoint. 'And if we decide to fuck you, then you'll get fucked up that arse of yours whether you like it or not.'

Drusus came up to Marc and gave him a playful slap on the arse. 'You too, pretty boy,' he drooled, an evil smile on his bearded face. 'I'd love to feel my cock pushing its way in and out of your hole.'

'The boy is mine from now on,' Decius said firmly, in a voice that brooked no argument. 'You've all had your pleasure with him, and that's good enough for Romans like you. Do what you like with the barbarian filth – he'll probably love it anyway. But no one touches the boy, is that clear?'

Drusus's face fell, but he and the other two legionaries muttered their agreement. Marc wasn't sure what to make of it: their lives had been saved, but what was going to happen to them? The idea of being a slave to the whims of Decius and his men wasn't that bad – as long as Karl was with him. But Decius's natural dislike of 'barbarians' meant that Karl – especially given the German's antagonism – could be in danger. Their only chance was to look out for each other – and look for some means of escape.

'Good – I'm glad that's sorted out,' said Decius, and relaxed his grip on Marc's arm slightly. 'It'll be dawn in a few hours' time. Our camp is a short walk from here: we'll get some sleep there before we start off.'

'Start off?' Marc asked. 'To where?' But somehow he knew the answer. It was obvious, if you thought about it.

He was right. 'To Rome, of course,' said Sulla. 'You didn't think we'd just let you go, did you? Rome needs pretty boys like you. Rough types, like your boyfriend here, as well. You'll fetch a good price in the auctions. Then your new owners will screw both of you out of your senses before they're through with you.'

'Enough of this discussion,' said Decius. 'We've had our fun: it's time to go home. Time to make for camp; then we introduce these two to the glory of the Roman Empire.'

As the party left the clearing for the legionaries' camp and sleep for the few hours of night left to them, Marc glanced at Karl and caught him smiling at him. Karl was obviously confident, but why? Did he have a plan, or were they both destined to become nothing more than victims of the slave trade?

Six

They reached the camp in about ten minutes, and Marc was surprised – and not a little horrified – to realise how close to the Romans he and Karl had bedded down for the night. No wonder they had been discovered!

Once they reached Decius's encampment, the Romans left Marc and Karl alone for what remained of the night – but they ensured that their newly found slaves were hobbled and secured to a stake before they retired. For warmth they'd provided them with red short-sleeved tunics, similar to the ones they wore themselves. Whatever notions Marc might have had that this was a sign of kindness on Decius's part were quickly dispelled by Sulla, however.

'We don't want your balls dropping off before we reach Rome,' he'd drawled when he'd been pulling tight the rope that bound Marc's feet together. 'Big-balled slaves we can trade. Eunuchs we've got no time for.'

Marc guessed that the encampment was about an hour's walk from the small town he and Karl had spotted earlier. Actually, encampment was probably too grand a word for the place that they found themselves in. It was hardly impressive – Marc decided that it must have been a miracle that Karl had seen it in the first place when he had been on his earlier recce – comprising as it did little more than two small tents, erected around a campfire. Sulla, Drusus and Andronicus slept in one of the tents and Decius alone in the other: the four of them seemed to make up the entire camp. A small oil lamp burnt in Decius's tent, but the other was dark, and from within there came the sound of heavy snoring.

A stake had been driven into the ground, and it was to this that Marc and Karl had been tied. A little way off, a horse was tethered to a tree, idly munching on a clump of grass. Marc's initial thought upon seeing the horse was that it was a packhorse, but its fine fetlocks and excellent conformation showed otherwise.

Karl – who was probably more familiar with horses than Marc was – confirmed Marc's opinion. 'That's a horse that belongs to a noble,' Karl muttered to Marc; Marc was leaning against a tree, still tied to the wooden post, unable to sleep.

'Decius's?'

The German shook his head. 'What would a legionary, even a general like Decius, be doing with a horse like that?' Karl asked. 'If he is a general, of course. Did you see his eyes and his blond hair, or were you just interested in having his cock inside you?'

This was the one conversation that Marc had been trying to avoid. Logic dictated that he had taken the only course of action that he could have done: anything else would have led to their death. But logic didn't sit easily with his feelings for Karl, and the knowledge that he might – in some strange way – have betrayed him. 'Karl, I –' Marc began awkwardly, but Karl chuckled and told him not to apologise.

'You did what you had to do,' he explained, assuaging Marc's guilt somewhat. 'Actually, I wouldn't mind having his cock in me sometime – when *I* choose, of course,' he said, and Marc found himself strangely excited at the thought of the dark barbarian being fucked up the arse by the blond soldier. Then Karl frowned. 'But he's not a Roman – not with that colouring. If I didn't know any better, I'd say he's from one of the German tribes in the far north.' Karl chewed his bottom lip – a curiously thoughtful gesture.

'He sounds like a Roman,' Marc remarked. 'He talks perfect Latin.'

Karl laughed sardonically. 'So do you, Marc.'

'That's thanks to Cimber,' Marc said, and the mention of his old teacher made him recall his first meeting with Gaius, and the fibula on his cloak. The same design as the one on Decius's cloak: the great god Pan, his massive phallus out of all proportion to the rest of his body. Suddenly it became clear. 'Karl: he knows Gaius.'

'Not necessarily,' Karl said reasonably. 'They might have just discovered him on the beach where we left him.'

'No,' Marc insisted, and thought back to when he was watching Gaius and Varus take Justin in the marketplace. 'The first time I ever saw Gaius, I heard him say that General Decius liked to keep all the "pretty ones" for himself. And later –' after Alexander had been murdered, he thought ruefully '– later, he stopped me from being raped by some of the Obsidian Legion's foot soldiers. He told them that Decius was still in Britain.' Marc frowned. 'But he couldn't have still been in Britain and got to Italy so quickly, could he?'

Karl put a reassuring hand on Marc's shoulder, and Marc felt a shiver at the longed-for contact. 'Look, Marc, this is all far beyond us, totally above our heads. We don't have to worry about all this imperial stuff: we just have to find a way to escape before we get auctioned off and separated.' A mischievous grin came over his face. 'Then again, you shouldn't have anything to worry about,' he said with mock cynicism. 'A boy like you could find himself in worse positions.'

'I'm not a boy,' Marc said defensively, almost as if Karl was impugning his masculinity.

'No, you're very definitely a man,' Karl replied with a smile that showed his memories of how he had taken Marc's long, hard shaft into his mouth by the pool. Marc knew that that had been only the first time – the first time of many.

'So Gaius and Decius know each other, and they both want their cocks up your backside,' Karl continued. 'That sorts that out. Let's have a few hours of sleep. It's a long march to Rome, Marc.'

But Marc wasn't going to leave it at that. 'When I last saw Cimber, he told me to beware of the Obsidian Legion,' Marc said. 'He said I had to warn his friend, the Emperor.' When Cimber had uttered those words, his voice weak with death, Marc hadn't really taken that much notice. But there was definitely something going on: the link between Gaius and Decius; the behaviour of the Obsidian Legion; Decius's where-abouts . . . And Marc owed it to Cimber – and to Alexander – to find out what was going on.

'Warn Nero? Don't make me laugh,' Karl said. 'You're getting above yourself, Marc. The closest we're going to get to Nero will be his face on the back of a sesterce. Now get some rest. It's going to be a hard day tomorrow, if we're heading for Rome.'

'You don't sound particularly concerned.' In a way, Marc was pleased. If Karl was so confident, Marc would be confident: they were together for the long haul – Marc knew that with a certainty.

Karl smiled, and Marc was even more hopeful. 'That's because I'm planning to escape,' he said. 'And, just like having a cock up my arse, it's me who's going to decide when and how.' He grinned. 'Sex, freedom . . . they're just the same really.'

And with that, Karl kissed Marc briefly on the lips, before dropping to his haunches and slumping against the wooden post. From the light snoring, it was obvious that he was fast asleep within seconds.

Even though he'd snatched only a few hours' sleep before being captured by Decius and the others, the thoughts flitting around Marc's mind made it impossible to fall asleep. They went all the way back to Cimber, and the warning that had come from his dying lips. To Alexander and his hatred of the Roman invader. To the god who had visited him in a dream. To Gaius, who had risked his life heading down to the slave hold when the *Cygnus* foundered on the rocks. To that strange look in Gaius's eyes when he had looked at Marc. It was a look that Marc thought he had spied in Decius's eyes as well. What linked them all together? What was the great secret? If only Cimber had lived a few minutes longer and had been able to tell him what he knew . . .

'Still not asleep, pretty boy?'

Marc looked up in surprise. He'd been so lost in his thoughts that he'd failed to notice the naked Sulla creep out of his tent towards him. The man's brutish features filled him with distaste, even though at the same time Marc couldn't resist feasting his eyes on his heavily veined muscles, made all the more prominent by his shaved and hairless body, even down to his tightly packed balls, between which nestled his cock. Marc wondered how it would feel to reach out and touch those rock-hard mounds of flesh and sinew, to have those hard, smooth thighs thrusting cock into him, feeling himself being dwarfed and crushed by Sulla's immensity. Even now Marc could feel a growing hardness underneath his tunic: the memories of Sulla's prick, filling his mouth with his manhood and his come. But he didn't trust the legionary, any more than he trusted any of the Romans – apart from Gaius, perhaps. But that was another story, for another time.

He looked defiantly into the legionary's eyes. 'What do you want from me?' he asked.

'What do you think?' Sulla said and his hand moved to his shaft, which was growing stiffer and stiffer by the minute. He started to rub it up and down, crooning softly as he pleasured himself with his own hand. 'I want you to take my cock in your mouth like you did earlier. And then, if you're very lucky, slave boy, I'll turn you around and ram it right up your arse, driving it all the way into you. How many cocks have you had up that arse of yours, pretty boy? Ten? Twenty? A hundred? I bet a good-looking slave like you has had hundreds of men queuing up, just waiting to spread-eagle you on the ground and stick it up your juicy hole, filling you with their creamy spunk. How many, boy? How many?' Before Marc could even come up with an answer, Sulla continued: 'Tell me how you loved it, pretty boy.'

Marc regarded Sulla with narrowed eyes, scarcely disguising his contempt for the giant of a man, even though the clearly visible bulge beneath his tunic must have said otherwise to the shaved legionary.

'Two,' he said truthfully – defiantly, even. 'And you're not going to be the third, Sulla.'

'You think not?' Sulla mocked, waving his cock in Marc's face. 'I'm part of the Obsidian Legion and you're just a slave. You do whatever I tell you to do'

Something inside Marc snapped. 'I'm a free man,' he said, and cast a sideways glance at Karl, who was still asleep. 'I'm nobody's slave.'

Sulla spat at Marc in contempt, before pushing his cock nearer to Marc's mouth. 'Once a slave, always a slave. Just because you escaped the wreck of the *Cygnus* doesn't change the fact that the Obsidian Legion captured you in Britannia. Once a slave, always a slave,' he repeated.

Marc turned his face away, willing himself not to succumb to the temptation of Sulla's vein-pumped cock. Sulla was tempting, but there was something about him that terrified Marc: a core of evil which summed up the Obsidian Legion. But it also fascinated Marc, and he knew that he would need all of his resolve if he wasn't to end up with Sulla's thick cock inside him. 'I'm not a slave – whatever you might think.'

'Of course you are,' he snorted. 'As soon as you get to Rome, you'll be a slave till the day you die: a rich man's plaything.'

That was it. 'Not if I escape first,' Marc exploded.

Sulla shook his head in amusement. 'Don't make me laugh. The way Decius is watching you, you'd never get far. And even if you did, the empire will always hunt you down. This is Rome, slave boy.'

'I'll take my chances, *Roman*,' Marc said, but he couldn't help licking his lips. Sulla's cock was right in front of him now, its purple helmet a feast too delicious to miss. He had enjoyed it so much the last time – what would one more taste of Sulla's thick moist prick matter?

'See reason, boy,' Sulla said, as he kept his cock just out of reach of Marc's open mouth, mesmerising him like some hypnotic snake. 'An arse like yours doesn't have to fight against Rome. See reason, boy.'

Marc didn't care to ask him what he meant: he could guess. Surrender your morals, surrender your hope: give up your soul and your arse to the glory of the Roman Empire. But what was wrong with that? Before he could even consider what he was doing, he was straining against the bonds securing him to the stake, craning his neck forward to taste Sulla's cock.

'So you do want it after all, you little British slave,' Sulla crowed, and rubbed the thick purple vein that ran along the length of his shaft. 'You liked it so much the last time that you want to try it again, don't you?' Sulla moved closer, he prick only inches away from Marc's mouth –

'What in hell do you think you're doing?' Decius was standing in front of his own tent, still dressed in his legionary garb, and his right hand was unconsciously fingering the hilt of his sword. He looked curiously at Sulla. 'What are you doing with the slave boy?' he reiterated.

'Nothing, General,' came the nervous reply; but Marc couldn't help but notice that Sulla was keeping his back to

Decius, trying to hide his erection until it subsided. 'Just making sure that he was secure.'

The tone of Decius's voice made it clear that he didn't believe a word of it. 'If I find out that you've been pawing him . . .' He paused and gave Sulla a very telling look. 'Well, you know what will happen to you.'

Sulla swallowed. 'Of course, General. It was just a bit of horseplay, that was all,' he said lamely, turning around. By now, his erection had subsided and his cock had become weak and flaccid: however, if Decius had been observant, he would have seen the telltale glistening of pre-come. But Decius was distracted: he ordered Sulla back to his tent before striding over to Marc. Marc was puzzled: there appeared to be a look of genuine concern on the general's fair-complexioned face.

Even more puzzling were his next words. 'Are you all right, Marc?' he asked.

There was no doubt it, Marc realised. Decius *was* worried about him. But why?

'I'm fine . . . sir,' he assured the Roman general. Best not to antagonise him.

'Because if he's so much as touched you –'

'I said I'm fine,' Marc interrupted while his mind raced. The Roman general was obviously infatuated with him: indeed, he must have been since the very first moment they had met in the forest – that would explain a lot. And now that he'd fucked Marc, it seemed to have become an obsession. Marc had learnt much from being with Karl even this short while, and a sly look appeared in his eyes. Perhaps there was a way to escape before they reached Rome . . . He looked up at Decius, trying to appear as innocent and vulnerable as he could.

'How long before we reach Rome?' he asked.

'We'll see the Capitoline Hill in two mornings' time,' Decius replied. 'So we'll be in Rome not long after.'

'And what will happen then?'

'You'll be sold to the highest bidder,' Decius replied, with clear regret in his voice.

Marc's eyes assumed a seductive softness: he was getting better at this! 'And that will be the last I see of you?'

'Yes.' There was now no doubt about the emotions that coloured Decius's voice. He bent down and pressed a tentative hand on Marc's shoulder, gently caressing it. 'I wish it didn't have to be this way, but there are more important things to worry about than passion,' he said.

Marc frowned, wondering what Decius meant. The key to this conspiracy, perhaps? But to ask would have broken the spell that he was so expertly exercising over the general; he just hoped that another opportunity would present itself. He shifted awkwardly in his bonds, careful not to awaken the sleeping Karl, and in such a way that the skirt of his tunic rose up, exposing his pants and the white flesh of his thighs.

Their eyes met, and Decius placed a hand on the inside of Marc's thigh. Marc marvelled at how Decius's tenderness contrasted so much with the roughness he'd shown when he had been fucking him earlier. Decius's hand rubbed up and down the inside of his leg; at the same time he looked longingly at the stiffness he could already see swelling under the cloth of Marc's pants. Marc's erection wasn't something he had to fake, though – Decius was an attractive man. For a moment, Marc wondered about this: how could he be attracted to two such different types of people – rough barbarians such as Alexander and Karl, and classically handsome men like Gaius and Decius? Realising that his newly born emotions would need a lot more thought, he put such considerations away and broke into a nervous grin. Decius smiled in response. It was working!

Marc closed his eyes for a second, a look of growing ecstasy on his face, and murmured indistinctly to himself. Decius was in his power now, he knew that, and he could bend him to his will as easily as a Roman master would his household slave. He moved his hips back and forth as much as his bonds would allow, teasing Decius with the sight of his growing penis, pushing it against the tight constriction of his pants.

'Let me help you,' Decius whispered, and he brought his hand on to Marc's hardness, pressing into it and moving his fingers up and down. Marc let him do so for several seconds, allowing the Roman general to feel the hard, long shaft and the tip, letting him wank him in his pants, driving Decius wild with desire.

Then he abruptly shifted away, and Decius's hand fell from his cock.

'No,' he said bluntly, and turned his face away from Decius. This was the dangerous part. If this went wrong, both he and Karl could be dead within minutes.

'What's wrong?' Decius asked, his voice heavy with disappointment and thwarted desire. 'Don't you want me? Don't you want to make love with me?'

Marc looked back at Decius, a hard cruel look now on his face. 'Make love?' The tone was mocking. 'What we did before was pure and simple fucking as far as I'm concerned.' There: blunt, insulting . . . enough to put Decius off his guard.

The general frowned. 'I could make you,' he said.

'Of course, you could,' Marc said knowingly. 'But you won't.' That wasn't what Decius wanted. Decius wanted Marc to surrender himself willingly. Any other way just wasn't enough.

There was a sudden gleam in Decius's emerald eyes: dangerous, angry. For a moment, Marc thought he might have overplayed his hand. And then Decius turned away, and Marc knew that he had won. The Roman general was under his command now, a slave to the teasing promise of Marc's cock, a promise that would be carried out when and how Marc decided. He knew that Karl would be pleased with him.

'Get some sleep, Briton,' said Decius as he stalked back to his tent. His voice was quiet: disappointed, frustrated –

enslaved. As he entered his tent, he said one last thing over his shoulder. 'We march for Rome tomorrow.'

They rose early the following morning, just as the sun was rising in the cloudless sky. It was a hard and scorching sun, a Roman sun, which burnt their backs as they left the woods and trudged across open land towards the hub of the empire: Rome, the Eternal City. The scent of olives and cypress trees was thick around them as they made their way towards the seven hills which defined Rome: all in all, it had a serene and sensual beauty. If only he and Karl had been free to enjoy it, Marc thought wryly. And then he thought of Cimber, with his promises of Rome. I'm going to see Rome, old friend, thought Marc. I just hope I get to see it as a free man and not a slave.

They had been untied once they had woken, but the ever-vigilant swords of Sulla, Drusus and Andronicus meant that there was little chance of escape. Not only that, but they were carrying the legionaries' heavy backpacks, which weighed them down. Trying to escape under these circumstances would have been futile. Especially since Decius could have ridden them down in moments.

General Decius was riding the horse that they had seen tethered at camp, a fine chestnut stallion which was a good eighteen hands high. Karl, who claimed that he had ridden many horses back home in Germanica, agreed with Marc's opinion: the horse was that of an aristocrat, or a man of some standing at the very least. Even the name of the horse spoke of dignity: Bucephalus. The legendary war horse of Alexander the Great. Whoever Decius was, he wasn't a common legionary. Like Gaius, thought Marc.

At midday they rested on the banks of a river, taking cover from the noontime sun. The legionaries stripped off and bathed in the cool running waters, but Decius held himself aloof. He stood watching his fellow Romans wrestle naked in the river, their cocks semihard in an unashamed display of horseplay.

From time to time, he would turn his gaze away from them and look at Marc and Karl. Or rather, at Marc. Karl wasn't slow to notice the fact.

'He's besotted,' he remarked, with a mixture of amusement and jealousy. 'You could use that to your advantage.'

'I intend to,' Marc told him in a half-whisper. 'When the time's right.' He hadn't yet had a chance to tell Karl about what had happened the previous night, with Decius's failed approaches to him.

'So, you'll tease him, and drive him mad, until he'll do anything you want him to do.' Karl smiled. 'You're no longer the innocent Briton I met on board the *Cygnus*.'

Wasn't that the truth? 'I've changed, Karl – I had to,' Marc replied. 'Wouldn't you do what I'm doing if you had the chance?' Marc felt a twinge of worry: his stratagem for Decius was based on what he thought Karl would do. He wanted Karl to be proud of him, for the gods' sake!

The German nodded, and placed a friendly hand on Marc's shoulder. 'Of course I would Marc: if it were *me* that Decius was lusting after,' Karl replied. 'Remember: sex is power.'

'You wouldn't let him fuck you up the arse, though, would you?' Marc asked. 'If your freedom depended upon it?'

'Maybe. Maybe not. Every situation is different. But I'd do it solely to ensure my freedom. You're different. You just will.' A trace of spite entered his voice, and Marc wasn't sure he liked it. 'You can't get enough of that feeling of hot hard male inside you. I saw you when you were being fucked by Decius. You were loving every minute of it.' His voice suddenly grew soft – soft and affectionate. 'I'm just glad that I was the first one.'

Marc couldn't help but remember what he had thought, that night in the hold with Justin: Wait for someone special, Marc, or you'll regret it. He had waited, waited for the big, brutal German to take him, steal his innocence before paying him back with the special bond that now existed between them.

'I wouldn't have had it any other way, Karl,' Marc said softly. 'You have to believe that.'

Karl smiled softy. 'I do, Marc. I do.'

Before they could continue, Marc noticed that Sulla, Drusus and Andronicus had finished their horseplay in the water and were climbing back on to the bank to dry themselves off. They looked over at the watching Marc and Karl, muttering and laughing to themselves.

'What do you reckon, boys?' Andronicus asked the others. 'Should we take that barbarian's arse? Each one of us in turn?'

'I say we should fuck him till he screams for mercy,' said Drusus. 'Fuck him till he surrenders himself, cock, balls and arse, to imperial Rome. Show the barbarian how we built an empire.'

Karl's peaceful demeanour instantly changed at the insult; he looked defiantly at the three taunting Romans, challenging them to take him on. The dark look in his barbarian eyes told them that they wouldn't fuck him and live.

Decius strode forward. 'There'll be time to teach the slave proper respect for the empire later,' he told them. 'Our agent will be waiting for us in Rome. We must make all haste.'

Sulla frowned. 'We can still have some sport with him now,' he said resentfully. Marc wondered why Decius put up with such disobedience. For a second, he thought of Gaius – both he and Decius seemed unsure in command, as if this wasn't their true position in life. More mysteries to be solved.

'We make for Rome now!' Decius snapped back, and Marc and Karl looked knowingly at the general: pressure of time wasn't the reason why Decius was forbidding his men to satisfy their immediate cravings with Karl. It was the thought of seeing his men take their pleasure with the more-than-willing Karl while at the same time knowing that he could never have Marc in the way he wanted. Marc's plan was working: with Decius enthralled by him, they had virtually ensured their safety – until they reached Rome.

Grumbling among themselves, but not prepared to voice their dissent to their leader, the men dressed themselves and then dragged Marc and Karl to their feet, loading them down once again with their heavy backpacks. As Andronicus handed his to Karl he sneered.

'Tonight, barbarian, I'll make you pay for your insults to Rome and the empire,' he threatened. 'I'll stick you like a pig till you scream for mercy.'

'Go hang yourself,' Karl snarled as he pulled the backpack onto his shoulders. 'And your precious Emperor Nero as well.'

Andronicus smiled a secret smile. 'Believe me, barbarian, he very soon will.' But the Roman didn't elaborate: he walked off and took his place next to Bucephalus as Decius mounted the fine stallion.

Once he was seated on Bucephalus, Decius ordered them to start off again. He led the way on his chestnut mount: Andronicus to his side, with Marc and Karl behind him, and Sulla and Drusus following behind them.

As they left the river, Marc pondered over Decius: he didn't fit into this Obsidian Legion, but he was obviously part of its machinations. How did it all fit in with Cimber's deathbed warning? Suddenly, reaching Rome in one piece had become of paramount importance. And if that meant betraying Decius's confidence, then so be it. Marcus Lucius, son of Claudius Lucius, owed it to his family, to Alexander, and to Cimber to discover the truth. He just hoped that he and Karl would survive the experience.

As night fell, the little group pitched tent and rested in a small wooded glade scarcely five leagues from the Seven Hills of the Imperial City. Throughout the journey, Decius had been unusually taciturn, occasionally turning around to look at Marc, who returned his gaze with a warm yet elusive stare, promising delights that were never quite defined. Soon he would strike,

Marc decided, and strike with the sweetest and deadliest weapon of them all.

As darkness consumed the glade, Sulla, Drusus and Andronicus were sitting around the camp fire, playing a game of dice. Decius was once again in his own tent, and Marc and Karl were tied up to the trunk of a tree.

A shout of disgust came from the gamblers around the fire, and Andronicus stood up, throwing the dice to the ground in disgust. Sulla and Drusus laughed at him.

'Call yourself a Roman?' snapped Drusus, scratching his beard.

'I've seen barbarians play better than that!' laughed Sulla, running his hand across his now stubbled scalp. He cast a dismissive glance at Karl. 'I bet even that savage could beat you.'

'Fuck you!' shouted Andronicus. It was clear that this was simply the latest in a series of rivalries that existed between the two true-bred Romans and Andronicus: Marc guessed it was something to do with Andronicus's obvious non-Roman origins. From his looks, Marc reckoned that the blond-haired legionary was probably a German like Karl: if so, Marc decided that he would have been ashamed of his origins, and the digs from the other two were nothing more than put-down reminders that they were better than he was.

Suddenly Karl called out a single phrase.

'*Unrein! Schmutziger Bauer!*'

Marc didn't understand a word of it, but Andronicus obviously did and, from the dark look on his face, it was clearly an insult.

'*Was sagen Sie?*' he spat.

'*Du bist ein schmutziger Bauer, Unrein.*' Karl gestured towards Sulla and Drusus. '*Sie sind treue Römer – Du bist nur Scheiße!*'

Andronicus's reaction was immediate: he strode over to Karl and slapped him round the face, once, twice –

The third time, Karl grabbed his wrist and held it. 'Just what

I would have expected from one of the *Unrein*,' he hissed in Latin. 'Not man enough to fight me on equal terms.'

'If it's a fair fight you want, it's a fair fight you're going to get.' Andronicus leant down and loosened the bonds that secured Marc and Karl to the tree. As soon as the ropes were free, Karl leapt up, ready to knock the legionary to the ground. But Andronicus was too quick for him, and drew the dagger from the sheath at his side, pointing it not at Karl, but at Marc.

'Touch me, *barbarian*, and your pretty little boyfriend gets it,' he threatened. 'Won't look so pretty with a gash across his face then, will he?'

Karl bowed his head. From his expression, Marc could tell that Andronicus had found and struck at his one weak spot: part of him was moved by the big German's behaviour, but part of him was disappointed. Why didn't he fight him? Marc could look after himself. But there was nothing that Marc could do. He sat there as Andronicus resecured Marc to the trunk, and then turned back to Karl. Replacing his dagger in its sheath, he took Karl by the hand. There was gentleness in the action, but definitely none in his next words.

'You and I have unfinished business, slave,' Andronicus said with a sneer, and then glanced over to his two companions, who were still playing dice around the fire – although they had been watching the disagreement with amusement. Decius was nowhere to be seen.

'Any trouble from you, and it'll be the worse for the boy. I hope you understand.'

Karl glared at the Roman. 'I understand,' he said through gritted teeth and let himself be led away by the Roman into the trees. Marc watched them disappear into the moonlit woods, and tried to work out how he felt. Was he afraid that Karl would be killed? Or was he jealous that his barbarian lover was about to pleasure another man? He just couldn't decide.

★ ★ ★

Andronicus stopped Karl once they reached a small clearing, not dissimilar to the one in which he and Marc had bedded down the previous night.

'Right – strip off. I want to see you naked again.' He wasn't speaking Latin, though, but the Germanic tongue which Karl had used earlier: a reminder of Andronicus's heritage. Now that they were alone, however, the language was no longer an insult: it had become a bond between them. Karl sensed that his countryman missed Germanica almost as much as he did.

Karl looked knowingly at the Roman, teasing him as he slowly unbuckled the belt around his waist, and let it fall to the ground. He tugged at his tunic, pulling it over his head, first revealing his leather shorts, bulging with his growing erection, and then his midriff, abdominal muscles tight and powerful, and his chest, the nipple ring gleaming in the moonlight. He brought one hand up to his right biceps and stroked the blue-black tattoo provocatively.

Andronicus watched, transfixed by Karl's display, and took his cock out of the folds of his tunic. It was already hard and stiff, and Andronicus spat in his hand before massaging the engorged helmet.

'All of it,' he grunted. 'Take all of it off.'

Karl bent down, never taking his eyes off Andronicus, and peeled off his leather pants. He stood up, and started to fondle his cock, bringing it to a stiffness that he knew Andronicus would long to take into his mouth. Playing with his nipples, licking his lips, he was teasing Andronicus with his prick, his arse, his mouth and his fist.

'Now you,' Karl said, his bearing suddenly assuming a new dominance. 'Let me see you naked.'

Andronicus didn't need to be asked twice. Karl guessed that getting off with a countryman – even one from a tribe such as Karl's, which had a traditional enmity with Andronicus's people – was a rare treat for the big blond legionary. Andronicus ripped off his tunic; Karl knew that he was desperate to get his massive hands on Karl's cock, to pump it up and down, to bring him to climax, before turning him over on to his belly, and fucking him, ignoring his protests, ignoring his struggles, just pleasuring himself like some rutting animal.

Andronicus came over to Karl and took his hand off his penis, replacing it with his own hand. He started to stroke it as Karl reached out and pulled on Andronicus's cock. Karl groaned with pleasure, as he felt the strong fingers massage his willing man-flesh, and he reached up and caressed Andronicus's chest, feeling those massive chest muscles and the nipples, red and hardening under his touch. He bent town and pinched each of them in turn with his teeth, flicking his tongue back and forth.

'You taste so good,' he breathed, and buried his face in Andronicus's chest, licking it with his tongue, and leaving a trace of saliva in the cleft between the pectorals. 'I want to feel you in me, fucking my mouth.' And he did smell and taste good: a reminder of what had been taken from Karl when he had been torn from Germanica and put into slavery.

Without thinking, Karl went to his knees, and his tongue snaked out, licking Andronicus's trembling cock from the balls, huge and covered in blond hair, along the shaft, up towards the tip of his meat. Andronicus's fingers reached down and entwined themselves in his hair, pushing him on to his waiting cock, willing him to take him.

Karl reached out behind Andronicus and dug his fingers deep into his fleshy buttocks, pressing them and kneading them, before pushing Andronicus right into him, swallowing his entire meat in one crazed and frenzied gulp, sucking all of him into his mouth, every last inch, from the tip to the balls, revelling in the sensation of the adopted Roman's cock thrusting in and out, in and out of him, his balls slapping against his chin.

Andronicus pulled out momentarily and Karl looked up with a manipulative smile at the legionary towering above him. Then he blew on the glistening head of his cock, and grinned as the sudden coldness sent shivers of delight throughout Andronicus's body. He went down once more on Andronicus, jaws aching as he savoured every inch of his flesh, sucking on him like he wanted to suck the very life out of him.

Andronicus reached down and dragged Karl to his feet. He glared menacingly at Karl, and pulled hard on his nipple ring. 'Now I'm going to fuck you like you've never been fucked before.'

'Fuck you, *Roman*,' Karl said and spat in Andronicus's face. Andronicus glared evilly at him and raised a hand to strike him: the insult hadn't been lost on him. Karl grabbed his arm, stalling the blow. 'We've been through this before . . . *Unrein*.' The word meant *unclean* – it was Karl's people's name for the tribe that he guessed Andronicus came from. To reinforce the insult, he spat in his face once again. 'That's what I think of any *Roman* who wants to get his filthy whore-son's hands on my arse.'

'You deserve a lesson, barbarian,' Andronicus said, as he pulled away at his own prick.

'Fuck you.' Karl clenched a fist and slammed it into the Roman's shoulder. Andronicus grappled with him, pulling him to the floor, where they rolled around in the dirt and the leaves, each of them trying to gain the upper hand. Andronicus was far bulkier than Karl, and could easily have overpowered him, but both men knew the game they were playing.

Karl was on top of Andronicus now, pinning his arms to the ground, his knee prising apart his heavily muscled thighs. He glowered at his countryman, spat in his face again and again and again.

'You treacherous bastard,' he growled. 'If you want my arse then here it is.'

He crawled up Andronicus's body and squatted over his face, lowering his arse on to Andronicus's face, experiencing the warm and slinky feeling as Andronicus's tongue explored the crevice of his arse cheeks, before sliding into the pink and puckered opening, slipping in and out, sucking on his hole.

'You're good,' Karl said as he moved up and down on Andronicus's expert tongue, the legionary licking him out, savouring his dark maleness, biting away at the tiny hairs in the crack of his arse.

Karl stood up, and Andronicus made no effort to move, lying on the ground spread-eagled and waiting, eager and ready for Karl's long thick cock, and the come that was barely restrained in his full and bursting balls.

'Look at you, you pathetic bastard,' Karl said and spat in Andronicus's face again. Andronicus licked his lips, drinking in the spit. 'Begging for it. Begging for me to come all over you, and inside you. Wiping my creamy spunk all over your face, making you drink my come like the thirsty pig you really are.'

A slave to his desires, Andronicus reached greedily out for Karl's cock, taking it in his mouth with practised ease. He slurped on it, fondling the balls that were banging away at his forehead with his hand, massaging them, teasing them, willing them to shoot out their precious fluid into his mouth, to feel the taste of man on his tongue, on his lips.

Karl thrust his hips back and forth, fucking Andronicus's insatiable mouth, which opened and closed on his cock, sucking him into him, blowing him out, bringing him almost to the point of release, and then bringing him down again, wanting him inside him for as long as he could take it.

Karl leant forwards, his own mouth again searching out Andronicus's cock, fastening his mouth hard on it, burying his face in the small bush of blond-brown hair around the beautiful prick. Rocking back and forth together. Taking each other in their mouths. One creature now, one wild and rampant animal, fucking and sucking on the forest floor.

Karl reached out behind Andronicus, and clasped his arse cheeks in his hand, lifting them off the ground, thrusting him deeper and harder into him. His hand slid into the furrow between the cheeks, and he fingered Andronicus's arsehole. It was wide and willing, a hole that had been fucked many times before, a hole that had known hundreds of hardened, hot and juicy cocks inside it. A whore's hole. The hole of a man who had turned his back on his country for the decadence of the *Pax Romana*.

Karl stood up abruptly, leaving Andronicus aching and gasping for another taste of him inside him. He stared down at the legionary with contempt, placing a sandalled foot on him, increasing the pressure on his heaving chest, pushing him down, keeping him pinned to the ground, enjoying the power of domination over him, knowing that this legionary was his to control, his to command, his to fuck for ever.

'Turn over, you bastard,' he said, and took his foot off Andronicus's chest. He gave him a gentle kick in the side, and Andronicus obediently turned over, obedient to his new master, kneeling on all fours, offering him his arse and his hole, to fuck, to lick, to do with whatever Karl wanted.

Karl brought his hand down hard on Andronicus's buttocks, and he yelped in pain.

'You like that, don't you?' Karl said, and when Andronicus grunted he took that as a yes. He grabbed hold of the leather belt he'd discarded, and slapped Andronicus's white arse cheeks with it. The force of the blow pushed Andronicus down into the ground, his face in the dirt.

'That's right, traitor,' Karl said, as he brought another stroke of leather down on Andronicus. 'Eat dirt, like the dog you are. What are you?'

'A dog . . .'

'That's right, a filthy Roman dog, fit only to be fucked and thrashed,' Karl said and brought the leather belt down once more on Andronicus's arse. 'You're enjoying this, aren't you? Enjoying the feel of leather on your backside, reminding you of the scum you really are.' Another slap of leather on flesh. 'Traitor!'

'Yes . . .' Andronicus was groaning now, enjoying the humiliation, revelling in the reversal of roles that had made Karl his master and him his slave, to do only as he commanded.

'Your arse looks good,' Karl said, and slapped the cheeks one last time, before putting his hands on Andronicus's heaving backside and pulling the buttocks apart – no, not pulling them apart but *tearing* them apart, until Andronicus whimpered in pain, which spurred Karl on to dig deeper and harder into his fleshy arse. Karl lowered his head and spat in the arse cleft.

'Please, fuck me,' Andronicus moaned. 'Ram your hard cock all the way in me. Rip me up. Treat me like the miserable dog I am.'

'Dog!' Karl said, and whacked Andronicus on the arse with his hand. 'Did I say that you could speak? Did I give you permission to fucking speak?'

Andronicus shook his head. 'No . . .'

'No what?'

'No, master.'

'That's better,' Karl sneered, and pushed one finger into Andronicus's arsehole. It slipped in easily, sucked in by the legionary's hungry sphincter, and then he inserted another and then another.

'How big is your arsehole, *Roman*?' Karl asked and jerked on his own cock. 'How many cocks have you had up there? How many men have shot their come all the way up you? How many did you have in Germanica before you sold out to the empire?'

'Fuck me now,' Andronicus begged, squirming on Karl's hand, pushing down so hard that Karl could have sworn that nothing would have pleased Andronicus more than to take his whole fist, even up to the wrist, and beyond, up to the fucking elbow itself, thudding away inside him.

'Yes, I'll fuck you,' Karl said, and reached between Andronicus's open legs for his balls, which he pulled back, squeezing them and twisting, inflicting equal amounts of pleasure and pain

148

on the sex-crazed legionary. 'I'll fuck you till it hurts. Fuck you for what you did for my country. Fuck you till you cry out for mercy. Fuck you for turning your back on our country!'

'Yes!' Andronicus screamed out as Karl pulled his arse cheeks even wider, opening him up, entering him roughly and mercilessly with his hard engorged tool. Shoving the Roman to the ground, pressing his face in the dirt, making him fuck the very earth itself. Karl's arms encircled Andronicus's waist, pulling him further on to his cock, pushing his way into his hot centre.

Andronicus reached behind, slapping Karl's heaving buttocks, inciting the German to even rougher, even more merciless penetration. Karl increased the force of his thrusts, wanting to hurt Andronicus, wanting to pleasure him, wanting to fill him up with his cock, with his come. Feeling the Roman's huge biceps, the thudding of his arse into his groin, his sphincter drawing him in, swallowing him up whole.

'No!' Andronicus cried, his protests serving only to excite Karl even further, 'No more, please, I can't take it any more.'

'You'll take it as long as I give it,' Karl commanded, and lunged once more deeply into Andronicus's aching, grateful arse.

'It's too big,' Andronicus moaned. 'I can't take it all in me! It hurts . . .'

'Who cares what you think?' Karl shouted, throwing his head back in a frenzy, a wild maniacal glaze in his dark eyes. 'You're made to be fucked, you're made to pleasure me. Nothing more. And nothing less. Take it, you bastard. Take it until you can't take it any more!'

'Yes, oh, yes,' cried Andronicus, eyes watering at the torturous ecstasy of Karl taking his revenge on him with his cock. His arse rammed deeper and deeper on to Karl's thick cock, as the German increased his pressure, driving deeper and deeper into the German who had embraced Rome.

Karl slapped Andronicus on the cheeks as he felt himself

close to release. He pulled his cock out of Andronicus's arse, provoking a sigh of pain from Andronicus at the sudden emptiness of his arse passage, and jerked himself over the man's naked and muscled body, over the arse bucking up and down, over the sight of the hated Roman invader in helpless thrall to his passions.

'Feel me come all over you, you bastard,' Karl cried out as he found he couldn't hold himself back any longer, and his cock spurted out its thick and precious load all over Andronicus's heaving back. Karl continued to pump up and down, coaxing every last drop out of his throbbing prick, shooting the last of his load between Andronicus's cheeks.

Karl took a foot to Andronicus's arse. 'Get up, you whore,' he ordered, and Andronicus did as he was told, turning over, and getting to his knees. His hand was stroking his own cock, and there was an expectant look on his face. His mouth was open wide, and his tongue was out. Still begging for it, Karl thought, and he knew exactly what it was that Andronicus wanted. It was what pigs like him always wanted.

'You look hot, *Roman*,' he said. 'I think it's time you cooled down.'

Karl took hold of his now flaccid cock, and aimed a shower of water towards Andronicus's mouth, filling it up with his piss. Andronicus drank thirstily, the golden liquid welling up in his mouth and then running down his chin, over his chest and belly. He jerked on his cock, enjoying Karl's humiliation of him, rubbing the shower of Karl's piss all over his body, the liquid shining in the moonlight. He was covered now with Karl's sperm, with his piss, and he pulled faster and faster on his cock until he came too, dropping his load at the foot of the man who now in his moment of orgasm was his lord and master.

Marc was dozing fitfully when Karl returned to camp; he was at swordpoint, Andronicus behind him. The legionary pushed

Karl to the ground at the base of the tree where Marc was tied up, unfastened the rope holding Marc to the tree, and used it to resecure Karl beside him.

'You're a good whore,' Andronicus said to Karl, as Marc turned to listen. 'Perhaps I'll use you again before this journey's out.'

Karl spat at the ground beneath Andronicus's feet, and, with a satisfied smile on his face, the legionary returned to the tent where his other comrades had already turned in for the night. Even now the sound of their snores could be heard on the evening air.

'I was worried about you,' Marc said after Andronicus had entered his tent.

'There was no need to be,' Karl said gruffly. 'I was just teaching that turncoat bastard who's the real boss around here. Not him, but his cock. He's like the rest of his legion: he can't live without it. Remember what I told you earlier, Marc – sex really is power. Use it while you still can. Has Decius been here yet?'

'No,' Marc said and glanced over to the general's tent, in which an oil lamp was still burning. 'He didn't even appear when you had your . . . your fight with Andronicus.'

'He will,' Karl said confidently. 'He will.'

Had he been awake, Karl would have known that he was proved right an hour later, when the flap to Decius's tent opened and the general stepped out. He looked over first to his men's tent, then to Bucephalus, tethered to a tree, and finally to the figures of Marc and Karl, apparently sleeping in their bonds, backs resting against the tree trunk.

With the light of the moon shining on the metal strips of the armour he was still wearing even at this hour, Decius crept silently to where Marc and Karl were sleeping.

He paid no attention to Karl, who was snoring softly, but instead stretched out his hand to touch Marc's cheek, letting his fingers rest gently on its soft complexion. He stroked his cheek and, as he did so, Marc's long eyelids fluttered gently and a smile played along his lips.

'So beautiful,' Decius muttered to himself. 'So beautiful . . .'

He traced a line with his finger down from Marc's cheek to his lips, letting it stay there for a minute. Even though his eyes were still shut, Marc's mouth opened and he bit on the general's finger, and then sucked it gently, taking it in his mouth, drawing him into his mouth tenderly, just as before he had allowed himself to be entered much more violently. The result was just the same, and there was an obvious stiffening beneath Marc's pants equal to the one beneath Decius's tunic.

Marc opened his eyes and stared curiously at Decius, who quickly withdrew his probing finger, even though it had been Marc who had invited it into his mouth in the first place.

'Why are you doing this?' Marc asked, a look of surprise and uncertainty on his face from being stirred from his sleep. 'What do you want with me?'

'I'm sorry,' Decius said. 'I didn't mean to wake you.'

'It's all right,' Marc said sleepily and then repeated his question: 'Why are you doing this?'

Decius seemed flustered by the question: but why was a grown man unsettled by the artless questioning of a boy?

'You remind me of someone,' he finally said, trying not to look at Marc's boyish features, and failing.

Marc fixed him with a knowing look. 'A lover, then?'

'Yes. A lover,' Decius admitted, snatching a brief look at Karl. He seemed to be sleeping soundly, and his snores were louder now, loud enough to drown out the noise from the legionaries' tent.

'He left you?' Marc guessed and, when Decius nodded, continued: 'I can't imagine anyone leaving someone like you.'

'What do you mean?'

'Leaving the security of those firm and muscular arms that could keep you safe for ever,' Marc said, lowering his voice to a seductive whisper, so that Decius had to lean down to hear what he was saying. 'Missing the feel of your body against theirs, your legs wrapped around theirs, your lips on theirs . . . I know that I certainly couldn't ever give up something like that: I'd want to keep hold of something like that for ever, never let it out of my sight . . .'

Marc's words were having an unbelievable effect on Decius. After the boy's earlier comment that what they had experienced together was just a fuck – plain and simple, nothing more than that – Marc's expression of his feelings for Decius came like a bolt out of the blue for the general, a shaft of light sent down from the gods from their palaces on high Olympus. Decius felt his heart bound with hope: hope that Marc might have some sort of feeling for him, that Marc could replace that which he had lost.

'I didn't know that you felt like that,' he murmured and smiled to himself. A general of the Obsidian Legion, now putty in the hands of an eighteen-year-old boy. What would his comrades think?

'You never asked.'

Decius let his hand drop down between Marc's thighs, and he began to run his fingertips along the swelling in his pants. Marc groaned with delight, opening his legs wider so that Decius could feel his balls beneath the cloth.

'I want you,' Decius said. 'I want you now.'

Marc looked slyly at him. 'Not here,' he said and nodded over to the sleeping Karl beside him. 'In your tent. We won't wake anyone there.'

Decius untied the ropes that bound Marc and Karl to the tree trunk, his hands trembling. Once he had helped Marc up to his feet, he started to tie the sleeping Karl up again. Marc shook his head, and rested a hand on Decius's shoulder.

'Leave him,' he said, and raised his hand to Decius's cheek, which he caressed like the lover the general hoped he would soon become. 'He's fast asleep – he won't wake. And I need you now. I need to feel you next to me, your flesh rubbing against mine, your cock against mine . . .'

Decius needed no further encouragement, and he took Marc by the hand and led him towards his tent. Once inside, Marc took Decius's face in his hands, kissing him full on the mouth, tenderly even, running his fingers through his short blond hair, pressing his body against the metal strips of his breastplate, rubbing his leg up the inside of Decius's naked thigh.

'You're so beautiful,' Marc said softy, as he ran his hands down Decius's bare arms, feeling the naked power contained in the muscles there. 'How I'd like to feel you hold me tight, never letting me go . . . Feel you on top of me, having your flesh on my flesh, feeling you move inside me, your long beautiful cock, buried in me . . .'

Decius was about to say something but Marc hushed him with a kiss on the lips. His fingers started to unlace the leather straps which held the strips of his breastplate together, fingers moving expertly over the dark, soft leather. One by one, he unfastened them, until Decius was standing before him wearing only his tunic, open to the waist, his sheathed sword hanging by his belt, and his leather sandals.

Marc slipped one hand inside Decius's open tunic, and started playing with his hard nipples, while the other pressed hard on the general's erection, which was clearly visible even beneath the loose-fitting skirt he was wearing. Suddenly Marc stopped, and looked nervously towards the tent opening. He took his hand off Decius's cock, and Decius pulled him back.

'What's wrong?' asked Decius.

Marc frowned. 'I thought I heard a noise.'

Decius hadn't heard anything – but then again, he had been rather preoccupied. 'It was just the wind in the trees.'

'No.' Marc was insistent. 'Perhaps it's Sulla, or Drusus. What if they find us here?'

'What if they do? I'm their commanding officer. What I do is no business of theirs.'

Marc looked at him, and Decius guessed that those rich brown eyes must have melted the hearts of many a girl in his home town – and more than a few of the men's, he would have wagered. The look of concern in them was hard to ignore. 'Please . . . go out and see. I'll still be here for you when you come back,' Marc insisted.

Decius shrugged: what harm would it do to indulge him? He smiled, and kissed Marc, reluctantly leaving him alone in the tent while he checked outside.

Marc's expression of concern evaporated immediately. The moment that Decius stepped through the door of the tent, Marc started to look around, to see if there was anything that could help him and Karl to escape. There was little out of the ordinary: a rough horsehair blanket, on to which Decius had tossed his cloak, a leather water bottle and a food bowl, a mattock for digging ditches – all the standard content of a legionary's pack. Apart, that is, for one thing. A roll of parchment was just visible, poking from the top of Decius's pack – a pack that Decius always insisted on carrying himself. In a time when few legionaries could even read or write, a parchment was unusual, to say the least, although Decius, like Gaius before him, had already proven himself to be not the likeliest of Roman soldiers. Marc slipped the scroll out of Decius's pack and unrolled it.

It appeared to be a map of Rome, showing the location of all the most important buildings in that mighty town: the Forum with its magnificent temple dedicated to Castor and Pollux, the twin sons of the King of the Gods; the Circus Maximus, the largest racetrack in the world; and, of course, the official residence of the Emperor himself, the great Nero, Emperor of the world for more than a decade, more ruthless and tyrannical than even the mad Caligula. Or so some people dared to say.

Marc recognised the places on the map from the charts

Cimber had shown him during his lessons in that stone hut in Britain – the hut that had now become the final and bloody resting place for both the old man and Alexander. However, some of the buildings were unknown to him, and he presumed these to be the townhouses of local dignitaries, consuls and senators, the privileged elite, although why Decius should have a plan of these he had no idea.

The houses circled the imperial palace, clutching on to its security like ducklings nestling around their mother, their occupants dependent on the grace and favour of the Emperor, knowing that at the merest whim the Emperor could have them all killed just as coldly as he had his first wife, Octavia, and even Agrippina, his own mother, dispatched.

As Marc replaced the scroll into Decius's pack, he noticed another piece of parchment tucked in among the general's other possessions. He drew it out, and scanned its contents, expertly translating the formal Latin in which the letter was written. It bore an official seal, and, as Marc read it, his eyes widened with horror. Before he could read the name signed at the bottom, he heard Decius's footsteps outside the tent. Hurriedly he put the letter back into the general's backpack, making sure that there was no sign that it had been disturbed.

'It must have been the wind, or an animal in the woods,' Decius explained. 'There's no one out there.'

'I must have been mistaken then,' Marc said and, as Decius stepped towards him, he motioned for him to extinguish the tiny oil lamp that was burning in the corner of the tent.

'Why?'

Marc paused. Was there a note of suspicion in Decius's voice, a sense that everything wasn't quite right?

'The others might wake and see us,' Marc whispered and stroked Decius's chest. 'I want to be left alone. With you.'

The explanation seemed to satisfy Decius, who immediately went over and snuffed out the light. Marc came over to him in the darkness, and reached up to stroke his beardless face, ran his fingers lightly over his cheek, tangled his fingers in his hair.

'You feel so beautiful here in the dark,' he said. His hands travelled down the side of Decius's body, and undid the buckle of his belt, dropping it and the attached scabbard to the ground. He took the hem of the Roman's tunic, and pulled it over his head, leaving long and lingering kisses on his thighs, his belly, his nipples and his neck as he did so.

Marc reached down and touched Decius's cock, gently at first, with just his fingertips, then with his whole hand, stroking it up and down with light teasing caresses. In the darkness it seemed even longer, the contours more defined, the vein along the side of the shaft thicker. Marc longed to have it in his mouth, ached to lick its whole length with his tongue.

'You've got such a beautiful prick,' he whispered, as he pulled on Decius, and Decius kissed him tenderly on the neck. 'Long and hard and tasty. You don't know just how much I want it in me again. How much I want to feel you pounding away inside me with that gorgeous, beautiful, marvellous cock.'

'Take off your clothes.'

Marc shook his head and kissed Decius briefly on the lips. 'Not yet,' he said. 'Let me suck you first. Then you can fuck me.'

Marc knelt down and kissed Decius's sandalled feet, taking each of his big toes in his mouth in turn. Worshipping at the feet of his lord and master. Then his tongue trailed up Decius's muscular calves, then to his inner thighs. Decius pressed his legs together, holding Marc's head there, running his fingers through the boy's silken hair.

Marc looked up at Decius. His huge erection was clearly visible even in the darkness of the tent. It stood out from his crotch, a proud expression of his masculinity.

'It looks so good,' Marc said and licked the underside of it with darting flicks of his tongue, causing the prick to twitch involuntarily, and Decius to sigh with contentment. 'Let me taste it, Decius, let me taste that wonderful cock. It's already been in my arse. Now let me take it in my mouth.'

Marc held Decius's cock by its base, and gently guided it towards his mouth, sucking it all into him, before taking it out, and teasing its head with the tip of his tongue, leaving trails of saliva all around the tiny slit which was already moistening with pre-come.

Marc began to tug gently on the legionary's penis, while at the same time moving his mouth up and down on the tip of his cock, occasionally gently pinching it with his teeth until Decius was close to coming, close to shooting his seed into Marc's mouth. Again and again, Marc brought Decius to the brink of orgasm, sensing the Roman's balls tightening. Then he would stop, leaving Decius gasping and trembling.

Marc kept Decius's cock just this side of coming for what felt like hours, using just the touch of his lips and his flickering tongue. Finally he stopped and looked up, but continued to stroke him, making Decius desperate for the full and blissful release.

'Can you feel it, Decius?' Marc asked. 'All that come welling up inside you? You can't wait for it to shoot out of you, to spurt out all over me, drenching me with it. Just feel my tongue, licking you up and down. Licking. Up and down, up and down. Oh, you taste so good. So very good, Decius. Let me have it now. Let me see you come, let me taste it all, Decius, every last drop of it until you're dry, let me have it, Decius!'

'Yes!' cried Decius, as Marc's words, Marc's hand, Marc's mouth, finally brought him to the wonderful, longed-for climax. 'Yes! Yes! Take it all! I'm coming, oh gods, oh Marc, I'm coming, I'm coming, I'm coming *now*!'

A gout of thick come shot from Decius's cock, covering Marc's face and shoulders; Marc clamped his mouth over the twitching, throbbing helmet, determined not to waste another mouthful as he eagerly fed on Decius's load.

He tugged harder on Decius's cock, milking it for every last drop of spunk, licking and sucking the head until Decius wept with ecstasy, unable to control the trembling in his body at the exquisite sensation of release.

Decius fondly stroked Marc's head as the final shudders of his orgasm coursed through him. 'Oh gods, Marc, that was so wonderful –' he began, and then frowned as he saw Marc stand up in the darkness. Strong arms grabbed him from behind. Arms that weren't Marc's.

'We're glad you enjoyed it, Roman,' said Karl, who had crept unnoticed into the tent while Marc had been bringing Decius to orgasm – unnoticed by Decius, but not by Marc. 'Perhaps I should give you another taste of my cock?'

Decius struggled in Karl's arms, but the barbarian was too strong for him as he led him to the corner of the tent. Unable to struggle, unable to move, Decius had to submit to being tied up with the same rope as had previously bound Marc and Karl.

'You fooled me,' Decius hissed angrily, bitterly, as Karl ripped off a strip of cloth from the legionary's tunic before stuffing it into his mouth to stop him calling out to Sulla and the others.

'You fooled yourself,' Karl said. 'Why would someone like Marc want a Roman bastard like you?' He yanked the rope tight, and Decius grunted, even through the makeshift gag.

'Don't hurt him,' said Marc, as Karl finished tying the general up. Marc knew that they had to escape: not just for themselves, but to carry out Cimber's promise – especially in light of what he had just read – but something inside him wasn't proud of deceiving Decius. Decius wasn't a bad man – that was obvious. Unlike some of his brutal comrades, he had a decency about him, a solid core of goodness that Marc couldn't help thinking he'd betrayed. He just hoped that he would live long enough to make it up to him. Somehow.

Leaving Decius behind, Marc and Karl exited the tent, and stood for a second in the clearing.

'What now?' Marc hissed, careful not to disturb the legionaries in the other tent.

'What now?' Karl laughed. 'I would have thought that was obvious. He nodded at the horse. 'We take Bucephalus and make for Rome.'

Marc nodded. *Yes, Rome.* After reading the scroll in Decius's tent, getting to Rome and warning Nero had to be their priority. Because, if they didn't, the results could bring down an empire.

'Our hospitality not good enough, boys?' The gruff voice cut across the silent clearing, rooting Marcus and Karl to the spot. They turned to see a familiar figure silhouetted in front of the other tent: the thickset build of Drusus. Behind him, Sulla and Andronicus were stirring.

Marc looked at Karl, silently asking him what to do, but the expression on the young German's face made it all very clear.

We've lost.

With an involuntary shudder, Marc allowed himself to be led meekly back to the tree. Rome still lay before them. But so did slavery.

Seven

Compared with the events of the last few days, the final day spent reaching Rome was uneventful. Once again, Marc and Karl followed behind Decius atop his horse, which was flanked by Drusus and Sulla, while Andronicus stood guard behind them. The only difference between the previous days' marching and today's was the behaviour of Decius.

Nothing had been said that morning. After a brutal kick in the side from Sulla, Marc and Karl had awoken to a fresh, sunny morning – and a quiet, reflective Decius. None of the general's previous interest in the two potential slaves was evident: especially not his covert glances at Marc, which had been replaced by a reluctance even to meet his gaze. No reference was made to Marc's earlier betrayal, but to Marc, none needed to be made. Any warmth that had existed between him and Decius was gone, replaced by an icy silence, a coldness that seemed to begin somewhere deep within Decius. It was almost as if Decius were a spurned lover . . .

And for that reason – which Marc couldn't quite fathom – he seemed hurt.

★ ★ ★

As they marched the last few hours towards the seven hills of Rome and the glories of the Eternal City, Marc looked back over the last few days – especially his own feelings, his own behaviour. It was as if the influx of emotions that he had never felt before had opened up a side of him at which he had never dared to look.

Less than a week ago, he had been a scholar in far-off Britannia, his only thoughts revolving around Cimber's lessons and his vague promises of seeing Rome. Then the Obsidian Legion had arrived and, in destroying his life of ordered calm, had unlocked feelings and emotions inside him that he had denied for far too long. The simple act of witnessing Justin's submission to Gaius and Varus had changed Marc irrevocably: for the first time, he had been able to face up to his feelings for other men. The first had been Alexander, faithful friend of his father – he had died because of his own feelings towards Marc. Then Karl: would Karl be here, bruised and battered and unable to escape a life of slavery, if it hadn't been for his love of Marc? How many people had died or suffered because of Marc? And how many were yet to come? Who knew what sort of an ally Decius could have become if Marc hadn't betrayed him?

'Are you all right?' Karl said softly, trying to keep his voice down in case one of the Romans overheard.

Marc sighed. 'I was just thinking how badly things have gone since I left Britannia.' He hesitated for a second: dare he reveal any more of his emotions to Karl, and risk his being hurt even more? But Marc needed a friend more than he needed anything else at that moment, and Karl was definitely that. 'Everyone I've cared for – everyone who's cared for me – has been hurt because of it. You included,' he added.

Karl shrugged. 'We live in troubled times, Marc. I know you see me as a barbarian: uneducated, uncivilised, with primitive beliefs and primitive feelings. But my own people are a proud race. Seeing everything that we believe in, everything we are, taken away from us by Rome, has made us hard. We fight because we have to.' He frowned, as if weighing something up in his mind. Then he continued. 'I have seen you look at this often.' He touched the fish-shaped piercing in his navel. 'You don't know what it is, do you?'

Marc shook his head. 'I guess it's more than just decorative.'

'It represents my own beliefs. The gods of Olympus are not my gods, Marc. I believe in a God who sent his son to us. A son who later died for all of our sins. That is my belief, and I am willing to die myself for that belief. I am willing to die so that the others who share my beliefs can live and spread His message. I am willing to die before I will allow these Roman bastards to crush that. You are disturbed because you are beginning to question your own feelings, your own beliefs.'

Marc was shocked: Karl's words had struck a raw nerve. Just as he had with Alexander, Marc had seriously underestimated Karl. He was far from being a barbarian: Marc would even have gone so far as to call him . . . spiritual? Was this what being part of the Roman Empire did to a person? Taught them to see everyone else as an inferior? Karl was anything but inferior. Indeed, at that moment, it was Marc who felt inferior. He didn't even deserve the German's friendship.

Suddenly, everything crystallised in Marc's mind. If it hadn't been for the Roman Empire, if it hadn't been for his father and Cimber and all of the others who saw Rome as idealised perfection, Marc wouldn't be in this situation, and Alexander and Justin would probably still be alive. It all became clear to Marc. The Roman Empire was to blame: and Decius and Gaius's plan would make sure that it suffered for everything that had been done to Marc, to his people, to the whole world.

With that thought burning in his mind like a beacon, Marc remained silent for the rest of the short march to Rome. To the future.

★　★　★

Rome was beautiful: even with his new-found hatred of the empire still burning away, Marc could see that. Perhaps Decius had deliberately chosen the route by which they approached the Eternal City, or maybe it was more by luck than design, but Marc's first view of the city had been as breathtaking as it had been unexpected. The party had been marching through a valley, its top obscured by groves of thick, sweet-smelling cypress trees. They had finally reached the end of the valley and made their way through one last copse of trees, only to emerge at the foot of the seven hills.

Rome was built on seven hills; Marc knew this from his lessons with Cimber. But little was visible of the hills themselves: Rome was a vast, sprawling city of marble and wood, stone and statues. Buildings rose above them, the like of which Marc had never even imagined, let alone seen. He had always thought that his father's villa in Britannia was impressive, but it was nothing more than a hut compared with the villas that he could see around him. And not only villas: there were temples, rows of shops, fountains . . . Marc shook his head. How could Rome have failed to conquer the world, when the empire had grown from something like this? A last gasp of his old devotion to the empire, and then he remembered his mission. The empire was evil, and had to be destroyed. All Marc had to do was keep his mouth shut and wait. His unspoken promise to Cimber – to warn the Emperor – was instantly broken: Cimber was no better than the other debauched degenerates who lived in this monument to conquest and power. Marc glanced round at Karl, and was taken aback to see that the German was also in awe, his eyes wide at the magnificent sight in front of them. But beautiful buildings didn't mean beautiful people: put a pig in a palace and it was still a pig.

Marc's reverie didn't last very long: Decius was urging Bucephalus onwards, towards an ornate set of gates surrounding a large stone building that could just be seen beyond them, and a shove in the back from Andronicus urged him forward.

'The auction pit,' muttered Karl.

Marc frowned. 'How did you learn so much about Rome?' he asked sarcastically.

'What else could it be? You don't have to have a Roman education to work that out,' Karl sneered.

Marc smiled: Karl had a point.

The party stopped in front of a smaller door set into the big wooden gates. The door immediately opened, to reveal two more legionaries. Or were they? Cimber had touched upon the different orders of soldiers in Rome, and had tried to explain to Marcus how to tell them apart simply by the subtle difference in their armour and clothing. At the time, Marcus hadn't paid much attention to Cimber: why would he ever need to know something like that? Now he knew only too well.

The major difference between the four members of the Obsidian Legion who surrounded Karl and Marcus and the two inside the auction pit was the colour of the plumes on their helmets: Decius and his men used black feathers, while the others wore white plumes.

Despite clearly being from different legions, the two in the pit obviously knew Decius. After the general had dismounted his horse, a few minutes were spent in small talk before the party was allowed to continue.

The inside of the auction pit was huge: a vast open space, surrounded on three sides by tall white stone buildings. As well as a large number of legionaries, there were even more people who were clearly not members of the Roman army: people in simple togas and tunics, others in clothing that Marc didn't actually recognise. If that hadn't been a sufficient clue to these people's identities, the various skin colours definitely were. Many were olive-skinned Romans, it was true, but there were countless others with the fair skin tone of the northern provinces, or the ruddy colouring of the Picts. There were others whose like Marc had never seen, only ever heard about: people whose skins were as black as ebony. Marc guessed that these were slaves from the southern states of Rome, such as the Nubians that Cimber had talked about.

A yank on his arm interrupted his thoughts: Andronicus once more.

'This is where we say goodbye, boys,' he said with a sneer. 'You've been a lot of fun, but you're worth more to us as someone else's slaves. I just hope your new masters don't mind used goods.' With that he shoved the two of them towards one of the other legionaries. 'All yours, Sebastian.'

Sebastian nodded. He was of the same type as Drusus – perhaps even stockier. His body was solid and extremely hairy: tufts of it were visible above the red of his uniform tunic, while his face was virtually covered with a close-cropped back beard. But his eyes lacked the cruelty that permanently burned in Drusus's; if anything, he looked quite friendly. Friendly for a slaver, Marc thought bitterly.

Sebastian turned to Decius and saluted him. 'Your runner wasn't lying when he said you had two which would fetch a good sum, old friend. I can think of at least three senators who will pay handsomely for the German, and I'm sure we can both guess who'll want the pretty one.' Marc frowned: *that* sounded ominous.

Decius smiled, but Marc could see that there was no humour in his face. 'I'm glad to have been of service, Sebastian.'

'What are your plans now?' Sebastian asked. 'Back to Britannia?'

Decius shook his head. 'Some business to take care of in Rome,' he said, briefly touching the fibula which fastened his cloak: the same Pan-symbol that Gaius and Cimber had worn. The knowledge that Decius would be continuing with his plan to destroy the Roman Empire made the thought of slavery bearable. *Almost* bearable, Marc corrected.

With that, the four members of the Obsidian Legion grouped together. Only then did Decius finally look at Marc with some of the feeling that he had shown previously. 'You are tenacious,

Marcus Lucius. I wish you luck with your new life.' And then he was gone, leading Bucephalus and his men out of the auction-pit gate. As the door in the gate shut, Marc looked at Karl.

'So, this is it. Rome.'

Karl's reaction was unexpected: he burst into a grin that Marc had never seen before. 'Just where I wanted to be, Marc. This is where it begins.' With that, he allowed himself to be led away by Sebastian.

The next few hours were pleasant enough – for potential slaves. Marc and Karl were taken to a large dormitory, big enough to sleep over a hundred slaves. As they had made their way there, Sebastian had explained the procedure: they would be given a chance to clean up, be given fresh clothes, a hearty meal and a night's sleep, and then sold into slavery the next morning at the daily auctions. Sebastian was careful to impress upon them the importance of the next day's auction, though. Whereas six of the daily auctions were open to everyone, the one held on the fifth day of the week – tomorrow – was open only to the highest echelons of the Roman Empire: consuls, senators, senior members of the Roman army. Only the best slaves were put up for auction on the fifth day, but Sebastian had said he had no doubt that Marc and Karl would qualify. As he put them into the charge of one of the slave masters, his tone changed, but only briefly; Sebastian ran his auction pit with a gentle hand. But escape – or the attempt to escape – was punishable with a single sentence: death.

Marc and Karl had been given adjacent beds – if the word could be applied to the rough straw mattresses on the cold stone floor. Still, they promised a lot more comfort than the base of a tree or the cramped hold of a slave galley.

Thomas, the slave master who was responsible for their last few hours of freedom, watched them silently. He was a large man, over six feet tall, with cropped blond hair and a tailored beard which only covered his chin. He was well-built, even larger than Sebastian or Drusus, but his frame spoke of solidity rather than aggression: an immovable object rather than an irresistible force.

'Not quite the villa you're used to, I expect,' he said suddenly. 'Don't worry: this time tomorrow you'll be with your new masters. And given the people who come to tomorrow's auction, you'll be living in luxury – until they tire of you, of course.'

'What do we do until then?' asked Marc, getting a bit tired himself: tired of the little veiled threats that Sebastian and Thomas were so fond of dropping into the conversation; tired of the fact that everyone seemed to know who he was and where he came from. Since the only person who knew this was Gaius, Marc was surprised that the Roman wasn't there to greet them in person. A twinge of sadness hit him; somewhere deep inside, Marc had thought that Gaius actually cared about him. Now it was clear that he was nothing more than a bit of British trash, a distraction from the elegance and culture of Gaius's proper Roman friends. Someone to laugh at. Slightly angered, he glared at Thomas. 'Any chance of some food?'

'My, aren't we the impatient ones?' Thomas laughed. He folded his strong arms over his broad, tunic-covered chest. 'You're going to need a good hosing down before we try to sell you off, that's for certain. You two smell like street urchins from the gutter.'

'I'm sorry if our barbarian smells offend your fine Roman nose,' Karl said coldly.

Thomas raised an eyebrow. 'Not at all: I quite like it. But some of our clients are a bit . . . choosy. It's always best to show our wares in their best light, don't you think?' He beckoned for them to follow him. 'You'll be given food later on this evening. For now I want you to relax and get yourselves cleaned up. I'll have clean clothes ready for you when you come back.'

'Back?' asked Marc. 'Back from where?'
'From the steam room.'

In contrast to learning about the differences between the legions, Marc had taken notice of Cimber's lessons regarding Roman sanitation. Even Cimber's normally nonchalant tones had mellowed into a nostalgic reminiscence when he had described the way that Roman houses had running water, facilities for disposing of your daily toilet which didn't involve buckets and ditches, underfloor heating which made every day like the middle of summer, and the wonders of the steam room. At the time, Marc hadn't quite seen the attraction. A room full of hot steam sounded less like relaxation and more like punishment.

Now he could see why Cimber had liked it so much. Thomas had led the two of them down a windowless, torch-lit corridor, down winding staircases and even more corridors, until they reached a heavy wooden door: a door flanked by two guards.

'This is the only way out of the steam room, boys, so don't get any ideas about escaping. Anyway, I feel like a break, so I'll be keeping an eye on you.' From Thomas's tone, it was obvious what he meant by that. He nodded at one of the guards who pulled the door open; Marc was almost knocked off his feet by the blast of scalding air which hit him. 'After you,' instructed Thomas.

Unlike the rest of the auction pit, which was built predominantly of wood or rough stone blocks, a lot more effort – and money – had been spent on the steam room. Marc and Karl found themselves in some kind of atrium, a marble-floored hall with about twenty marble benches. A large wooden tub stood in the middle of the atrium.

'Since it's unlikely that you would have ever seen a place like this before, I'll explain it to you. The baths are through there –' Thomas gestured towards an archway on their left. 'Spend some time in there getting the grime off. Then you go through to the steam room –' The archway to the right was indicated. 'That'll refresh you. Then it's back to the baths, and then out. That should clean up even a couple of barbarians like you.' He pointed a finger at Marc. 'Clothes off.'

'What?'

'Those shorts are even grubbier than you. Take them off and throw them in the tub. You too,' he added to Karl.

Well aware of Thomas's interested gaze, Marc pulled down his shorts, which he had to admit were absolutely filthy with the dirt and sweat of his recent travels. As he bent to remove his sandals, he couldn't help glancing at Karl, and was pleased to catch a glimpse of the German's thick cock. He wondered if and when he would ever see it erect, or feel it sliding inside his arse once more. All the evidence suggested that Marc and Karl would be parted for ever tomorrow, but Marc still trusted the special bond that he knew existed between the two of them. Something inside him said that he and Karl would be together when their mutual dream came true: they would stand together, hand in hand, and watch Rome burn.

'Right,' said Thomas. 'Into the baths.' As Marc and Karl set off through the archway, Marc was aware that Thomas was removing his own tunic. For a second, he wondered whether seducing the Roman would assist their escape. Then he remembered Decius, remembered what Rome had done to Marc himself . . . and reconsidered. The baths would be just that: a chance to rest before his new life of slavery began.

The baths were even more impressive than the atrium: the ceiling was a high dome of arched black marble, decorated with a white marble bas-relief. Marc guessed that the only reason that the baths were underground was to allow for the dome. Such extravagance was understandable when you realised that the slave trade was one of the most lucrative parts of the Roman economy. The Roman Empire ran on slavery: without its slaves, it would collapse. With that thought warming him, Marc looked at the other occupants of the baths.

About ten other men were in the water, but there was no way of telling if they were fellow slaves or slavers: the baths seemed to be making everyone equal, if the yells of enjoyment and excited horseplay from the far end of the room were anything to go by. Further investigation made it clear that something else was making them equal as well: sex. The majority of the others in the baths were in groups of twos and threes, hands touching and stroking, mouths licking and sucking, cocks being wanked and arses being fucked. Marc felt his own shaft beginning to stir, and decided that he ought to do something about hiding it.

Without waiting for Thomas's instructions – indeed, he really wanted to hide it before Thomas joined them – Marc walked over to the side of the baths. Marble steps led into the gently steaming water, and Marc began to descend.

The water was as warm as it looked, warm and relaxing, more relaxing than Marc could remember. The villa in Britannia seemed centuries away – a past life that was becoming more and more distant with each new turn of events. To survive, Marc would have to forget that he had ever had a previous life as a scholar. As he submerged himself in the baths, he allowed the waters to wash away the old Marc, the scholar, the Briton.

He felt a comforting hand on his shoulder and looked round to see Karl next to him. It did nothing to stifle his erection.

'I am worried about you, Marc,' he whispered. 'You do not seem the same since last night.'

Marc shook his head. 'I'm not. But don't worry: it's time to make a new start, and this is where it happens. Let's just enjoy the baths.'

'That's right, enjoy yourselves.' Both Karl and Marc looked round: Thomas was stepping into the waters. Without his clothes, Marc could see how big he really was: the extremely broad shoulders and chest, solid arms and legs. He had obviously been very well-muscled in his youth, and this was just beginning to turn to fat. All this did was take the edge off him, making his large frame look less threatening. His entire body was covered with a light covering of dark-blond hair: chest, back, arms and legs, with a dense forest of it around his cock, which was beginning to stiffen as he stared at Karl and Marc. When fully erect, it was going to be both long and thick. Thomas looked familiar, and suddenly Marc realised why: he looked like Marc's vision of Jupiter in his dream. Fired by this, Marc briefly entertained the idea of sucking it, sucking it until the slave trader came in his mouth. But that once again reminded him of Decius, and he banished the thought. He would save himself for his new master: that way, he could persuade his conscience that he had no choice but to enjoy himself, pleasure himself. And if his master got hurt, well . . . it was his master's fault.

'You're new.' A boy, no older than Marc, had waded over towards them. 'I'm Cletus,' he said in an amicable manner. 'Here for the auctions?'

Even though this was a rather pointless thing to say – what else would they be there for? – Marc decided that Cletus was simply trying to be friendly. 'I'm Marc and this is Karl. I'm from Britannia and Karl's from Germanica. And you?'

Cletus shrugged. 'I'm from a village outside of Rome. I've been here for about five weeks now. No one wants to buy me, I'm afraid.' And he did look Roman: there was an olive tint to his skin, and his hair was black. The beginnings of what Marc guessed would one day be an impressively hairy chest was just visible around the nipples and on his flat, well-defined stomach. His face was angular, with chiselled cheekbones and a strong chin. Marc looked into the boy's wide brown eyes and could see hope mixed with a sense of hopelessness; he wondered whether the same emotions were visible on his own face.

'Why not?' Marc asked.

'Because he's Roman,' said Thomas, butting into the conversation. 'Roman slaves aren't fashionable at the moment. Those with money want something a little more ... exotic, shall we say?' He moved through the water towards Cletus, and there was genuine concern in his voice when he addressed him. 'Poor old Cletus is on his last chance now.'

'Last chance?' asked Marc.

'Rules of the slave trade,' said Cletus softly. 'If you aren't sold after five weeks, you're obviously not going to be sold.'

A horrible thought occurred to Marc. 'You're not going to be ...' He left the sentence unfinished.

Thomas looked shocked. He placed a big hairy arm around Cletus and squeezed him affectionately. 'Of course not. What do you think we are – barbarians? I'm putting Cletus up for tomorrow's auction. If he isn't picked for that, he's given a chance to become a free man.'

'He becomes a gladiator,' stated Karl flatly. 'And dies.'

Thomas pursed his lips. 'There is always that chance, yes. But I have every confidence that if it comes to that, Cletus here will acquit himself perfectly.'

Marc was puzzled: Thomas was genuinely fond of the boy. Then he thought of Gaius and Decius. For both their sakes, Marc just hoped that neither of them hurt the other like he had hurt Decius.

'Anyway, enough of this,' said Thomas. 'Cletus, I'm showing our new boys the steam room. Care to join us?'

It was hot, hot and humid, and Marc had never known anything like it. The steam room was a huge chamber with a very low ceiling, although the far reaches of the room weren't particularly visible through the warm fog. The steam room was obviously more popular than the baths: Marc lost count of the number of shadowy figures shrouded in the steam.

Suddenly he felt a hand grab his cock, bringing it to full

erection in moments. Looking round, he saw Thomas next to him.

'You're a good-looking boy, Marc. You have no idea of the number of boys who arrive at the auction pit that I would buy myself.' Thomas sighed. 'But that just isn't to be. All I can do is make sure that you're well looked after until I hand you over to someone else.'

Marc smiled sheepishly. Unlike his earlier, faked naïveté with Decius, Marc really didn't know what to do. Thomas was obviously attracted to him, and Marc found that the slave trader's huge, muscular body and friendly, trusting face, the strong hairy arms and long, thick cock, were making his own body respond despite himself.

With Gaius and Decius, with Karl and with the others of the Obsidian Legion, it had been the cruelty, the domination, that had attracted him, that had turned him on. But there was a tenderness about Thomas that reminded Marc of someone else.

Alexander. Somehow, the Pict had managed to combine strength and warmth; while Karl embodied Alexander's strength, the warmth was here, here inside Thomas.

Reaching out, Marc grasped Thomas's cock, which was warm and moist with the steam, but hard as iron. Marc glanced over Thomas's shoulder and saw Karl and Cletus standing very close to one another. It was clear that they had the same thing on their minds as he and Thomas.

Thomas smiled. 'That's right: squeeze it. Wank it, Marc.'

Marc obliged: he slowly but firmly pulled Thomas's foreskin back, revealing the large, reddened helmet, already coated with pre-come. Still grasping tightly, he rubbed his thumb over the velvet softness of Thomas's helmet, massaging the leaking slit and making the slave trader gasp with the sensation. Then he pulled the foreskin forward, then back, until he had built up a rhythm, his thumb still driving Thomas wild with its slow, circular motions. Thomas let out a tiny groan as Marc continued. 'Suck it, Marc. Please, suck it.'

Marc didn't need any more encouragement: he'd wanted to take Thomas's thick meat since he'd first seen it. Dropping to his knees on the damp marble floor of the steam room, he leant forward and reached out with his tongue. He flicked the end of Thomas's helmet, taking a droplet of sweet pre-come into his mouth. Then he started to tease at the slave trader's dick slit, forcing it open with his tongue, continuing where his thumb had left off. He heard Thomas groaning above him, groaning for him to stop, but he wouldn't – he couldn't. It felt too good, tasted too good, for him to stop now.

He moved one of his hands so it was resting amongst the fur on Thomas's stomach; he stroked the thick hair, his fingers entwined in it, even as he took all of Thomas's helmet in his mouth and ran his tongue all over the hot, salty skin. Then his hand climbed up Thomas's body, from the stomach to the solid, muscled chest. He sought out one nipple, then the other, and teased them, squeezed them, turning Thomas's groans of pleasure to sharp cries of pain.

As he was doing this, he peered through the steam; Cletus had his back to Karl, while the German had his hands on the Roman's shoulders. Marc felt a sudden pang of jealousy: he wanted Karl's cock inside *him*, not someone else. Then he heard Thomas's groans become stronger, more insistent, and Marc knew that Thomas's release was close. Still squeezing Thomas's nipples, Marc put his other hand on Thomas's big balls and tightened his grip. His mouth slid further down Thomas's shaft, taking as much of it as he could before pulling back, then sliding down it again. One hand searched through the chest hair for the slave trader's nipples, the other squeezed the hairy ball sac, urging Thomas to come, urging him to shoot his load in Marc's impatient mouth.

With a deep cry, a roar that was swallowed up by the steam, Thomas finally came, his hips grinding his cock even further into Marc's mouth with violent, forceful shoves. Marc thought he would choke with the thick cock filling his mouth and the spurts of salty come that hit the back of his throat, but he managed to swallow it, swallow every drop that shot from Thomas, not wanting to waste any of it. Finally Thomas's thrusts ended, and he gently pulled his cock from Marc's mouth, its hardness already subsiding. Marc looked up at him and smiled warmly, aware of the dribble of come on his chin.

Thomas stroked Marc's hair and gave him a grateful smile in return, wiping off the come with a finger and holding it to Marc's lips. Marc drank the last of Thomas's come and sighed.

'Thank you,' said Thomas. 'Once again, I find myself saddened that one of my charges has to leave me. Unlike poor Cletus, I don't think that there's much chance of your being left on the shelf at tomorrow's auctions.'

Marc was taken aback: that had been the first time that sex had been so tender, so free of domination and of power. He had never realised that it could be that way and still feel so good, and he hadn't even come yet. Even as he considered what to do about his own orgasm, the answer was given to him.

'Perhaps you'd like to join your friend and Cletus,' Thomas added almost wistfully. 'They might like a little company.' As Marc got to his feet, Thomas vanished into the steam.

Karl's cock was teasing Cletus's ring, the engorged, moist helmet stroking the black hairs, pushing gently forward, just enough to make the Roman slave gasp at the slight penetration, before Karl pulled away completely. Karl was enjoying this: another Roman to dominate, another Roman to fuck. He would keep teasing Cletus until the boy could no longer stand it, then Karl would drive his cock into the Roman's tight, virgin arse until he was filled with Karl's spunk.

'Karl . . .' said the voice in his ear. At the familiar tone, Karl pulled away from Cletus and span round to see Marc standing next to him.

'Finished pleasuring your Roman master?' he sneered, more

176

spitefully than he had intended. Part of him was disappointed –
jealous, even – that Marc had chosen to have sex with their
slave trader. Tonight would probably be the last night that they
spent together, and this was probably the last chance that they
would have to have sex, but Marc chose to –

He stopped as Marc put his finger on Karl's lips. 'No words,
nothing. Tonight's our last chance, Karl. After tonight, we
won't ever see one another again.'

'But . . .' Karl nodded in the vague direction of Thomas,
although he couldn't see anything through the fog.

Marc shook his head and gestured at his erection. 'I've saved
it for you, Karl. All of this is yours.'

In that moment, Karl realised that Marc had done what no
one else had ever done. He had suspected it from the moment
that he had seen him boarding the *Cygnus*, but had refused to
think about it, refused to consider it. He was Karl of Kuster,
with a mission to bring down Rome. Nothing else mattered
. . . nothing else apart from this Briton who had invaded every
single moment of his thoughts, of his life.

Marc had touched Karl's soul, without Karl realising it. And
now it was too late. Too late to stop it, and too late to do
anything about it. He was vaguely aware that Cletus had moved
away, drawn into the steam by the promise of someone else,
but Karl didn't care. The person he wanted was standing in
front of him. The knowledge that, in a few short hours, he
might never see him again was enough for him to reach out
and grab him, squeeze him tightly.

'I . . . I love you, Marc,' he whispered. The words came
from a place buried so deep inside him that he had doubted
they would ever surface. But Marc had reached him, touched
him there.

'I know,' Marc replied. 'Just hold me.'

For long moments, the two of them grabbed onto each
other, both sharing the knowledge that this could be the end,
but both with their own reasons for the strength of the emotion

between them. For Karl, it was anger: anger at himself for waiting so long to open himself up to Marc. For Marc, Karl suspected that it was also anger, but anger at the empire, which was tearing something beautiful apart before either of them had had a real chance to experience it.

Karl knew that he wasn't as educated as Marc; he knew that he wouldn't be able to find the words necessary to explain all of this to the man he loved. But he knew something that would explain it more clearly than words; something which he knew Marc would understand.

'Marc: I want you to fuck me.'

The expression on Marc's face made it clear that the Briton understood perfectly. I *decide when I get fucked. Not you and not anyone else. Do you understand?* Those had been the words that Karl had used after they had first had sex. The truth was, no one had ever fucked him. Ever. Just as he had taken Marc's virginity, now Marc was going to take his. And brave Karl, hero of the Germanic battlefields, found that he was nervous, as nervous as a young girl.

Marc grabbed Karl's hand tightly and pulled him into the humid fog: there was no violence, just impatience, as if Marc couldn't wait another moment. It was a feeling Karl not only understood, but shared. Other shapes were around them, and Karl could just about make out men fucking, wanking, sucking – a feeling of desperation in the air, as if they all knew that this was the last time that they were going to see their friends, their comrades, their lovers. But no one else mattered: as far as Karl was concerned, the steam room could have been empty of everyone apart from him and Marc. Finally, after a frantic search, they found an empty bench.

'Lie down,' said Marc softly. There was none of the usual submission in Marc's voice, but nor was there an air of domination. Before, they had had sex. Now they were making love.

Karl lay down on the damp but warm marble, trying not to

slide off – the heat of the steam room meant that both he and Marc were covered in sweat. He moved so that his arse was level with the edge of the bench; it was up to Marc to decide exactly what position he wanted.

Marc placed his hands beneath Karl's thighs and lifted them up and apart, and Karl pushed his arse forward. Slowly, Marc came closer, his erection so hard that it was almost vertical against his taut stomach. Karl could see the helmet glistening, though whether this was with sweat or pre-come he didn't know, and didn't care. All he wanted was to feel the man he loved inside him, completing him.

Marc's helmet brushed the hairs around Karl's ring, and Karl felt a shiver of wonderful anticipation run through him. Without thinking, he pushed his arse even further towards Marc's cock; at the same time, he relaxed his arse muscles, inviting his lover's shaft to enter him.

Marc obviously didn't need to be asked twice: gently, he continued to exert pressure, pushing his body forward, sliding his sweat-and-pre-come soaked cock into Karl's arse.

As the helmet passed through Karl's ring, he gasped: the pain was unbelievable. But he didn't want Marc to stop; he wanted him to carry on, to drive all of his cock inside him. Despite the pain, he forced his arse onto Marc's shaft, forced him to enter him, inch by inch.

'I want all of your dick inside me, Marc,' Karl gasped. 'I want to feel you become part of me.'

'Oh yes,' said Marc. 'All of it, all of my cock in your arse.' Less gently, more forcefully, he pushed even harder, and Karl felt more and more of his lover's meat in him, filling him up. The pain continued to grow, and Karl – tough warrior Karl – wasn't sure that he could take much more of it. Only his desire to feel all of Marc inside him made him carry on – until the pain stopped. But it didn't stop: suddenly it wasn't pain, it was a total, utter satisfaction that filled him from head to toe. He knew that Marc was inside him: all of him. They were together.

Then he felt Marc slide out: not completely, but the sensation was exquisite. Karl's hand reached up to tug on his nipple ring, pulling on it, squeezing on his tit, amplifying the pleasure that he was feeling. His other hand rubbed his sweat-soaked stomach and chest.

Marc suddenly slammed his cock into Karl, who gasped with the pleasure-pain of the hard stroke. Marc pulled out then drove back in, fucking Karl with a building rhythm. As he did so, he reached out and took Karl's stiff, ready cock in his hand and started to wank him, pulling him with strokes that were timed with his deep fucks.

Karl lay on the bench, experiencing a pleasure that he had never felt before: his lover was inside him, fucking him, filling him with his long, thick cock; his lover was wanking him, squeezing his cock with a tight, measured grip. And now Marc's other hand was tugging and twisting his tit-ring, pinching the nipple then pulling on the ring.

Karl could feel himself losing control; he could feel his climax building up in his balls, in his stomach. His body began to tingle, waves of pleasure that washed over him, each one bringing him closer and closer. Karl, veteran of the battlefield, the man who would topple Rome, started to whimper with the overwhelming sense of completeness, of utter release.

For a brief second, he was aware of Marc's breathing: short, hard grunts. Marc was close, and Karl tightened his arse around Marc's cock, squeezing it and releasing it in time with Marc's deep strokes. Marc's balls were slamming into Karl's arse, his hands were touching him, tugging at him, wanking him . . .

With a deep, guttural cry, Karl came, knowing as he did so that Marc was coming inside him at exactly the same time. With wave upon wave of his own orgasm, Karl could feel Marc's dick pulse within him, shooting into him, filling him. With each spasm of Karl's cock, with each gout of white come that landed on his stomach and his chest, Karl let out another groan, a groan echoed by Marc, until there was nothing left inside him except total satisfaction. He slumped back on the wet marble and sighed. It was a sigh like no other: a sigh of total, utter contentment.

Marc gently pulled his cock out of him and then straddled him, sitting on Karl's stomach. Then he leant down and kissed him, deeply, passionately, until they were one person, one person in body and soul.

'Time to leave, I'm afraid.' Thomas was standing next to them, a look of kindly concern on his face. 'You've a big day tomorrow.'

As Marc clambered off him, Karl sat up and sighed. But it wasn't a sigh of pleasure. Finally, he had met someone who made him feel complete. And tomorrow they would be torn apart. For ever.

Eight

The mid-morning sun was sweltering as Marc and Karl were led from the dormitory into the wide open arena which marked the end of their lives as free men, and the beginning of their true slavery. There were ten of them in today's auction: as well as Marc and Karl, there was Cletus – looking extremely forlorn – three Nubians, two blond giants who looked like countrymen of Karl, and two whose origins Marc couldn't place. Leading them into the arena was Thomas, who displayed none of his good humour of the previous day; Marc guessed that Thomas's feelings for Cletus were a lot stronger than he let on.

About fifty people were standing in front of the podium on to which the prospective slaves were to be marched. From the look of their clothes and their general demeanour, they were exactly what Thomas had led them to anticipate: the rich and the powerful, the movers and shakers of Roman society. The presence of royal purple – a colour that could only be worn by senators or the Emperor himself, on pain of death – proved that.

You may be a slave, but you're going to be a slave in luxury,

Marc told himself. Then he glanced at Karl, and saw just what he had seen since they had woken that morning, entwined in one another's arms: a cold, hard stoicism, as if the emotions that he had shown the previous night had once more been locked away beneath that iron German exterior. This was Karl's way of dealing with it – and there was nothing that Marc could do about it.

They reached the foot of the podium, where they were told to wait by Thomas. The slave trader mounted the wooden dais and addressed the crowd who, despite their high-born status, were making the noise expected of any rabble.

After a few obsequious words to silence them, Thomas brought the first slave on to the podium. Marc was pleased – and not that surprised – to see that it was Cletus. As much as Thomas would undoubtedly miss him, Marc would rather know that he was safe as a slave than fighting for his life in the gladiatorial arena.

The next hour both flew past and crawled. The auction went by in the background, with slave after slave either being sold or sent back to the dormitory; Marc was dimly aware that Cletus had been bought by someone of status, but that was all. Thomas seemed to be leaving him and Karl to last, although whether that was to give them time together, or simply because he hoped that they would remain unsold and offer him a repeat performance of the previous night, Marc didn't know.

But Marc's attention was focused on Karl. The man he loved, the man who had professed his own love, was like one of the marble statues which were dotted around the arena: cold, unmoving . . . without a soul. No amount of conversation, no gentle touches or stolen glances, provoked even the slightest reaction. Marc was still trying to get something out of him when Thomas indicated for him to come up on the podium.

As the price went up and up, Marc didn't notice. He was still staring at the silent Karl when he realised that he had been sold. He looked at Thomas, who nodded his head at a grey-haired, distinguished-looking man in the white-and-purple-trimmed toga of a senator.

'Senator Flavius, Marc!' Thomas hissed. 'He's one of the most important men in Rome – second only to the Emperor!'

Marc shrugged, but said nothing. His old life was at an end, and nothing made that clearer than Karl's emotionless, expressionless face as Marc allowed himself to be led away. Led away to his new life.

He never even noticed when Karl was sold.

Flavius's villa was almost beyond Marc's ability to describe. It was at least ten times the size of his father's villa, as far as he could tell: it wasn't as if he was given a guided tour. What made it even more breathtaking was the knowledge that this was only the senator's town house. His country home was even bigger.

After Marc had been marched to the villa – Flavius had been carried in a silk-covered litter, hefted on to the shoulders of four huge slaves, while Marc had marched behind with the other two slaves that his new master had purchased – he had immediately been put in the care of one of the established slaves: Philip, a very large man with light ginger hair and a beaming smile.

Philip had made no bones about it: Marc was there to serve, was there to do everything that Flavius asked of him. Marc suppressed a shudder. Flavius might have been rich, he might have been powerful, but there was something about him – an oiliness, an untrustworthiness – that Marc had picked up on immediately, and that repulsed him. He was resigned to the fact that he would be forced to have sex for his master's enjoyment, but the thought of Flavius's hot heaving body above him filled him with disgust.

After being shown through the impressively large atrium, Marc was led through to the rear of the villa: the slave's section of the house. From Philip's dry delivery, Marc gathered that this was where the real work in the house was carried out: the kitchens, the stables, the private baths . . . all of them were the province of the huge army of slaves that Flavius and his wife, Julia, kept around them to shield them from the unpleasant necessity of getting their hands dirty. Marc doubted that they knew how to cook, or how to sew, or how to do any of the things that he and his family had to do in their day-to-day lives. But that was how Rome functioned, he reminded himself: without slaves, the empire would collapse. If only, he thought, as Philip showed him to his room, before wondering how Decius and Gaius were getting on. He started to think about Karl, but banished the image immediately. Karl was the past; indenture to Flavius was his future.

Marc's room was simply decorated, but clean, with a comfortable bed and something he had never seen before: running water. As he looked at the clean, cold water flowing through the copper pipe into a marble bowl, he was hypnotised.

'Flavius likes to tell everyone that even his slaves have running water: nothing like flaunting your wealth for improving your status in the Senate.'

Marc continued to stare at the water until Philip turned it off. 'You share this room with the other three members of . . .' He laughed. 'The bedroom elite.'

'Bedroom elite?' Then Marc had to laugh too. The meaning was obvious, and that part of his new role was hardly unexpected. 'Who are the others?'

'Maximillian, Tavius, Constantine and Cletus. The first three are doing their day jobs –'

'Cletus?' Surely it couldn't be the same one?

'You know him? I suppose Lord Flavius bought him at the same auction as you, so you should know him.'

'So why wasn't he marching with me and the others?' Marc asked.

Philip raised an eyebrow. 'Sometimes, even the great Lord Flavius can't wait that long.' With that, he looked out of the window at the sun. 'Anyway, it's well past midday. If you want something to eat, you'd better come with me to the kitchens. Everything's going to be a bit busy in a couple of hours.'

'Why's that?' asked Marc, following the tubby Roman slave out of his new bedroom.

Philip stopped and smiled – an enigmatic smile. 'The master is having one of his affairs,' he replied, before hurrying off down the mosaic-covered corridor.

It didn't take much to guess what one of Flavius's 'affairs' entailed: the hooded looks from the other slaves when he entered the kitchen were indication enough. Marc was another of Flavius's 'entertainments', something for which he was legendary. While he was eating – and he had to admit that the food was better than anything that he had ever tasted – one of the female slaves took it upon herself to befriend him. There was obviously a camaraderie amongst slaves, a friendship based upon their shared circumstances, and Marc found it most welcome. Without Karl, he was alone: Flavius's extended family of slaves was now *his* family, and he was grateful for it.

Pontonia was probably the oldest woman Marc had ever seen: she claimed to be over fifty years old! But she was filled with a compassion and a love of all things, and Marc found her to be enjoyable company. Pontonia was the head cook. No meal ever went to the *triclinium* – the ornate dining room in which Flavius and his family ate – without Pontonia's last-minute inspection, and there were certain meals that were never left to Rubia or the other under-cooks. 'Lord Flavius always asks for me,' she said proudly.

'So,' said Marc, wiping up the last of the olive oil with a slice of Pontonia's delicious bread, 'what's going to happen to me?'

Pontonia's lined face concertinaed into an expression of kindly concern. 'You've been brought here to replace poor young Janus. He was a lovely boy,' she reminisced.

186

Almost afraid to hear the answer, Marc asked the obvious question. 'What happened to him?'

'That is not for us to know, Marc,' said Baius, the head of Flavius's slaves and Flavius's personal manservant. 'While you are here, you will be better treated than any other slave in Rome – as long as you do what Lord Flavius asks of you.'

And that was that. Philip took Marc back to his room, explaining that tomorrow he would be told his roster of duties throughout the week. For now, he was to rest. After the master and his guests had dined – something which would take hours – Marc would be called. A clean toga was lying on the bed; Marc was expected to wear it.

Philip left, and Marc realised that he had nothing else to do but wait. And wonder. Lying on the soft bed, the warm afternoon sunshine pouring through the window, he closed his eyes and thought about Karl – even though he knew he shouldn't. Where was he? *How* was he? Was he missing Marc as much as Marc was missing *him*? Perhaps they could still meet: slaves were often sent into town on errands, and maybe . . .

'Marc! Marc – wake up!' Marc shook his head, realising immediately what had happened. He opened his eyes, and was shocked to see a familiar face leaning over him: it was Cletus!

'Cletus!' he cried out, glad to see someone he knew, however slightly. 'How are you?'

'There's no time for that!' Cletus said, panic clear in his voice. 'They've finished their meal and are about to start – well, whatever they're starting. Philip sent me to fetch you. Put on your toga! Quickly!'

Marc hoped that he wasn't going to make both of them late. He wasn't exactly clear about what was expected of them in Flavius's 'affair', but he knew that being late – for a slave – was not the way to a long and healthy life.

'Are we late?' he asked, pulling off the toga that Thomas had given him and wrapping the new one around him, noticing immediately the quality of the cloth. Was it silk?

'Not if you hurry, no. But I know that I don't want to be late for my first –'

Marc coughed. 'First? I wasn't the one in the litter.'

Cletus gave an embarrassed smile. 'All right, second then. But we mustn't be late – we mustn't.'

His toga around him, Marc placed a friendly hand on Cletus's shoulder. 'We're not going to be. Calm down and lead the way.'

The villa was empty. Cletus explained that all of the slaves were confined to their rooms for the rest of the day, until Flavius's festivities were over. The marble-floored corridors, their fabric-draped walls only broken by the regular alcoves filled with busts of gods and long-departed family members, echoed to the sound of the two slaves' bare feet slapping against the mosaics.

'Are you nervous?' asked Marc.

'Of what?'

'I know you've already had sex with Flavius, but –'

Cletus stopped him. 'No, I haven't. Flavius isn't interested in men, Marc.'

Marc was surprised. 'He isn't? So –'

'He was talking to me. He'd learnt that my brother was a slave in Nero's court, and wondered if I still had contact with him. He was quite disappointed when I said no.'

'So what are we walking into?' If Flavius wasn't interested in having sex with them, what were his 'affairs' all about?

Cletus sighed. 'You still don't get it, do you? Then again, I only know because Flavius told me. The *triclinium* is playing host to about a dozen members of the Senate. Not everyone shares Flavius's interest in women . . .'

He trailed off as they reached the curtained archway which Marc assumed led into the *triclinium*.

'What now?' Marc whispered, looking at the curtain with

188

something approaching dread. He was about to become the plaything of the highest echelons of Rome! A small part of him wondered what Cimber would have thought of it – then he decided that he would have been proud. And very, very jealous.

Cletus shrugged. 'We wait.'

They didn't have to wait for long. The curtain parted to reveal Philip, now wearing a far more ornate tunic. 'Ah, boys – on time, I'm pleased to say. The others have already started: you're being kept in reserve. Fresh blood, for when their eminences' interest begins to wane.'

'Bring them on!' came the cry from the *triclinium*.

He gave the curtain a gentle pull. 'You're on!'

The *triclinium* was impressive. The floor was black marble, veined with white, while the walls were covered with tapestries which Marc guessed were from Egypt. The thick patterned fabric obscured the windows, leaving illumination the sole responsibility of the oil lamps which were placed at the corners. The ceiling was low and decorated, but details were lost in the gloom which even the oil lamps could not penetrate.

And the room was full.

Reclining on the soft couches which were arranged against two sides of the *triclinium*, half the Senate appeared to be present. But their attention was fixed on what was going on in front of them: four slaves, naked and shining with oil, were wrestling with one another on the black marble. Many of the senators were gently wanking themselves, while others had clearly already spent their passion on the floor.

The only person not obsessed by the spectacle was Flavius, his hawk-like face focused on the man sitting next to him on the couch. Flavius should have been sitting in the third place of the *medius* – at the top of the couch at the juncture of the two rows. That was his right, as master of the house. But he had forsaken his place for the man with the purple toga who was slowly pulling on his penis, watching the four slaves. A young man with short golden hair and a thin face with a fruity, indulgent expression. The only man in the Roman Empire who could unseat a master from his position.

Nero: Emperor of Rome.

Marc swallowed. Even if he hadn't recognised the Emperor from the etchings and coins that Cimber had shown him, the fact that his toga was totally purple was clue enough. Flavius and his fellow senators could edge their togas in the royal colour, but only the Emperor was permitted to wear it in all its glory.

A sudden hand-clap made the slaves stop their wrestling: for a second, they stood like statues, not sure what to do, before they were led from the floor by Philip. Marc guessed that at least two of them belonged to one of the senators.

'Your Imperial Majesty,' said Flavius grandly, rising to his feet. 'Let me introduce you to my newest acquisitions: Marcus Lucius of far Britannia, and Cletus Claudius Minimus, brother of your own favoured manservant, Dominus Claudius Maximus.'

Nero stood – none too steadily, Marc noted. 'Brother of my dear Dominus, eh?' he asked. Marc knew that Nero was only twenty-five, but he looked far, far older: the weight of the Roman Empire, the constant fear of assassination, all of that had taken its toll on the young Emperor. 'I hope you prove as lively as he does.' Then he looked at Marc, and Marc felt the entire force of Nero's majesty burning into him.

'From Britannia, Marcus Lucius? And how am I revered in my distant province?'

Marc swallowed, but forced himself to answer. 'The empire is everything to us, Your Imperial Majesty. Everything I was taught by my mentor, Cimber –'

Nero held up his hand. 'Cimber, you say? Old Cimber? Cimber the randy old goat who couldn't keep his hands off me?'

Marc nodded.

'How is the old reprobate?' Nero asked warmly. 'Enjoying the British rain?'

Marc hesitated: should he answer? But he had no choice. He owed it to Cimber. Even if he couldn't – wouldn't – warn Nero of the plot against him, he still owed it to his old mentor and friend. 'Cimber is dead.'

'Dead?' Nero's voice was quiet. 'How?'

'Killed by the Obsidian Legion, Your Imperial Majesty,' Marc answered – but his attention wasn't on Nero . . . it was on Flavius. The man was definitely discomfited, but why? What did he have to do with the Obsidian Legion? According to the scroll that Marc had read in Decius's tent, the plan was the sole responsibility of the army . . .

Nero sighed. 'The Obsidian Legion! How many times will I hear of their perfidy?' He shook his head. 'Poor Cimber. May he rest with the gods on Olympus.' Sitting down on the couch once more, he stared into the distance. 'Why do I bother?' he muttered. 'Emperor of the entire world, and I cannot even protect my own teacher. Empire? What is the point?' He turned to the senator next to him. 'Have you got an answer, Polonius? No, I hardly thought you would.' An odd expression came over his face. 'All is nothing, and nothing matters.' For long moments, he sat there, deep in thought. Was this the man who ruled the Empire? thought Marc. But Nero was speaking again: this time, his tone was firm.

'Well, Marcus Lucius and Cletus Claudius . . .' Nero smiled. 'I order you to fuck one another.'

But Cletus needed no encouragement: he dropped to his knees and greedily pushed his face into Marc's groin, pressing on to Marc's growing erection. Marc responded by undoing his own toga, urgently pulling it off and leaving it unravelled on the marble floor.

For a moment, the two of them remained still, both of them

naked apart from their shorts. Then Cletus reached up and undid Marc's shorts, allowing them to fall to the floor.

Marc's erection sprang free, and Cletus wasted no time in taking it in his mouth. Marc gasped as Cletus's probing tongue explored his sensitive helmet, licking the rim, probing his dick-slit. As Cletus did so, his fingers began to explore Marc's arse, stroking the hairs around his ring.

Cletus moved on from Marc's helmet, taking more and more of his length into his mouth until he had the whole shaft, his lips brushing against the dark bush of pubic hair at the base. Then he slid back up Marc's cock until only his tongue was still touching the red end, already leaking pre-come.

Stepping back, Marc pulled the boy to his feet and returned the favour. Ripping off Cletus's shorts, he was delighted by what he saw: Cletus's lower body was dusted with black hair, but around his impressively sized shaft it was a thick forest. Marc wasted no time in dropping to his feet and licking Cletus's large balls, taking each one of the hairy sacs into his mouth in turn. Cletus gasped with pleasure, so Marc intensified his efforts, sucking and nibbling even more furiously. His hand moved up Cletus's thigh until it found his arse, but unlike Cletus's gentle exploration, he forced his forefinger into the boy's arse, pushing into his ring and making him groan with pain. Further and further he went, opening Cletus up so that he would take all of Marc's cock when the time came.

While he continued to finger-fuck Cletus, Marc moved on from Cletus's balls to his cock, running his tongue along the thick shaft until he reached the helmet, which was wet with glistening pre-come. Marc hungrily drank it, licking it off until the only moisture was Marc's spit. Then he took the shaft in his mouth and ran his lips up and down, up and down, in time with the pressure of his finger up Cletus's arse.

Finally he knew that Cletus was ready. He forced the boy on to his back, before lifting his legs into the air to reveal his hole, which was noticeably larger than it had been: large enough for Marc to slide his cock into.

Placing both hands on Cletus's shoulders, Marc manoeuvred himself so that his cock was level with the boy's ring. Then he touched his helmet to Cletus's hole and exerted the slightest amount of pressure, and was glad to see that the first inch of his cock went in easily. Slowly, he fed more and more of his meat into Cletus's willing arse, until all of his length was inside him. Then he pushed with all of his weight, and Cletus groaned. Marc pulled out, slowly, deliberately, until he was half withdrawn, then drove himself back in. He increased the speed, pulling out then forcing his way back in, until he reached the rhythm that he enjoyed. One of his hands moved down Cletus's chest until he found his nipple. Taking the bud between his fingers, he squeezed it, tighter and tighter and harder and harder, before suddenly releasing it.

Cletus's cries of pleasure increased, so Marc squeezed it once again, delighting in the sounds which were being forced from the boy. He moved his other hand down, past the solid stomach, down towards the navel and then following the thin trail of black hair till he found Cletus's cock. Grasping it, he started to wank it in time to his fucking, while his other hand continued to grip the boy's nipple. All the time, his cock forced its way in and out of Cletus's arse, in and out, in and out. Marc knew that he was close, and Cletus's heavy breathing suggested that he was too. Marc increased his speed, fucking him faster and faster, more and more desperately, until he could feel his climax growing inside him.

Just as it began to explode, Marc pulled his cock from Cletus's hole and, taking his hand from Cletus's nipple, aimed his meat at the boy's chest. With a yell of release, Marc came, shooting one, two, three gouts of warm load over Cletus's chest and face. At the same time, he continued to wank Cletus, and was pleased when, with a groan to rival his own, Cletus shot out thick droplets of come which mingled with the thin dusting of hair and the pools of Marc's own come.

Marc slumped on to the floor in exhaustion, before realising that someone was clapping. It was Nero. He looked up and saw that many of the men watching them had also come, covering the marble floor of the *triclinium* with drops of white.

Marc and Cletus got to their feet and bowed to the Emperor, before Philip came forward and whispered to them.

'Well done, lads. Go and relax in the baths. If you are needed again, I will fetch you. Now run along.'

With that, Marc and Cletus left the room, still drained from their efforts.

'This isn't the way to the baths,' Marc hissed. 'They're on the other side of the villa.'

'I know,' said Cletus. 'But there's another room I want to look at. I saw it earlier, but there were too many people about. Old Flavius has given all of the servants the night off apart from Philip, so we should be safe tonight. Ah – here it is.'

They had stopped in front of a large wooden door, ornately carved with a handsome face. Marc recognised it immediately.

'Cletus, this is the family shrine: the shrine to Apollo, looking at that carving.'

'I know – I just want to see what sort of a shrine a villa like this has.' And he pushed the door open.

The room was large, with mosaic-covered flooring and walls draped in rich tapestries, each one depicting a scene from legend. But the room was dominated by the lifesize golden statue which stood at the far end: proud and handsome, it was Apollo.

'This is beautiful,' gasped Cletus, walking over to the statue. 'Hey – this is what I was looking for!'

Marc followed him over. Cletus had picked up a large golden goblet that was full of deep red liquid. Before he could say anything, Cletus took a deep mouthful.

'This is wonderful, Marc. Try some.' He held the goblet out to him, but Marc hesitated. Should he be doing this? Why not? he decided, taking the goblet and drinking from it.

The wine was heavy and tasted of rich spices. The moment he finished swallowing it, he felt light-headed, and had to sit at the base of the statue before he fell over. He looked over at Cletus, and could see that the boy felt the same way; he was reaching out to steady himself, but failed, and slipped to the floor.

Marc tried to reach for him, but the wine overcame him too, and he fell backwards, lying on the cold marble, staring into the golden face of Apollo. Suddenly the face grew larger and larger, until it filled his entire vision.

Then it spoke, words that burnt in the air. The words of a god.

This is not how it ends, Imperator. *Rome will end in fire, and that will be your beginning!*

Before Marc could ponder the meaning, he felt consciousness slipping away. The last thing he was aware of was the sound of the door being opened, and loud angry words. Was it Philip?

And then there was nothing, as merciful blackness overcame him. Nothing save the words of Apollo: *This is not how it ends,* Imperator. *Rome will end in fire, and that will be your beginning!*

Marc awoke and rubbed his forehead. What had Cletus been thinking of? Why had he brought him to Flavius's family shrine? Then he remembered: the wine. Cletus had thought it would be a good idea.

But that was about all he could remember. Then another thought invaded his mind. The words of a god . . .

This is not how it ends, Imperator. *Rome will end in fire, and that will be your beginning!*

The words burnt in Marc's mind like fire on marble: those had been the words imparted by Apollo in Marc's dream.

Marc sat up, immediately realising that he was naked. But

where was he? He wasn't in his quarters, nor was he in Apollo's shrine. And it was cold . . . Marc looked up and saw the stars, dim pinpoints only just rivalled by the cloud-covered moon – suddenly he knew where he was. Not in his quarters; not even in the villa. He was outside, in the courtyard.

Then he remembered why. Philip had come to find them: Marc and Cletus, drunk on the drugged wine of the shrine to Apollo, unaware of its potency. Philip had dragged both of them through the marble corridors, shouting at them, screaming at them. They had disgraced Flavius in front of the Emperor, and would be lucky if they saw the next sunrise. He was going to leave them by the *impluvium* until they sobered up. Then they would be dealt with.

But Cletus was nowhere to be seen. Not that Marc could see very far: it was almost pitch-black, the moon obscured by clouds. What was he going to do? Go back into the villa and face Philip's – and Flavius's – wrath? Or turn his back on slavery, and go on the run?

Before he could consider the options, he heard the voice. A woman's voice, high and haughty: Julia, the arrogant wife of Flavius. She was talking to someone . . . and Marc suddenly realised that he knew the identity of the other person.

It was Decius.

'Nero is relaxed, now – off guard,' she was saying. 'Are your men in position?'

'They are, Lady Julia.' Decius sounded different from normal, and it took Marc a few moments to realise why: fear. He was afraid of Flavius's wife! Then again, from some of the chit-chat Marc had picked up from the other household slaves, that was with good reason: Flavius might have been known as the most powerful man in Rome, but the true power came from the scheming, manipulative Julia.

'Nero's honour guard has been . . . removed,' Decius continued. 'How is the Emperor?'

Julia's tone betrayed her arrogance. 'Enjoying his last night on Earth, General Decius. In just a few hours, we will be rid of him – well rid of him.'

'Rid of the whole empire, my lady. Long live the republic.' As the sound of Decius's boots hitting the marble of the courtyard faded, Marc smiled to himself, and remembered the contents of Decius's letter – specifically the last few lines:

The empire is corrupt, Decius. You and Gaius have successfully used the Obsidian Legion to diminish the name of Rome, making Nero's position untenable. Once you return to the Eternal City, you can perform the final act. Without Nero, the empire should fall, but there are those of us who know how to catch it, and will forge a new republic from the ashes.

May Jove watch and protect you.

F.

F – *Flavius*. Marc realised that fate had placed him in at the exact point where he could watch the evil of the empire die, to be replaced by the justness of a new republic. He could see why Cimber had been so worried: Nero was his pupil, and the empire was his life. But it was a corrupt life, an immoral life. History would show that Flavius and his wife had had the best interests of the Roman people at heart.

'Simple-minded fool.' It was Julia. 'I can play him like a puppet.'

'Of course you can, my dear, of course you can. In two hours, Decius will be dead, dying as a traitor deserves. Rome will learn of their Cult of Pan, dedicated to the overthrow of Nero, and will rejoice at their death. If only poor Cimber hadn't realised what was really going on . . .' She trailed off, before continuing, her voice resolute: 'Rome will weep for their dead Emperor, and we shall step into the breach and take the reins of power. Emperor Flavius . . . it has a certain ring about it, don't you think?'

Flavius. Here, in the courtyard. But what was he saying?

197

'You deserve the power, my husband. The family line which started with great Augustus is all but exhausted. Nero is nothing but a perverted sybarite. We, on the other hand, will give Rome what it needs. A strong and mighty hand.'

'Without a single senator to stand against us, of course.'

'Of course,' said Julia, her voice silky. 'I'm sure that our friends in the Senate would be most distressed if their attendance at our . . . parties were to become public knowledge. It wouldn't do them much good.' She laughed a cruel, spiteful laugh, the laugh of a woman who knew she held all the cards.

Not all of them, Marc realised. With slow movements, he dragged himself away from Julia and Flavius and towards the dim light that would lead him back into the villa. If he could find Decius or Gaius, he could warn them that it was all a trap. He just hoped that they would believe him.

Decius stood in the doorway, in a position that allowed him full view of the *triclinium*, but which obscured him from the guests' prying eyes. His concentration was focused on Nero, sitting at the centre of attention, stuffing himself with food, watching boys fuck one another for his entertainment. It made Decius feel sick. For a moment, he thought of Marc, and wondered where he was. Who had bought him? Did Marc think of him, or had it been an act? But then his thoughts turned to Gaius, standing just beside him, his own slave at his back. Gaius, the only man that Decius had ever loved: would Decius ever have the strength to admit that to him, knowing that he couldn't face being rebuffed?

He took a deep breath and fingered his sword, still sheathed. There would be time for such reflections once the deed was done. Nero would die this night, and a new republic would rise. And Decius would be made a hero for his part in it.

He turned to Gaius, and couldn't help admiring his strong features, his masculine bearing. How he longed for Gaius to grab him, take him, pin him to the ground and force his thick cock into him. Decius felt his own cock beginning to harden at the image. He tried to ignore it and whispered to Gaius:

'Any moment now: the signal will be a clap from Flavius. Nero will think that Flavius is calling on the next entertainment.'

'Entertainment,' laughed Gaius softly. 'The entertainment that comes at the point of a sharpened sword.' Gaius turned to his second. 'Are you prepared?'

'I am,' was the simple answer.

The clap rang out from the *triclinium*: a simple sound that would herald the end of an empire. Gaius, Decius and the others unsheathed their swords and strode into the *triclinium*.

'What is the meaning of this!' snapped Nero, jumping to his feet.

'The end of your tyranny!' bellowed Decius. 'For too long, you and your family have bled the empire dry to satisfy your lusts. It stops now: you are the last of the Caesars, Nero.' Decius stepped forward.

'No!'

Decius turned to the source of the noise and was rendered speechless. Marc was standing there, sword in his hand, walking with determination towards Nero. To protect Nero.

'Marc – what are you doing?' Decius realised that it was Gaius's slave talking.

Karl.

Marc stared at him, and even Decius could see the confusion in the boy's eyes. *Yes, Marc – what are you doing?*

Marc froze: Gaius, Decius *and* Karl. Was this some kind of sick joke? Was this Jupiter's revenge on him for something? He knew what would happen unless he could persuade them. But how?

There was only one weapon left to him. Not the sword, but the truth. If the bond between him and Karl was as strong as he believed it to be, it was the only answer. He just prayed that he hadn't been mistaken.

'Karl!' he shouted. 'You must listen to me, and you must believe me. You know that I have little love for Rome, but what you are doing here – all of you – is wrong. Flavius wants Nero dead, but not to forge a new republic. Why would Flavius create something which took away his own power? Flavius and Julia want Nero dead so that they can take over. I heard them talking in the courtyard: you'll all be blamed for Nero's murder, and Flavius will become Emperor. Nero might have his faults –' Marc glanced at the Emperor, who was standing in shock, realising that a single British boy was trying to save his life ' – but who knows what Flavius would be like. Especially since the true power isn't Flavius at all, but Julia. Please Karl,' he begged, 'you have to believe me.' He stared at Nero once more. 'In a vision, Apollo told me that this isn't the way you should die. He told me: *This is not how it ends, Imperator. Rome will end in fire, and that will be your beginning!* Would you defy a god?'

In the silence that followed, Marc stared at the German, trying to read his eyes. If Nero died, Rome would be damned for ever. He *had* to believe him, he *had* to.

Karl broke rank and strode over to Marc, his sword still unsheathed. He stopped less than a foot away.

'Your word against everyone else's, Marc. But that's enough for me.'

In a single, fluid movement, he ran Flavius through with his sword. Before anyone could react, the same fate befell Julia – at Decius's sword.

Marc let out the breath that he realised he had been holding for far too long. 'You believed me,' he whispered.

Karl smiled. 'Of course I did.'

The next few hours were chaotic. None of the senators were supporters of Flavius – at least none of them would admit it in front of Nero – and they all re-swore their allegiance to the Emperor. Marc and Karl were given the freedom of the empire by Nero, and Decius and Gaius were given their release from the Legion: an act which also gave them land and a small fortune. Marc was a bit confused – hadn't they been about to kill Nero? – but Karl pointed out that the best way for Nero to assure his continued survival was to move the danger further away. As citizens, Decius and Gaius would no longer be able to call on the Obsidian Legion or any of the other armies to help them – and Nero was relying on their gratitude to control them.

Marc stood in the courtyard, watching the first fires of the sun burn over the horizon. Karl came up behind him and hugged him.

'So, you have changed your mind about the empire, have you?' he said with affectionate mockery. 'My little rebel now conforms?'

Marc shrugged. 'Perhaps Nero will learn something from this. And besides, all the things I blamed the empire for were caused by Flavius and his wife – not Nero, and not the empire.' He looked at the brightening sky. 'A new dawn. Let's make the most of it, Karl.

'Together.'

Karl looked into the dawn and smiled. 'Amen to that.'

Nero sat in the now empty *triclinium*, his face dark. He had survived, that was true, but it was time to make his mark on history. Time to become truly great. But how?

Then he remembered, and a smile crossed his face.

'In fire . . .'

Epilogue

M arc stood on the balcony of his villa, high on the Palatine Hill, and looked out on the inferno raging on the adjacent Capitoline Hill. Only an hour ago, the smell of smoke had roused him and Karl from their sleep, and moments later the reason had become clear.

Rome was on fire.

Karl came up behind him and placed a protective arm around his waist. 'The wind is blowing away from us, thankfully. There isn't much danger of it reaching here.'

Marc watched the flames as they continued to consume the centre of the city – the centre of the Roman Empire – and felt mixed emotions. Two years ago, when he and Karl had first met, he had been in awe of Rome. Soon after he had come to hate it, to want to see it fall. But, given the chance to destroy the empire, he had finally realised that the empire was the best that they could hope for. Seeing the Eternal City in flames had once been his goal; now it was heartbreaking.

'Do you think he did it?' asked Karl, remembering Marc's words. *This is not how it ends,* Imperator. *Rome will end in fire, and that will be your beginning!*

'Nero?' Marc replied. Then he shrugged. 'Perhaps he thought that this was how he would attain godhood. But whether he did start this —'

'He did,' came a third voice. Karl and Marc turned to see Gaius walking on to the balcony, Decius close behind. 'I have it on good authority that he started that fire himself, just so that he could build a new city in his image.'

Gaius shook his head. 'As we always suspected: the Emperor is mad.'

Marc smiled. Despite all the evidence — all the *proof* — that Flavius was nothing more than a puppet of his manipulative wife, a small part of Gaius still regretted that the plan of the Obsidian Legion hadn't come to fruition. It was an ongoing argument that often entertained them all when the four of them dined together — which was quite often. Not surprising, since Decius and Gaius lived in a villa only a few minutes' walk away.

'You would have preferred weak Flavius and his power-hungry wife, would you?' Decius teased. 'Anyway, we came to see whether you two were all right. They think that the fire will be out by morning, although the flames have already spread to the Viminal Hill. So long as the winds don't change, you should be fine.'

'Would you care to dine with us?' asked Marc. 'We have plenty of food.' Karl and Marcus were well known in Rome for their good treatment of both their friends and their own slaves.

Gaius looked at Decius. 'Sounds a good idea to me.'

Decius nodded. 'A good meal with friends: what more could a man ask for?'

'Us on the guest list, that's what,' came another familiar voice from the atrium.

Marc couldn't help grinning: they hadn't seen this particular couple for nearly a year!

'Thomas! Cletus! How good to see you both again.' Marc

hugged them both in turn, before releasing them to the affections of the others. After Flavius's 'execution', his slaves had automatically become the property of the auction pits, since Flavius and Julia had had no offspring. But Thomas had been prepared: with his savings, he had bought Cletus – and then released him as a freedman. Hoping against hope, the bearlike slave trader had been overjoyed when Cletus had admitted his own feelings, and the two of them had also joined Marc and Karl's group of friends. But they had been missed for the last eight months: Thomas had taken Cletus to Egypt – to broaden his mind, Thomas had claimed. Their return was as welcome as it was unexpected.

The evening wore on. Eventually, the drama of the fire passed, and Gaius and Decius and Thomas and Cletus made their way home, leaving Karl and Marc alone on the balcony.

Karl wrapped his arms around Marc's waist and squeezed him, and Marc couldn't help thinking how different the German was from when they had first met. Two years of living in Rome had allowed Karl to express his emotions, and he had slowly but surely opened up to Marc, admitting his feelings and showing his love.

Not that Karl had forgotten his heritage. He still practised his religion – Christianity, he called it – having found others in Rome who shared his beliefs. It had to be performed in secret, because it was illegal in Rome, but Marc suspected that added to it in some way. And Karl's warrior side found release in the gladiatorial arena, where he taught the gladiators. Karl's prowess with the sword was legendary, and his gladiators were the most feared in Rome.

And Marc? Marc had followed in the footsteps of Cimber: he was now a teacher, well loved by all of his pupils. He sometimes wondered whether Cimber would have been proud of him, and realised it was a stupid question – Cimber had *always* been proud of him.

Karl turned him around to face him. 'It was good to see Thomas and Cletus again.'

Marc smiled. 'They're part of our life now. Our new life.'

Karl said nothing. He pulled Marc close and kissed him on the lips, his tongue exploring Marc's mouth, finding his tongue and entwining with it. For long moments, they stayed like that, their arms around each other, squeezing one another, holding one another.

Then Marc stepped back and took hold of Karl's tunic. In one easy move, he pulled the garment off, revealing Karl's toned and muscular body. He still wore his two piercings: the ring through his nipple and the fish in his navel. Marc reached out and stroked the dark tattoo around his biceps, his fingers tracing the curves and loops. Then his hand moved to Karl's chest. He ran his fingers through the thickening dark chest hair, down towards his taut stomach, and finally to Karl's cock, which was already stiffening. His fingers gently teased the thickness, along the shaft and to the darker helmet.

Karl responded by pulling off Marc's tunic. For a second, they just looked at one another: then Karl knelt down and took Marc's shaft in his mouth. He swallowed all of it, taking it deep in his throat, and Marc gasped with the pleasure of it, thrusting forward with his hips to force even more of it into his lover's mouth.

Karl pulled back, his lips sliding along the shaft, until he released it. Then he stood and gently urged Marc to the ground. Marc knelt, turning Karl around as he did. Karl bent forward slightly, and Marc pulled his cheeks apart to reveal his arse. Greedily, he put his face between the cheeks, and reached out with his tongue, licking at the hairs around the ring, nibbling on the soft flesh and eliciting a cry from Karl. His tongue explored further, into the hole, tasting Karl. Marc's tongue darted in and out, while his hands kneaded Karl's buttocks, gently at first, then more forcefully, pulling Karl on to him as Marc pushed himself forward.

Then he turned Karl around and started on his cock: he took the helmet in his mouth and licked it, tasting the hot, sweet pre-come which dribbled from the slit, drinking it, delighting in it. As he sucked, he grabbed his own cock, but Karl took his hand away immediately. The meaning was clear: *that's for me to do.*

Karl took him by the wrist and led him into the *triclinium*, gently pushing him on to the couch. Then Karl lowered himself on to the couch, so that their cocks were at each other's mouths. Without saying a word, they took what was offered. Marc swallowed Karl's shaft, moving his mouth up and down as he did so. Karl did the same, and Marc groaned as he felt his lover's tongue running around his helmet, teasing at the rim and the slit.

As Marc sucked, he moved a hand so it was resting on Karl's arse; he started to finger Karl's hole, gently probing the hot ring, still moist with Marc's spit. Karl's tongue was still running up and down Marc's shaft, but it was joined by Karl's strong hand, which grasped Marc's cock and started to wank him. With firm, regular strokes, he wanked, while his mouth played with the sensitive red helmet. Marc knew that he wouldn't be able to hold out for long, so he increased his probing, forcing his finger further and further into Karl's ring, trying to find the spot that he knew would have Karl groaning with overwhelming pleasure, while Marc's mouth continued to suck at Karl's meat, sliding back and forth over him, faster and faster.

Karl came without warning. Marc almost choked as the hot wave of come hit the back of his throat, but he swallowed all of it, his mouth urging every last drop from Karl. At the first taste of Karl's salty warm load, Marc abandoned himself to his own release: his hips bucked as he delivered himself into Karl's mouth, driving his cock further down the German's throat.

Finally they were both drained. Karl rolled off Marc and sat on the floor next to him, gently stroking his hair, damp with sweat.

'I love you,' he said softly.

Marc smiled. That was all he wanted to hear. For a moment he thought of Alexander. But that had been lust, a boy's first obsession. This was real, and Marc knew that.

For, despite his freedom, Marc knew with a certainty that he was still a slave. A slave to Karl.

A slave to love. And he didn't mind a bit.

IDOL NEW BOOKS

Also published:

THE KING'S MEN
Christian Fall

Ned Medcombe, spoilt son of an Oxfordshire landowner, has always remembered his first love: the beautiful, golden-haired Lewis. But seventeenth-century England forbids such a love and Ned is content to indulge his domineering passions with the willing members of the local community, including the submissive parish cleric. Until the Civil War changes his world, and he is forced to pursue his desires as a soldier in Cromwell's army – while his long-lost lover fights as one of the King's men.

ISBN 0 352 33207 7

THE VELVET WEB
Christopher Summerisle

The year is 1889. Daniel McGaw arrives at Calverdale, a centre of academic excellence buried deep in the English countryside. But this is like no other college. As Daniel explores, he discovers secret passages in the grounds and forbidden texts in the library. The young male students, isolated from the outside world, share a darkly bizarre brotherhood based on the most extreme forms of erotic expression. It isn't long before Daniel is initiated into the rites that bind together the youths of Calverdale in a web of desire.

ISBN 0 352 33208 5

CHAINS OF DECEIT
Paul C. Alexander

Journalist Nathan Dexter's life is turned around when he meets a young student called Scott – someone who offers him the relationship for which he's been searching. Then Nathan's best friend goes missing, and Nathan uncovers evidence that he has become the victim of a slavery ring which is rumoured to be operating out of London's leather scene. To rescue their friend and expose the perverted slave trade, Nathan and Scott must go undercover, risking detection and betrayal at every turn.

ISBN 0 352 33206 9

WE NEED YOUR HELP . . .

to plan the future of Idol books –

Yours are the only opinions that matter. Idol is a new and exciting venture: the first British series of books devoted to homoerotic fiction for men.

We're going to do our best to provide the sexiest, best-written books you can buy. And we'd like you to help in these early stages. Tell us what you want to read. There's a freepost address for your filled-in questionnaires, so you won't even need to buy a stamp.

THE IDOL QUESTIONNAIRE

SECTION ONE: ABOUT YOU

1.1 Sex (*we presume you are male, but just in case*)
     Are you?
            Male   ☐
            Female   ☐

1.2 Age
            under 21   ☐   21–30   ☐
            31–40   ☐   41–50   ☐
            51–60   ☐   over 60 ☐

1.3 At what age did you leave full-time education?
            still in education ☐   16 or younger ☐
            17–19   ☐   20 or older   ☐

1.4 Occupation _____

1.5 Annual household income _____

1.6 We are perfectly happy for you to remain anonymous; but if you would like us to send you a free booklist of Idol books, please insert your name and address

_____

_____

_____

_____

SECTION TWO: ABOUT BUYING IDOL BOOKS

2.1 Where did you get this copy of *The Slave Trade*?
    Bought at chain book shop ☐
    Bought at independent book shop ☐
    Bought at supermarket ☐
    Bought at book exchange or used book shop ☐
    I borrowed it/found it ☐
    My partner bought it ☐

2.2 How did you find out about Idol books?
    I saw them in a shop ☐
    I saw them advertised in a magazine ☐
    I read about them in _____
    Other _____

2.3 Please tick the following statements you agree with:
    I would be less embarrassed about buying Idol
    books if the cover pictures were less explicit ☐
    I think that in general the pictures on Idol
    books are about right ☐
    I think Idol cover pictures should be as
    explicit as possible ☐

2.4 Would you read an Idol book in a public place – on a train for instance?
    Yes ☐   No ☐

SECTION THREE: ABOUT THIS IDOL BOOK

3.1 Do you think the sex content in this book is:
    Too much ☐   About right ☐
    Not enough ☐

3.2   Do you think the writing style in this book is:

        Too unreal/escapist   ☐   About right   ☐

        Too down to earth   ☐

3.3   Do you think the story in this book is:

        Too complicated   ☐   About right   ☐

        Too boring/simple   ☐

3.4   Do you think the cover of this book is:

        Too explicit   ☐   About right   ☐

        Not explicit enough   ☐

Here's a space for any other comments:

SECTION FOUR: ABOUT OTHER IDOL BOOKS

4.1   How many Idol books have you read?

4.2   If more than one, which one did you prefer?

    _____

4.3   Why?

SECTION FIVE: ABOUT YOUR IDEAL EROTIC NOVEL

We want to publish the books you want to read – so this is your chance to tell us exactly what your ideal erotic novel would be like.

5.1   Using a scale of 1 to 5 (1 = no interest at all, 5 = your ideal), please rate the following possible settings for an erotic novel:

        Roman / Ancient World   ☐

        Medieval / barbarian / sword 'n' sorcery   ☐

        Renaissance / Elizabethan / Restoration   ☐

        Victorian / Edwardian   ☐

        1920s & 1930s   ☐

        Present day   ☐

        Future / Science Fiction   ☐

5.2 Using the same scale of 1 to 5, please rate the following themes you may find in an erotic novel:

Bondage / fetishism ☐
Romantic love ☐
SM / corporal punishment ☐
Bisexuality ☐
Group sex ☐
Watersports ☐
Rent / sex for money ☐

5.3 Using the same scale of 1 to 5, please rate the following styles in which an erotic novel could be written:

Gritty realism, down to earth ☐
Set in real life but ignoring its more unpleasant aspects ☐
Escapist fantasy, but just about believable ☐
Complete escapism, totally unrealistic ☐

5.4 In a book that features power differentials or sexual initiation, would you prefer the writing to be from the viewpoint of the dominant / experienced or submissive / inexperienced characters:

Dominant / Experienced ☐
Submissive / Inexperienced ☐
Both ☐

5.5 We'd like to include characters close to your ideal lover. What characteristics would your ideal lover have? Tick as many as you want:

Dominant	☐	Caring	☐
Slim	☐	Rugged	☐
Extroverted	☐	Romantic	☐
Bisexual	☐	Old	☐
Working Class	☐	Intellectual	☐
Introverted	☐	Professional	☐
Submissive	☐	Pervy	☐
Cruel	☐	Ordinary	☐
Young	☐	Muscular	☐
Naïve	☐		

Anything else? _____

5.6 Is there one particular setting or subject matter that your ideal erotic novel would contain:

_____

5.7 As you'll have seen, we include safe-sex guidelines in every book. However, while our policy is always to show safe sex in stories with contemporary settings, we don't insist on safe-sex practices in stories with historical settings because it would be anachronistic. What, if anything, would you change about this policy?

_____

_____

SECTION SIX: LAST WORDS

6.1 What do you like best about Idol books?

_____

6.2 What do you most dislike about Idol books?

_____

6.3 In what way, if any, would you like to change Idol covers?

_____

6.4 Here's a space for any other comments:

_____

_____

_____

_____

Thanks for completing this questionnaire. Now either tear it out, or photocopy it, then put it in an envelope and send it to:

Idol
FREEPOST
London
W10 5BR

You don't need a stamp if you're in the UK, but you'll need one if you're posting from overseas.